Praise for the Bear Collector's Mysteries

The False-Hearted Teddy

"With a quick-moving plot that's neither too cozy nor too hard-boiled, a likable sleuth, and an original premise, Lamb has another honey of a mystery."
—*Richmond Times-Dispatch*

"A fast-paced trip . . . Mystery fans will follow the twists and turns of this tightly woven tale with pleasure."
—*Teddy Bear and Friends Magazine*

"A fast and fun romp into murder and mayhem . . . An enjoyable read."
—*Armchair Interviews*

"Both story and dialogue are fast-paced . . . I finished *The False-Hearted Teddy* in one lazy afternoon because I couldn't put it down."
—*Cozy Library*

The Mournful Teddy

"Once you start, you can't bear to miss a teddy mystery."
—Rita Mae Brown, *New York Times* bestselling author of the Mrs. Murphy Mysteries

"A smart debut."
—*Mystery Scene*

"A fascinating look at teddy bears . . . [Lamb] provides readers with a delightful whodunit that more than just bear collectors will enjoy."
—*Midwest Book Review*

continued . . .

"An exceptional mystery . . . Skillfully blends elements of the traditional cozy with the gritty instincts of a tough but tender ex-homicide detective . . . *The Mournful Teddy* is one teddy bear you won't take for granted."

—Ellen Byerrum, author of
the Crime of Fashion Mysteries

"*The Mournful Teddy* is a cozy police procedural, an unusual but not unheard-of combination. The author has pulled it off well—and with subtle humor . . . [it's] more than satisfying . . . I look forward to many more in the series."

—*Mystery News*

"Entertaining . . . a fun romp . . . Fans will need to bear patiently the wait for the Lyons' next outing."

—*Richmond Times-Dispatch*

"*The Mournful Teddy* is a fur ball of fun. There'll be no hibernating once you start reading it."

—*Harrisburg (PA) Patriot-News*

"The unique mystery surrounding collectible teddy bears provides this cozy an element of fun that is hard to find."

—*The Romance Readers Connection*

"True to his roots as an investigator, Lamb masterfully weaves reality with fiction in *The Mournful Teddy*."

—*The Massanutten (VA) Villager*

"A wonderful entry in this new cozy series."

—*Reviewing the Evidence*

The Crafty Teddy

John J. Lamb

BERKLEY PRIME CRIME, NEW YORK

THE BERKLEY PUBLISHING GROUP
Published by the Penguin Group
Penguin Group (USA) Inc.
375 Hudson Street, New York, New York 10014, USA

Penguin Group (Canada), 90 Eglinton Avenue East, Suite 700, Toronto, Ontario M4P 2Y3, Canada
(a division of Pearson Penguin Canada Inc.)
Penguin Books Ltd., 80 Strand, London WC2R 0RL, England
Penguin Group Ireland, 25 St. Stephen's Green, Dublin 2, Ireland (a division of Penguin Books Ltd.)
Penguin Group (Australia), 250 Camberwell Road, Camberwell, Victoria 3124, Australia
(a division of Pearson Australia Group Pty. Ltd.)
Penguin Books India Pvt. Ltd., 11 Community Centre, Panchsheel Park, New Delhi—110 017, India
Penguin Group (NZ), 67 Apollo Drive, Rosedale, North Shore 0632, New Zealand
(a division of Pearson New Zealand Ltd.)
Penguin Books (South Africa) (Pty.) Ltd., 24 Sturdee Avenue, Rosebank, Johannesburg 2196,
South Africa

Penguin Books Ltd., Registered Offices: 80 Strand, London WC2R 0RL, England

THE CRAFTY TEDDY

A Berkley Prime Crime Book / published by arrangement with the author

PRINTING HISTORY
Berkley Prime Crime mass-market edition / November 2007

ISBN: 978-0-425-21885-3

BERKLEY® PRIME CRIME
Berkley Prime Crime Books are published by The Berkley Publishing Group,
a division of Penguin Group (USA) Inc.,
375 Hudson Street, New York, New York 10014.
The name BERKLEY PRIME CRIME and the BERKLEY PRIME CRIME design
are trademarks belonging to Penguin Group (USA) Inc.

PRINTED IN THE UNITED STATES OF AMERICA

10 9 8 7 6 5 4 3 2 1

*For my beloved wife, Joyce,
who showed me a previously unsuspected universe of
love, joy, and teddy bears*

One

I awakened to Kitchener, our Old English sheepdog, growling quietly as he lay on the floor by my side of the bed. Although he weighs in at over a hundred pounds and is named after a famous British army field marshal, our dog is an utter coward. Ironically, one of the things he's most afraid of is sheep, the very creatures he was bred to herd. He's also prone to nightmares, so at first I thought he was having a bad dream about commando sheep, rappelling on ropes from the roof and through our open bedroom windows, intent on *baa*-baric acts. Kitch has an overactive imagination.

The growling stopped and I listened. It was a warm and still May night and the only sounds were the murmuring waters of the South Fork of the Shenandoah River, which runs in front of our house, and the desultory chirps of a couple of crickets. Then Kitch growled again. I leaned over to wake him up and froze. I heard soft footfalls outside on the gravel walkway leading to our front door downstairs.

My first inclination was to dismiss the noise as an animal:
a clumsy deer headed for the midnight buffet in our flower
garden, or perhaps even a big raccoon. However, I had
to abandon that comforting theory when someone—
definitely human and wearing shoes—began slowly creep-
ing across our wooden porch.

Now it was my turn to feel a nasty little rush of fear, because I knew the front door was unlocked. People are
friendly here in our country town of Remmelkemp Mill,
Virginia, but they don't come to visit in the middle of the
night. I listened intently, but the only sound now was the gentle breathing of Ashleigh, my wife, asleep beside me. Then
I heard the squeak of the downstairs screen door being
slowly opened.

I glanced at the LCD display of the alarm clock on Ash's
nightstand. The orange numerals read 2:45 A.M. It's a good
thing I'm not superstitious, or I'd have viewed the time as an
evil omen: Section 245 of the California Penal Code is the
definition for Assault with a Deadly Weapon, a tidbit of information that comes from my quarter century as a San
Francisco cop, the final fourteen years as an inspector in the
Robbery Homicide Division. That was before I received a
crippling gunshot wound to my left shin and was medically
retired from the force.

I'm not as old as I look. Really. The stress of getting
shot and suddenly losing my very satisfying career in police work has savagely aged me. In fact, I think I look old
enough to have voted for Nixon—when he ran against JFK
in 1960. But even though my hair is the same shade of gray
as the USS *Missouri*, the networks of creases on the sides
of my eyes look like relief maps of the Ganges River delta,
and I stump around with a blackthorn cane, I won't be
forty-eight until July.

The only positive thing I can say about my physical

appearance is that I weigh about fifteen pounds less than I did a couple of months ago. It was either drop some tonnage to reduce the pressure on the titanium hardware the doctors had used to rebuild my left shin or go shopping for one of those little electric carts for old folks that they advertise on daytime TV. The idea of accompanying a gorgeous woman like Ash out in public while riding in one of those powered go-carts was too disturbing for words, since strangers already automatically assume she's my trophy wife. So, I began to eat less and exercise more and the pounds just melted away. And if you believe that, I've got some Pan American Airways stock for sale, cheap.

Much as I wanted to leap into action like Errol Flynn, I had to proceed cautiously. There was something about lying in bed that often put my injured left leg to sleep. Slowly rolling myself into a sitting position, I flexed the muscles in my calf and gingerly rotated my ankle until the pins and needles began to go away. I got up from the bed and grabbed Kitch's nylon collar, because I didn't want to trip over him in the dark.

Although I was trying to be quiet, Ash woke, sat up, and brushed some strands of golden hair from her eyes. In spite of the impeding emergency, I paused for a second to admire her in the dim orange glow of the alarm clock's numerals. Ash has Delft China blue eyes, a sweet heart-shaped face, and a firm hourglass figure that never fails to command my complete attention. Tonight she was wearing a lilac-colored sheer nightgown inset with lace. If there hadn't been a burglar downstairs, I would have crawled right back into bed with her.

She sleepily asked, "What is it, honey?"

"Don't turn on the light. We've got a possible four-five-nine in progress downstairs," I whispered, using the California Penal Code section for a burglary.

"What?" Ash was instantly awake.

Doing my best to creep around the bed on my bum leg, I found her hand in the dark and guided it to the dog collar. "Call nine-one-one and hang on to Kitch."

"Why? What are you going to do?"

"I'm going to hunt a wascally wabbit," I said in my best Elmer Fudd voice as I opened my dresser's sock drawer and grabbed the Glock .40-caliber semiautomatic pistol I'd carried for many years as a cop.

Ash got Kitch to jump up on the bed and then jerked the cordless phone receiver from its base-station cradle. "Brad, honey, wouldn't it be safer if you stayed up here?"

I chambered a cartridge into the pistol. "Maybe, but I don't feel like letting some lowlife maggot pillage our house during the fifteen minutes it will take for the deputy to get here from Mount Meridian or wherever. Now, call the sheriff and I promise I'll be careful."

"You'd better be."

"Keep the door shut and don't come out until I tell you it's safe." I did my best to limp stealthily toward the bedroom door, deciding to leave my cane behind. I'd want both hands free to handle the pistol, just in case things got even more interesting than they already were.

"I will." There was a faint *boop-beep-beep* as Ash pressed 911.

I paused at the door to whisper, "And please tell the dispatcher to make sure the deputy understands that the guy in the turquoise nightshirt with the gun is the homeowner . . . although I hope they'll send us a cop who can puzzle that out without our help."

Next month, we'll have been married twenty-seven years and Ash knows I have a habit of making wisecracks when I'm nervous. "Don't worry, I'll tell them. I love you."

"Love you too, darling. I'll be back in a minute."

As Ash began talking in hushed tones to the dispatcher, I slipped out the door and slowly pushed it shut behind me. The house was as dark as Rob Schneider's chances of playing King Lear at London's Olivier Theatre—or anywhere else, for that matter. But after nearly a year of living in the 130-year-old farmhouse, I was able to navigate the hallway via a combination of touch and memory to the stairwell that led downstairs. I paused there for a moment to squint downward into the darkness and listen. Although I couldn't hear anything, I had to assume that, unless I'd made enough noise to spook the intruder, he was already in the house. I caught a momentary glimpse of pale reflected light, as if the burglar had just shone a small flashlight against a reflective surface. There was no doubt now, the guy was in the living room; yet I hesitated to start down the stairs.

Why? Because I'd suddenly turned into the Cowardly Lion. Standing there in the dark, with my left shin aching and a trickle of sweat running down my brow, I was painfully aware that I had no business trying to tangle with a burglar who was probably half my age and likely amped to the gills on methamphetamine. Hell, even Clint Eastwood knew when it was time to pass on the role of the action hero, so what was I thinking? Rationalizing my fear as good sense, I was ready to sneak back down the hallway to the bedroom. It was the most shameful moment of my life, because there was no denying that I'd just shown the white feather.

Then I heard what sounded like fabric being savagely torn. That's when I got mad, because I realized the son of a bitch was vandalizing one of the teddy bears from our collection of more than five hundred stuffed animals. We cherish all of them, but the really special ones—the antiques, those we'd given each other as gifts, and the one-of-a-kind artisan bears—are on display in the living room. I consider those bears a mohair and plush fur shrine to my joyful life with Ash, and now someone was desecrating it. Recovering a little of my nerve, I slowly started down the stairs, holding the pistol at the ready.

Three steps took me to a point where I could peek around the corner and down into the dark living room. I saw the silhouette of a man half-crouched near one of the tall glass and oak curio cabinets where we store some of our most valuable collectible bears. The crook's clothing was all black, and though I couldn't be certain, he seemed also to be wearing a dark-colored ski mask. This told me that the guy was probably a novice housebreaker. Professional "hot prowl" burglars almost never wear woolen masks, because they rely on speed, stealth, and an ability to hear whether they've awakened the victim homeowner. Anything that covers your ears also cuts down on your ability to hear, which explains why a crippled guy had managed to sneak up on this particular burglar in a house with hardwood floors.

I gingerly lowered myself into a kneeling position, using the banister as cover, and raised my pistol. There's an old-fashioned attitude where we live about the rights of decent folks to defend their homes and persons, so I was under no legal obligation to announce my presence or ask the burglar to surrender before giving him the St. Valentine's Day Massacre treatment. Still, I was incapable of just capping the guy in the back. A quarter century of cop work and obedience to the laws pertaining to the use of deadly force had taught me that just because something is legal, it doesn't necessarily make it right.

So, taking a deep breath in the hope that my voice

wouldn't quaver, I said, "Gee, I guess I missed the door-bell. Now, before you get any more stupid ideas tonight, take your filthy hands off our teddy bears and put them in the air where I can see them."

The intruder inhaled sharply and froze. *So far, so good,* I thought, but realized that I wasn't quite certain what my next move was. Back when I was a cop and physically ca-pable, I'd have gone over and hooked the guy up. But, along with lacking two good legs, I also didn't have any handcuffs. However, the problem of how to proceed was rendered academic when the burglar suddenly pivoted. I thought he was going to rabbit for the door, but he did something else first.

There was a blinding, yellowish-white muzzle flash, the deafening roar of a large caliber pistol being fired in our small living room, and the sound of the slug simultane-ously slamming into the wall just a couple of inches from my head. Now, there was no question of what I should do. I threw myself backward onto my butt and out of the line of fire. For an instant, I considered sticking my gun around the corner and blindly shooting back at the crook, but the last thing I wanted was a prolonged gun battle in our house with Ash upstairs. Better the gunman should escape than a stray round go through the wooden ceiling and endanger my wife. Upstairs, Kitchener was barking like crazy. I heard the burglar run across the wooden living room floor and out the door.

I pushed myself to my feet and had just started down the remaining steps when I realized that Ash was charg-ing down the stairs. It being dark, she ran smack into my back and I clung to the banister rail with my left hand to prevent us both from falling down the stairs. Something hard whacked my right shoulder blade and I realized that she'd armed herself with my cane. I didn't quite know how to feel: angry that she'd ignored my instructions to remain upstairs and out of harm's way, or profoundly humbled that she was willing to take on a gunman, armed only with a stick, because she thought I was in danger.

"Whoa, honey! Let's hang on here for a second until we can be certain the guy is in the wind," I said as we came to a stop a couple of steps short of the ground floor.

"Are you all right?" Ash demanded as her hand found my face in the darkness.

"Fine. He missed me."

"You're sure?"

"Absolutely. For God's sake, why didn't you stay upstairs?"

"If you think I'm going to hide in our bedroom while someone tries to kill you, you're completely fifty-one fifty," Ash said indignantly, using a California police expression she picked up from me to describe acute mental illness. "So I told the dispatcher what was happening and grabbed your cane."

"And then you came to the rescue. Thanks." I kissed her on the forehead.

"Where did the suspect go?"

"Out the front door."

"What do we do now?"

"Wait for the cops." Descending the final two steps to the ground floor, I added, "Stay here while I lock the front door."

"I'm coming with you."

"Is there any point in arguing about this?"

"No."

"That's what I figured. Then stay behind me."

I held the gun pointed in the direction of the front door

and we slowly crossed the living room. As we got to the front door, we heard a vehicle engine fire up somewhere down the long gravel driveway leading to our house. I pushed the screen door open to get a better look and saw the boxy silhouette of some sort of SUV—it could have been anything from an older model Jeep Cherokee to a newer Land Rover—back up into the lane. As the truck skidded to a stop, there was a momentary flicker of rectangular-shaped brake lamps and I noticed a small hole in the left-side light cover that showed bright white against the ruby background.

For a moment I considered firing at the SUV's rear tires to disable it, but just as quickly rejected the idea. It was so dark that I couldn't even see the wheels and the vehicle was perhaps fifty yards away, too great a distance to ensure I wouldn't accidentally send a round into the passenger compartment. Not that I had any objections to smoking the gun-toting burglar, but there might be another occupant in the truck and I couldn't accept the risk of shooting a relatively innocent person. The SUV took off down the driveway and turned right onto Cupp Road, where we lost sight of it. Somewhere in the distance to the north, a sheriff cruiser's siren was yelping.

After closing the door and locking it, I switched on the entryway light and a second later Ash gasped in shock. I turned and my jaw tightened with rage. Suddenly, I regretted my decision not to shoot.

The curio cabinet doors stood open and the floor around the display case was littered with the brutally torn arms, legs, torsos, and heads of three of our favorite teddy bears. Among the casualties was a sweet little girl bear made by Joanne Mitchell, that was attired in a maroon velvet dress; a large pink mohair bear made by Serieta Harrell that we'd gotten at a San Diego teddy bear show years before; and a café au lait–colored bear we'd purchased from Barbara Burke while attending the Har-Bear Expo in Baltimore two months previously. Each piece had cost several hundred dollars, yet the damage couldn't be measured in terms of money. Ash stooped to pick up a mohair leg.

I said, "Honey, please don't touch anything until the sheriff gets here."

"Why would anyone do this?" Her eyes were moist and red.

"To hurt us. This wasn't a run-of-the-mill burglary." I hooked a thumb in the direction of the DVD player. "The suspect wasn't interested in regular loot, because nothing else has been touched."

"But who could hate us that much?"

"Pick a name from the list of 'public servants' who either lost their jobs or went to prison because of us." I was referring to the events of the previous October when Ash and I solved a murder and recovered a stolen and very valuable Steiff teddy bear.

The siren was growing closer now and I said, "Hey, sweetheart, why don't you go upstairs and put some real clothes on? Call me old-fashioned, but I'm the only one who gets to see you dressed like that."

"I will in a sec—Oh God, the Farnell is gone."

"Damn it, you're right," I said, peering into the curio cabinet.

Ash began to cry and I gathered her into my arms, not quite certain how to hold her with the pistol still in my hand. The Farnell Alpha teddy bear—one of the most celebrated mass-produced stuffed animals in history—had been my gift to her on our twentieth wedding anniversary. Standing approximately two-feet tall with embroidered webbed paws, and made from golden-brown Yorkshire mohair, the bear was created by English toy manufacturer J. K. Farnell.

Its fame derived from the fact that back in 1921, Allen and Dorothy Milne purchased an Alpha bear from Harrod's Department Store in London as a first birthday present for their son, Christopher Robin. Yes, *that* Christopher Robin. And that teddy bear, christened Edward, was the inspiration for A. A. Milne's *Winnie the Pooh* books.

I'd found our Alpha bear in an antique shop in the California wine country town of Sonoma. The blue and white label sewn to the left foot marked it as being sometime between 1926 and 1945, yet it was pretty much in pristine condition, with only a little wear on the embroidered black nose. It had cost almost two thousand dollars at the time, so there was no telling what it was worth now. Yeah, it was insured, but at the moment that was scant consolation.

Murmuring what I knew were useless words of comfort, I looked out the window and saw the sheriff's cruiser slue into our driveway. With its rapidly flashing blue overhead emergency lights, spotlight flicking to and fro, and wig-wagging headlights, the patrol car was lit up like a Las Vegas marquee.

I said, "Honey, the deputy is here. Why don't you go upstairs and get dressed? Once you come back down, then I'll go up and throw some clothes on too."

"Okay," Ash sniffled.

"And please take this with you." I handed her the pistol. "I'll be down in a minute."

Ash padded up the stairs as the cop car slid to a halt on the gravel in front of our house. A few seconds later, there was a series of sharp raps on the door, as if delivered with a heavy-duty police flashlight, followed by the shouted announcement that it was the sheriff's department. I recognized the voice. It was our friend, Massanutten County Sheriff Tina Barron, who'd responded from her home in town and beaten her deputy to the call. I turned the porch light on and opened the door.

Tina had a large black flashlight in one hand and a stainless steel 9-mil pistol in the other. She'd taken over the reins of the sheriff's department in the wake of the Holcombe scandal and was elected by a landslide the following month. Since then, she'd labored ceaselessly to redeem her agency's tarnished reputation and had even won over some of the local Neanderthals who thought that women had no place in law enforcement. Tina was maybe an inch taller than me and in her late thirties, with curly brunette hair, kind brown eyes, and a cherubic face. Having left home in a rush, she wasn't dressed in her brown and tan sheriff's uniform. Instead, she wore a gray-colored McGaheysville Volunteer Fire Department T-shirt, blue jeans, a gun belt, and tennis shoes. As she came into the house, I saw another sheriff's unit turn into our driveway.

"Are you guys okay?" Tina asked.

"Nobody hurt."

"What happened?"

"We woke up to find the house being burgled. The suspect fired one round at me when I tried to detain him and then he bailed. He was last seen turning westbound onto Cupp Road, driving a SUV with the lights off. It was too dark to see the plates."

"Did you shoot back?"

"No, but I wish I had. Look what the son of a bitch did." I nodded downward in the direction of the vandalized teddy bears.

"That's just vile. Where's Ash?"

"Upstairs, getting dressed."

Tina gave me a slow once-over and for the first time seemed to realize that I was attired in nothing more than a thin cotton nightshirt that only came down to mid-thigh.

I raised my index finger in warning. "Not a word. I'm a crime victim tonight."

"I couldn't say anything even if I wanted to . . . and believe me, I do." Tina gave me a wicked grin. "But it'll take me a couple of days just to process this sight. After that we'll have some fun."

"How Gandhi-esque of you."

A male deputy came into the house and Tina excused herself for a moment to brief the cop on what had happened and then send him back out on the road to look for the suspect vehicle. Meanwhile, Ash came downstairs, dressed in khaki shorts and a purple T-shirt. She and Tina exchanged hugs and then Tina turned to me.

"So, where were you when he shot at you?"

"There on the stairs." I pointed to the place. "And the bullet has to be someplace nearby because I heard it hit the wall."

The three of us went over to examine the wall near the stairs and Ash was the first one to spot the round bullet hole a couple of inches beneath the crown molding. It wasn't much more than a half-foot from where my face had been at the time of the shooting but, not wanting to further frighten Ash, I said nothing. However, I noticed my wife's gaze as it flicked back and forth between the bullet hole and the stairs, measuring the distance. She turned to give my hand a squeeze, knowing how close I'd been to death.

Tina shined her flashlight at the cavity. "Pretty big. What do you think, a forty cal?"

I squinted at the hole. "Maybe bigger. A forty-five, I think. We won't know for certain until we dig it out of the wall when you process the crime scene."

"Whatever the caliber, I'll give the suspect this: He was brave."

Ash and I gaped in disbelief at Tina. At last, I said, "What the hell are you talking about, Tina?"

Tina chuckled dryly. "You don't hunt Lyons with a handgun—even a Lyon wearing a pretty turquoise nightshirt. That's just suicidal."

Two

Nearly two weeks passed and the investigation into the break-in was as stalled as the 101 Freeway during rush hour. It wasn't for lack of effort on Tina's part. She'd done a fine job processing the crime scene, but the intruder had worn gloves, so there weren't any fingerprints to work with and if anybody in Massanutten County knew anything about the attack, they weren't saying anything. This was a little surprising, because we strongly suspected the burglar was a local resident and there is no such thing as a secret in a small town. Indeed, almost everyone in Remmelkemp Mill now knew that I wore a turquoise nightshirt to bed.

The only new and slightly useful thing we learned about the crime was that Tina and I were both wrong about the size of the bullet that made the hole in our wall. It was a .41 caliber magnum hollow-point and was fired from the sort of large-bore revolver popular with police agencies back in the 1970s. Since it was a seldom-used type of ammunition, Tina followed up on the clue, checking gun and hunting shops throughout Massanutten and adjoining Rockingham County to see if anyone had recently bought a box of mini-artillery shells, but she came up dry.

Worst of all, there was no sign of the stolen Farnell Alpha Bear. Tina sent crime bulletins to law enforcement agencies throughout Virginia containing a digital photograph of the bear that we'd taken when it was insured. At the same time, I searched the online auction websites daily to see if it would show up for sale and contacted teddy bear shops all over the Mid-Atlantic region, asking the merchants to be on the lookout for a hot stuffed animal. I also posted messages on several Internet communities catering to teddy bear enthusiasts, telling of how we'd been burglarized and asking collectors to be on the lookout for a Farnell offered for sale by anyone who seemed especially vague as to how it came into their possession. Yet our work didn't produce a single useful lead.

Once we accepted the bitter fact that the bear was probably gone for good, our life slowly returned to normal. Ash did an amazing job repairing the damaged teddy bears and, unless you knew where to look, you couldn't see where she'd whipstitched the pieces back together. Meanwhile, I put in a claim to our insurance company, patched the bullet hole in the wall, and resumed work on my newest stuffed animal.

It's still a little hard for me to believe that after all those years of investigating murders I now spend my days making teddy bears with my wife. Some of my old friends from the PD think I've lost my marbles, but I have a great life. Creating teddy bears is a lot more fun than homicide work and there's the added bonus that nobody calls at two-thirty in the morning to have me come look at a corpse.

I officially unveiled the new bear for Ash one Saturday morning in mid-June. Marginally dressed in a gauzy white cotton nightgown, Ash was curled up on the quilt-covered sofa. She held her morning mug of hot cocoa and was faced toward the window, watching the birds gathered around the hanging feeder in our front yard. Kitch lay sprawled at her feet, which provided me with an excuse to keep my distance, because I really didn't want to breathe in any of the tendrils of steam rising from Ash's mug. I don't usually keep secrets from my wife, but I've never told her that the smell of chocolate invariably causes a teeth-gritting jolt of pain through the bone and titanium hardware of my left shin.

The pain is a psychosomatic effect of my having been shot in front of the chocolate factory and shop in Ghirardelli Square a couple of years ago. My old partner, Gregg Mauel, and I had been in foot pursuit of a murder suspect when he opened fire on us. I went down and Gregg smoked the guy. Now, my mind automatically links the agony of the crippling wound with the aroma of chocolate and although I understand it's a Pavlovian response, I can't control it. However, I'm not going to let my malfunctioning brain interfere with Ash's morning cup of cocoa.

Limping down the stairs and into our tiny living room, I lowered my voice a half octave and solemnly announced, "The bear you're about to see is new. Only the name has been changed to protect myself from a copyright infringement lawsuit." Then I whistled the famous nine-note fanfare that opened the old cop television program, *Dragnet*.

She looked up and gave me an excited smile. "He's done?"

"I finished him last night. That's why I was so late getting into bed." I held up the twenty-inch-tall teddy bear I'd been slaving over for nearly two months. Doing my best Jack Webb impression, I then began a variation on the prologue that preceded most *Dragnet* episodes. I jiggled the bear slightly pretending it was the one actually speaking. "This is the city, Remmelkemp Mill—"

"Actually it's a village, sweetheart."

"Excuse me, but nobody ever corrected Sergeant Joe Friday."

Ash's eyes were bright with merriment. "That's because he was a stickler for facts. He wouldn't have called Remmelkemp Mill a city."

"Okay . . . this is the *village*, Remmelkemp Mill, Virginia. It's a quiet community, full of hardworking people, but some are deeply disturbed at the idea of a grown man making teddy bears. When they call the bear artist's manhood into question, that's when I go to work. My name is Joe Fur-day and I carry a tiny badge."

"He's wonderful. Let me see him."

"Hang on a sec. I'm not done yet." I resumed channeling the spirit of Jack Webb. "Saturday, June seventeenth. It was sunny and warm in Remmelkemp Mill. I was working the Day Watch out of the Rob-bear-y-Homicide Division."

Ash winced at the bad pun. You'd think she'd be accustomed to my wretched one-liners by now. I handed Joe to her and sat down on the couch.

Back when I embarked on my new vocation of making stuffed animals, I'd struck on the idea of making bears that honored the fictional cops from television and film. My first effort was Dirty Beary, a mohair tribute to Clint Eastwood, and it had won an honorable mention at the Har-Bear Expo in Baltimore. I'd since given the bear to Tina as an inadequate token of gratitude for saving Ash's life and mine last October. With Joe Fur-day finally finished, I had to decide which bear I was going to make next, Steve Mc-Bear-ett, from *Hawaii Five-O*, or Inspector Ursa-kin from the old Quinn Martin *F.B.I.* series.

Joe Friday was a retro cop, so I'd made Joe Fur-day as a retro teddy bear. He was created from gunmetal gray mohair, had an old-fashioned seam running up the center of his head from his black nose, hockey stick arms with charcoal-colored felt paw pads, and a slight hump at the top of his back. His face and muzzle were shaved, which accentuated the stern appearance of the black glass eyes and grimacing embroidered mouth. In my commitment to authenticity, I'd even considered putting a tiny Chesterfield cigarette in the corner of Joe's mouth, but eventually decided against it, because these days, where there's smoke there's ire.

The bear was dressed in a gray suit, white shirt, tie, and a gray fedora—the clothing Jack Webb wore in the 1950s version of the show, which in my opinion was far superior to the 1960s incarnation of *Dragnet*, when Joe Friday was less a hard-nosed cop than a grouchy soapbox orator. There was even a leather holster on the bear's right hip that contained an inch-long replica of a Smith & Wesson snub-nose revolver that I'd carefully carved from balsa wood and painted metallic black.

"God, I love him," said Ash as she examined the bear.

"Really?"

"Of course, really. Look at how your work has improved since October."

"Only because I had a great teacher."

"Thank you. Can I pour you some coffee?"

"That'd be nice."

She placed the bear on the end table and went into the kitchen. Returning, she handed me a mug of coffee and said, "So, are you going to show him to the guild this morning?"

Ash was referring to the new club she'd organized back in April, the Massanutten Teddy Bear Artist Guild. There were about eleven local women in the group, including

Tina, and they met monthly at our house to socialize over coffee, discuss bear-making techniques, and work on stuffed animals. The club was an instant success and, if you didn't factor my creations into the judging pool, the quality of the bears being produced was nothing short of amazing. Although, in fairness to me, most of the members had been sewing since childhood.

For instance, Tina had already begun to experiment with giving her bears articulated limbs so that they could be posed. Then there was our neighbor, Missy Hendrix, who made whimsical large-eyed bears in bold and unorthodox colors, such as magenta and orange. Another artist showing great promise was fortysomething single mom Holly Reuss, who had never created a stuffed animal in her life. Up until she'd joined the guild, her forte was making hand-sewn quilts. Yet under Ash's tutelage, the quiet and reserved Holly had recently produced a superb cream-colored mohair teddy that was evocative of a Steiff bear from the 1920s. I'll admit I was a little envious. It had taken me nearly half a year to make something that could be identified as a teddy bear at a distance of over ten yards and, in a few months, a number of the women were producing masterpieces.

The other problem was that, after a few guild meetings, I was beginning to feel as if I needed a major testosterone transfusion. The Civil Defense siren-quality warning sign was when I found myself offering informed opinions on mineral-based facial foundation powder and four-hundred-thread-count sheets during discussions at last month's meeting. Afterwards, I worried if I was on the log flume ride to becoming a SNAG—a Sensitive New Age Guy—and wondered what the next manifestation would be. What if it was a craving to watch *Divine Secrets of the Ya-Ya Sisterhood*? The notion was enough to chill my blood.

I cleared my throat. "Actually, I was thinking of passing on the meeting today."

"Suffering from an overdose of girl cooties?" Ash gave me a gentle smile that told me she wasn't surprised by my announcement.

"Not yours. Never yours. But . . ."

"You're the only man there."

"Yeah, and I'm really dreading another Saturday morning listening to Rita Olmsted talk about how hard it is to find an underwire bra that fits properly."

"That *was* a little over the top." Ash saw my lips twitch and showed me her palm, signaling me to remain silent. "And don't say it, because I can see the thought bubble over your head."

"I'm certain I don't know what you mean."

"Oh? Tell me that you weren't going to say that Rita is always over the top . . . of both cups."

I assumed a look of injured innocence. "I'm stung that you think I'd pay the slightest attention to another woman's bust."

"Sweetheart, I love you more than life and trust you implicitly, but you're also one-hundred percent heterosexual male, which means you're genetically-coded to look. The first time we met, I could have drawn a dotted line from your eyes to my cleavage."

"As a matter of fact, you could do that right now."

"You have a one-track mind." Ash smiled and shook her head in mock disbelief, yet made no effort to obstruct my view. "But getting back to the guild meeting. The fact that the women discuss those things in your presence is really a compliment. It means they're comfortable saying almost anything around you."

"I know and I like them and I'm not quitting the guild. I just need a month's sabbatical from the ladies."

"I understand and, by all means, take a break."

"Thanks, my love."

"So, what will you do instead?"

"I don't know. Maybe go over to the Brick Pit and visit with Sergei until the lunch crowd starts coming in. We can talk about your basic brainless guy stuff. You know: monster truck-pulls, guns, and which country has the best main battle tanks."

"Wow. Men have all the fun."

Pinckney's Brick Pit was a barbecue restaurant owned and operated by Sergei Zubatov, my best friend in Remmelkemp Mill. Sergei was a former Soviet military attaché—which is a nice way of saying "godless Commie spy"—who'd immigrated to the United States shortly after the collapse of the U.S.S.R. Regardless of his past, I knew him to be a good and honorable man endowed with a wicked sense of humor and blessed with the talent to cook some of the most delicious North Carolina–style barbecue you've ever tasted.

However, I might as well admit that I hadn't told Ash the entire truth about visiting with Sergei. That's because— irony of ironies—our macho meeting was going to include me showing him some fabric swatches. Back in March, he'd commissioned me to make him a teddy bear costumed in the dress uniform of a Red Army Guards Tank officer from the 1970s, which I assumed was his alma mater before transferring to the intelligence service.

I'd finished the bear last week and was proud of it. The bear stood twenty-two inches tall, was made from cinnamon-colored velour plush, had hockey stick-shaped arms, and the ears were spaced wide enough so that it could eventually wear a military hat with a visor. Seeking to capture something of the essence of Sergei's droll alpha-wolf personality in the stuffed animal's face, I'd worked long and hard on the placement of the brown glass eyes and used distressed wool yarn to create a reasonable facsimile of his gray handlebar moustache. But now I'd come to the hard part of the project, making the bear's miniature clothing. Soviet army officers from that era wore a dark green woolen uniform and I needed Sergei to look at the samples and tell me which of the fabrics looked the most authentic.

One of the most challenging things about making the bear was that I hadn't been able to consult with Ash. Apprehensive that he'd forever lose his status as the town's cheerful cynic if it became common knowledge that he wanted a teddy bear, Sergei had sworn me to a dark and bloody oath of secrecy about the project. I'd agreed to the original vow of silence, with the proviso that I'd have to tell Ash about the bear at some point. That's because she was bound to notice it and, more importantly, I was going to need her guidance when it came time to make the uniform, which was going to be a quantum leap forward in complexity over anything I'd thus far attempted. The idea of making the hat alone was giving me night terrors.

Then, a month ago, Sergei had suddenly insisted that I couldn't tell anybody—not even Ash . . . especially Ash, because he was concerned that my wife might accidentally reveal the secret to other members of the bear guild. The idea she would betray a confidence is just plain crazy and I told him so. Yet Sergei was so unhappy and earnest, I eventually surrendered to his quiet pleas.

That meant we needed a cover story and the best I could come up with was that I was making a bear modeled after legendary western lawman, Bill Tilghman. This temporarily explained the handlebar moustache, but I didn't know what I was going to say once Ash noticed that my ursine frontier marshal was wearing a Soviet Army uniform.

"So, can I show him at the guild meeting?" Ash asked as she picked up Joe Fur-day and made a slight adjustment to the shirt collar.

"Of course."

"And when you meet with Sergei are you going to discuss that bear you're making for him?"

I took a sip of coffee. "Uh . . . what bear?"

"The one with the gray moustache that looks exactly like him. It's excellent work, by the way—maybe your best. But why the cloak-and-dagger?" Her eyes met mine and I was relieved to see that she wasn't annoyed, just curious.

"I'm sorry, honey. It was Sergei's idea. He's completely paranoid over people finding out he wants a teddy bear dressed as a Red Army colonel."

"But I wouldn't have said anything to anyone."

"I told him that, but he made this huge deal over being concerned you might slip and unintentionally say something to the women in the guild."

"The guild?"

"Yep. Pretty strange, huh?"

For some reason, Ash looked amused with me. She said, "You're right. It doesn't make any sense."

"And I have to ask a huge favor. Please humor me and pretend you don't know anything about the bear."

"What Russian Army bear?" She batted innocent blue eyes at me.

Three

I had another cup of coffee and some breakfast and then went upstairs to shower and shave. When it came time to get dressed, I put on an avocado-colored polo shirt and a pair of blue jeans. It was already in the low-eighties outside and short pants would have been far more comfortable, but I won't wear them anyplace except at home. That's because I have a puckered nine-by-four-inch cruciform-shaped scar on my left shin that looks as if Freddy Krueger was my orthopedic surgeon. People don't mean to, but they stare, and although I hate to admit it, I'm too vain to ignore their pitying looks.

Ash came in to take her shower and I gallantly offered to wash her back with some of our fancy waffle cone–scented soap. She declined with a coy and slightly regretful smile, reminding me that I'd never once managed to wash her back without getting undressed and climbing back into the shower with her, which was true. Ordinarily, that wasn't a problem—in fact, it was usually the high point of our day—but the guild members would be arriving soon and there wasn't enough time. She gave me a long slow kiss, told me to go and have fun with Sergei, and promised that I'd have her undivided attention later that afternoon.

Slightly dazed, I went into our combination office, sewing room, and teddy bear dormitory to collect the fabric swatches and a couple of reference books on modern military uniforms that I'd gotten from the Rockingham County Public Library. Then Kitch began to bark happily and barreled downstairs. I looked out the window and saw Tina's bronze-colored minivan rolling up the driveway toward our house.

Going into the bathroom, I said, "Sweetheart, Tina's here."

Ash stuck her head around the shower curtain. "And now aren't you glad I didn't let you wash my back?"

"Truthfully?"

She chuckled and flicked some water at me. "Tell her I'll be down in a few minutes."

"And I'll see you later this afternoon. Love you, Ash."

"I love you too, honey. Have a good time."

I went into the bedroom to get my cane, stuffed the fabric samples into my left front pants' pocket, and went downstairs. Kitch stood panting before the front door, his furry butt wiggling with joy. Tina was a frequent guest at our home and our dog loved playing with her three kids. He was going to be disappointed when he discovered that she'd come alone.

I pulled the door open before Tina had a chance to knock—not that she actually could have, since her arms were loaded with a couple of large and partially completed teddy bears, a rectangular Tupperware box packed with what appeared to be homemade chocolate chip cookies, and two canvas bags filled with mohair and what I assumed were sewing supplies. All that, plus a black nylon shoulder satchel that probably contained the tools of her trade: gun belt, semiautomatic pistol, handcuffs, and portable police radio. Massanutten County being small and rural, there were never any more than two deputies on patrol. That meant that if they needed backup, it was up to Tina to respond, even if she was off-duty and dressed in coral Bermuda shorts, a white poplin camp shirt, and tennis shoes, as she was today.

"Hi, Tina. Come on in."

"Thanks, Brad." Noting that Kitch was staring intently at the minivan, Tina added, "Sorry, Mr. Kitchener, but no kids this time."

Kitch peered at the vehicle for another couple of seconds and then his head drooped. I shut the door and followed Tina into the living room. Meanwhile, Kitch had gone to his sulking spot, underneath the kitchen table.

"Ash will be down in a minute. She's in the shower." I pointed to one of three folding tables that Ash had erected before going upstairs. "Why don't you put that stuff here?"

"Sorry. I know I'm early. It's just that I really look forward to these meetings."

"There's nothing to apologize for. Here, let me give you a hand with that." I slipped the black satchel from her shoulder and put it on the table.

"Thanks," she said as she put the bags, bears, and cookies on the table. "And thanks also for teaching that class. The deputies really got a lot out of it."

"My pleasure. It's nice having a fresh audience for my old war stories."

The class had been an eight-hour instructional workshop on the fundamentals of crime scene analysis and evidence collection that I'd given to Tina and seven of her deputies a few days earlier. Back in March, Tina had hired me as a consultant to the Massanutten Sheriff's Department. My duties were to periodically provide training to the cops and to be available for call out in the event of a homicide. Thus far, my biggest challenge as a consultant was keeping the deputies awake when a class resumed after the lunch break. There hadn't been a murder or suspicious death in the county since the previous October, not that I was complaining. After twenty-five years in San Francisco, one of the most attractive aspects of our new life in the Shenandoah Valley was the absence of routine carnage.

Tina picked up one of her bears and pretended to study the frosted raspberry fur. "Also, I'm sorry to tell you that I don't have any new leads on your burglary and I'm going to have to suspend the case."

"Hey, you did the best you could. There just wasn't any evidence."

She looked up at me. "I know, but it makes me so mad that someone broke into my best friends' house, destroyed your property, robbed and nearly killed you, and then I couldn't catch the guy."

"Tina, you conducted a first-rate investigation. But sometimes it isn't enough and when that happens you just have to let it go. You can't take it personally, or you'll end up eating antacids like they're salted peanuts."

"I'm allergic to peanuts."

"But you understand the concept."

She gave me a wry smile. "I suppose. So, how do you learn to let it go?"

"Beats me. I dispense excellent advice, but that doesn't mean I've ever followed it," I said, grabbing the Xterra keys from a wicker basket on our kitchen counter.

"Hey, aren't you staying for the meeting?"

"No, I woke up this morning wanting to sing 'I Feel

Pretty' from *West Side Story*, which was a clue that I needed a little R and R from the ladies."

"This from the man that wears a prettier and more revealing nightshirt than anything I own."

"You know, that sweet face of yours hides a cruel sense of humor."

"Thank you."

"So, I'm going to visit Sergei."

"Tell him I said hi."

With the reference books tucked under my arm, I went outside and limped across the lawn toward the garage. I heard the shrill and challenging call of a blue jay from the towering, hundred-year-old chinquapin oak which stands between our house and the river. The wild sound was a call to pause for a moment, take a deep breath of the warm morning air, and remind myself that I actually lived in a place of such astonishing beauty. Looking eastward, on the opposite side of the languidly flowing Shenandoah, was a rustic panorama of rolling yellowish-green hay fields dotted with old white barns, farmhouses, and the occasional huge black walnut tree. The undulating plain stretched for about three miles, coming to an abrupt end at the base of the forest-covered Blue Ridge Mountains, which were cloaked in a thin mist this morning.

I climbed into the Xterra and headed toward town. At the end of our driveway, I turned right onto Cupp Road and then, shortly thereafter, made another right turn, west onto Coggins Spring Road. The highway was lined with a colorful mosaic of white Queen Anne's lace, blue chicory flowers, yellow buttercups, and orange daylilies, all swaying in the gentle southerly breeze. As I emerged from the river valley, Massanutten Mountain came into view, some five miles to the west. Massanutten is an eye-grabber from almost any direction. The peak is shaped like the prow of a

Victorian era–dreadnought battleship and it juts dramatically 2,100 feet above the valley floor. However, the mountain's splendor was marred by a rocky summit bristling with microwave towers and tall antennae and upper slopes scarred with brown ski paths.

A few minutes later, I arrived in downtown Remmelkemp Mill, population 117, and the governmental seat of Massanutten County. The village is named after my wife's family, whose ancestors settled this part of the Valley before the American Revolution. It's your archetypal Southern small town, with a graceful Greek Revival courthouse, volunteer fire department and rescue squad, post office, and church. The commercial district consists of a small grocery market; a hardware and livestock supply store; an old-fashioned barber shop where they offer a RBH—Regular Boy's Haircut—with electric clippers for five bucks; a veterinary clinic; a combination tractor repair and video/DVD rental store; Pinckney's Brick Pit Barbecue Restaurant; and, mercifully, no businesses with golden arches, yellow happy faces, or green mermaids as their corporate emblems.

Ordinarily, Remmelkemp Mill is as torpid as a lizard in cold weather, but it being a Saturday, there were some tourists in town . . . although I wasn't certain why. Other than the river, there were only two things in the immediate area that might qualify as tourist attractions—and only if you were suffering from terminal boredom. The first was a bizarre-looking Civil War monument consisting of a bronze sculpture of a musket between two water buckets, which looks like the magical broomstick in the "Sorcerer's Apprentice" sequence from *Fantasia*. The other was the Massanutten County Museum of History, located in an old plantation mansion a couple of miles south of town on Wheale Road. Bottom line: neither place was going to supplant Colonial Williamsburg as Virginia's foremost tourist destination.

I parked in the restaurant's lot and went inside. Pinckney's Brick Pit—the business's name transferred to Sergei when he bought the eatery—is an amalgam of two separate historical buildings. The front portion of the structure, which houses the unpretentious dining room, was a largish dog-run-style wooden cabin built in 1822 that served as the village tavern for several decades. With the exception of the overhead electrical lighting and air-conditioning ducts, it hasn't changed much since then. The walls are roughhewn logs, there's a flagstone floor, and the two front windows are composed of hand-blown panes of glass nearly two centuries old. A brick addition was crudely grafted to the rear of the cabin in 1896 and this is where the restaurant's kitchen is located.

Inside, the air was redolent with the delicious aroma of slow-cooking meat. Two archaic Bose 901 stereo speakers were suspended from the ceiling behind the counter and I heard, "Take the 'A' Train," being played by the Dave Brubeck Quartet—Paul Desmond's saxophone was always instantly recognizable. Most folks listen to country music around here, but Sergei and I share a passion for vintage jazz from the 1950s and '60s.

Lunch was still nearly two hours away, so there weren't any customers in the restaurant. That was fine by me, because it meant we could examine the fabric swatches without Sergei getting all twitchy and acting as if I'd compromised the Manhattan Project. He was behind the counter, carefully chopping cabbage with a cleaver for his famous cole slaw. Sergei is about my height with a full head of silver curly hair, a handlebar moustache of the same color, high and strong Slavic cheekbones, and grayish-blue eyes that glitter with merriment. As is often the case with genuinely dangerous people, he doesn't look it.

He looked up while continuing to gently rock the knife back and forth on the cutting board. "Good morning, Bradley. I didn't expect to see you here this morning. Isn't there a meeting of the teddy bear guild at your house?"

"There is and I went AWOL."

"Absent Without Official Leave? That hardly seems the sort of thing you'd do to that lovely wife of yours." Although Sergei was as Russian as ugly modern architecture, his accent was melodious Oxbridge English.

"Agreed. That's why AWOL stands for Ash Was Okay with me Leaving."

"That isn't AWOL. It's AWOWML."

"You *did* go to university. Anyway, instead of making teddy bears with the girls, I thought I'd come over and harass you."

"How fortunate I am."

"And I brought these." I pulled the fabric swatches from my pocket and tossed them onto the counter.

"For the bear?" Sergei's eyes lit up.

"Yep, he's done. Now it's time to make the uniform."

"You didn't tell anybody?"

"Nobody except the teddy bear guild."

Sergei glowered at me as the pace of his cleaver strokes slowed perceptibly.

"Relax, you paranoid spook. I haven't told anyone."

"Including Ashleigh?"

"No, the cover story seems to be holding," I lied.

"Good."

"But, if she discovers the truth, should I sedate her and smuggle her to Moscow in a steamer trunk?"

Sergei's jaw tightened.

"Oh, I know . . . I'll jab her with an umbrella that has a poisoned tip."

"Brad, please be serious."

"*Me*, be serious? You've initiated a full-on clandestine operation—complete with need-to-know security restrictions, code words, disinformation, and secret meetings—to protect the identity of a teddy bear. In some parts of the world, those behaviors would be considered prima facie evidence of mental illness. Even worse, you've got me keeping secrets from my wife, which I really don't like."

Sergei gave a tiny sigh. "I know and I'm sorry. It's just that . . ."

"You don't want to look like a sissy boy to the locals like I do."

"No, it's because the bear is . . . going to be a gift and I want it to be a surprise."

"A gift, huh?"

"And don't bother asking who the intended recipient is."

Suddenly, some things began to make sense, including Ash's surreptitious amusement over my puzzlement at Sergei's insistence that the secret be kept from the teddy bear guild. There were only two persons in the club that he knew well enough to give a gift to and it didn't make any sense that he'd commission me to make a bear for Ash. That left the other person, which now that I examined the matter, made perfect sense.

A smile spread across my face. "You dog. You're sweet on Tina. Does she know?"

Sergei pointed the cleaver at me. "No, and *I'll* stab you with a poisoned umbrella if you say anything."

"Don't tell me you're shy."

"No, it's just that the last thing she needs in her life right now is me." Sergei's tone was melancholy. "Between raising her children and all the hours she spends at the Sheriff's Office, she hasn't got any time for romance."

"Maybe so, but do you want to take the risk that someone else isn't going to be so considerate? Tina is a very special lady—a close second to Ash—and you're a damned fool if you don't say something sooner rather than later."

"I know."

"So, when were you going to give her the bear?"

"Her birthday is in August. Will you be finished by then?"

"I guess I'd better be." I held the two books up. "The only thing holding me up is the uniform. I've looked at these for hours and can't decide which shade of green is best. You'll have to pick."

He meticulously scraped the pile of cabbage pieces into a stainless steel bowl, put the cleaver down, and wiped his hands on a dishtowel. "Some sweet tea?"

"That would be great."

Mark Twain once wrote that only Southerners know how to make truly delicious cornbread. Having married a Virginian, I agree with that statement and would add that the folks south of the Mason-Dixon Line are also the un-challenged masters of making sweetened ice tea. It doesn't taste quite as good anywhere else, which presented a co-nundrum the first time I sipped Sergei's brew. His sweet tea was magnificent—perhaps as good as Ash's, although I'd never admit it—yet, Sergei was a Russian. When I finally asked him how he'd acquired this talent, he informed me that he *was* a Southerner, after a fashion, having been born in Georgia . . . the one that used to be part of the U.S.S.R.

Sergei poured us big sixteen-ounce glasses of tea, put a wedge of lemon in his, and we sat down at a table. I slid the books across the table and he opened the top one. He grunted and mumbled under his breath as he leafed through the pages while holding the fabric swatches up against the color photographs and illustrations. Meanwhile, I sipped my sweet tea and enjoyed the music, which was now Brubeck's jazz classic, "Take Five."

As last, Sergei slid one of the fabric swatches across the table. "This one."

"Evening Evergreen," I read from the tag.

"And you know that the tank officers—"

"Wore black shoulder boards. Yes, you've mentioned that just a few times. There's one thing I think I should tell you about the bear, however."

"What's that?"

"It has a silver handlebar moustache and kind of looks like you."

Sergei blanched. "Good Lord, I can't give *that* to Tina. It, it . . ."

"Would say that behind that Cossack façade, you're a great big teddy bear. Believe me, she'll love it."

Four

Our conversation came to an abrupt halt as the front door opened and Reverend Terry Richert, the new pastor of the Remmelkemp Mill Apostolic Assembly, entered the restaurant. He and his wife Karen had come to the Shenandoah Valley from Alexandria in February, filling the vacancy left by Pastor Marc Poole when he suddenly abandoned his flock. I'd only encountered Richert a couple of times since his arrival, yet he'd impressed me as a quietly good and earnest man. This tallied with the things we heard from Ash's folks and some of our friends who were members of the congregation. They told us that even though Richert was from Northern Virginia, which practically made him a Yankee, he was a fine pastor.

The clergyman looked to be in his mid-thirties, which made me a little jealous because I knew that he was actually a couple of years older than me. Richert was about five-foot-ten, 190 pounds, with glossy brown hair, and a flawless white complexion he was shielding from the sun with the sort of huge straw hat that lifeguards wear on the beach. He also appeared to have enough sunscreen smeared on his face and arms to provide skin protection even if the sun went nova. I wasn't dense enough not to realize the surplus of SPF was one of the reasons Richert looked so much younger than me. Although I use it religiously now, I didn't during my early years as a street cop, and not because Ash didn't buy me tube after tube of sunscreen. The reason was idiotic: I got tired of the stuff liquefying as I perspired, dripping into my eyes, and making them sting.

Richert removed his sunglasses and hat. "Hi, fellas. It's a little hot out there. Mind if I join you for a few minutes?"

"By all means, pastor. Sweet tea?" asked Sergei as he closed the book and gave me a look that told me to put the fabric swatches in my pocket, which I did.

"Thank you, and I'd be a lot happier if you guys just called me Terry."

I pulled a chair out. "Then have a seat, Terry."

"I'll get the tea. Lemon?" Sergei asked as he went to the kitchen.

"Please." Richert sat down and put the straw hat on a vacant chair.

"So, what brings you to the Ptomaine Palace?" I asked.

"I heard that," said Sergei.

"You were supposed to."

Richert seemed oblivious to the silly verbal exchange. He grimaced slightly and I could tell he was a little uneasy. "Actually, when I saw your truck in the lot, I thought I'd come over and talk to you."

"Really? About what?"

"It might be a rather sensitive topic."

"You mean like why you've never seen me at church?"

"No, no, nothing like that."

"Then what?"

When Sergei returned, it was apparent he'd noticed Richert's uncomfortable demeanor and realized that the pastor wanted to speak to me privately. He placed the glass of sweet tea on the table and said, "I'd love to sit and chat, but I have to finish the cole slaw and turn the chickens over one more time before lunch."

Once Sergei was back behind the counter, Richert said diffidently, "I don't want to dredge up any bad memories, but can we talk about my predecessor for a couple of minutes?"

"Marvelous Marc Poole? Why?"

"As you know, he was very popular and some members of my congregation haven't come to terms with the circumstances of his departure. It's causing a rift and I'm searching for a way to heal the situation."

"Interesting. Ash's folks haven't said anything about a problem. They like you."

"Thank you and it isn't surprising that they haven't heard anything. They come to church to worship God, not gossip in the assembly hall afterwards."

"I'm still not quite certain how I can help."

"I need information. I just want some sense of what actually happened."

I shrugged. "Then you should ask Sheriff Barron to let you read the crime reports. It's all a matter of public record."

"I did read the reports, but they didn't really answer the questions I have. That's why I think it's so important to talk to you."

"Sorry, my brain is apparently working at half-speed this morning. Why me?"

"Because the reports only tell about the crimes that Pastor Poole apparently committed. I'm interested in his . . . relationship . . . with you and your wife."

At first I couldn't figure out what he meant and then the nasty answer hit me like a Three Stooges–quality smack to the face with a cast-iron frying pan. "Oh, don't tell me. Some of your flock told you that I framed Poole because I was insanely and irrationally jealous of his purely Christian love for my wife."

"I won't lie to you. I've heard that."

"And apparently you think there might be at least a kernel of truth to that idiotic story, otherwise you wouldn't have come over here to talk to me about it." My voice grew a little icy.

"As a matter of fact, I *don't* believe it."

"Because?"

"He stole every penny from the church treasury when he became a fugitive. A man that would do that is capable of anything."

I relaxed slightly. "Then, why the interest?"

"I'm tired of the gossip. My sermon tomorrow morning is going to be about bearing false witness against your neighbor." Richert paused to take a sip of sweet tea. "I want to kill that ugly story once and for all, but I need some facts from you to do that."

"Information about Poole lusting after my wife?"

"If that's what happened."

"That's exactly what happened. But I want to be totally accurate: He never overtly tried to romance her, because I think he knew that she'd have broken his neck. But Poole was utterly infatuated with Ash."

"How could you tell?"

"Well, for starters, he was always showing up at our house to visit and I can assure you, he wasn't interested in saving *my* soul." I drained the remainder of the sweet tea from the glass.

"Then what happened?"

"Ever seen a kid ogling the dessert counter at a buffet? That's the way he looked at Ash's . . . uh, figure, when he thought no one was paying attention. Also, whenever we met Poole, he wanted to give her a big hug."

"You know, to play devil's advocate, hugs can be a sign of innocent affection."

"Ash thought that for a long time too. But us guys know that hugs can also be a sneaky way of snuggling yourself up against a woman's breasts—not that you'd ever do such a thing, padre."

Richert pressed his index and middle fingers against his lips to half-conceal a tiny smile. "Not that I doubt you, but how could you tell which sort of hugs they were?"

"Trust me, he wasn't expressing platonic love and part of the proof is that he didn't even try to deny it when Ash jumped ten-eight in his face about those hugs and the vicious lies he'd been spreading around town about her."

"Ten-eight?"

"A California police expression. It's the radio transmission code for being in service, but it's also cop slang for reading someone the riot act."

"What was he telling folks?"

"That Ash had invited Poole over to our house one afternoon while I was in Harrisonburg at a doctor's appointment. The inference was that she was eager—panting almost—for a little laying-on of his hands."

Richert shook his head in disbelief. "Oh, no. I'm so sorry."

"Ash was incredibly hurt and ashamed when she found out what Poole had said." I tightened my hand around the plastic glass until my knuckles were white. "Nobody does that to my wife. And my only regret is that the randy reverend was in the wind before I could come back to conduct a little amateur dental extraction work on his front teeth."

"Well, come tomorrow I hope the Remmelkemp Mill Apostolic Assembly can begin to make some amends for my predecessor's behavior." Richert reached over to pat me on the arm.

Although Richert meant well, I thought his idea of discussing the false tale in church was a bad idea. People love gossip, so even though the purpose of his sermon would be to debunk the slimy story, the result would be like shattering a two-liter glass bottle of olive oil on a kitchen floor. The mess would spread everywhere and take forever to clean up. But before I could voice my misgivings, the door opened.

A stern-faced Asian man paused in the entrance to slowly scan the restaurant's interior through mirrored Ray-Ban sunglasses. He appeared to be in his mid-thirties, was about five-nine, kind of stocky, and had longish black pomaded hair. He was dressed in business casual: navy slacks, a periwinkle polo shirt, and a blue blazer that bore a small red diamond-shaped pin on the right lapel. I also noticed that he kept his right hand tucked inside the jacket pocket, which made me a little wary. Twenty-five years as a cop had drilled a vital lesson into my skull: watch people's hands and be cautious around someone deliberately concealing them. Without thinking, I reached out and took hold of my cane, ready to use it as a club.

Apparently deciding the restaurant was safe, the man— who was obviously either some sort of bodyguard or had watched far too many old Warner Bros. gangster films— held the door open for someone outside. That's when I got a look at his left hand and went into full alert mode. The tip of his pinky finger was gone. Most people wouldn't realize the significance of the missing bit of bone and flesh, but I did.

Mistaking my suddenly attentive demeanor for anger, Richert said, "I hope I didn't say anything to upset you."

"No, I'm just fascinated by the guy doing the bad George Raft impression," I murmured, and nodded toward the door. "And it would be best if you didn't turn around and stare at him."

"Why?"

"I'll tell you in a minute."

A second Asian man entered the restaurant and walked up to the counter, followed closely by his bodyguard. The newcomer looked to be in his mid-fifties with a plump physique, receding hairline, black hair that shone like the sealing wax nose of an antique Steiff teddy bear, and eyes invisible behind silver-framed eyeglasses with gray transition lenses. His clothing was similar to his bodyguard's, including the diamond-shaped lapel pin. However, he wore a twill shirt with a button-down collar. The man sniffed the air appreciatively, nodded, and softly said something to the younger man, who nodded and quietly barked, "*Hai.*"

I casually turned to take a quick look out the window at the parking lot and saw there was a third member of the group outside. The man was also Asian, was dressed in a brown business casual ensemble, and wore the inevitable mirrored aviator sunglasses. He stood in the scorching sun, smoking a cigarette next to a huge Hummer H3, an already ugly vehicle made even harder on the eyes because it was painted the same color orange as a highway roadwork sign. The Hummer had a Virginia license plate and I set myself to memorizing the alphanumeric sequence.

Sergei appeared through the doorway at the back of the kitchen and I guessed he'd been turning the chickens over in the brick pit. He looked first at the two newcomers and then glanced at me. Noticing my rigid posture and the cane in my hand, Sergei realized something was amiss. Calling out a cheerful, "Good morning," he strolled over to the cash register, where I knew he kept a loaded .45 semiautomatic pistol under the counter.

"Good morning and excuse me, please." The older man bowed slightly and spoke in Japanese-accented English. "We are visiting your wonderful country and have become lost. Please can you tell us how to get to the Massanutten Museum of History?"

"My pleasure. All you have to do is make a right turn from the parking lot and go down the road until you come to the stop sign. That's Wheale Road." Sergei pointed in the proper direction with his left hand while nonchalantly putting the right under the counter.

"Wheale Road." The older man nodded and looked at his bodyguard to make certain he understood.

"Turn left there and go about two miles through the farmland. You'll see the sign for the museum on your left. It's in a farmhouse."

"Thank you." The older man took another approving sniff. "And it is unfortunate that our schedule doesn't allow us to have lunch here. The food smells very good."

"Thank you. Perhaps some other time."

"Perhaps. Thank you, again."

The pair left the restaurant, the bodyguard walking backwards to keep an eye on us.

Once the door shut, I said, "Can I borrow a pen?"

Sergei tossed me a ballpoint pen that looked as if it had been stolen from the post office. Pulling a napkin from the metal dispenser, I wrote down the license number. Then I joined Sergei and Richert at the window. We watched as the Hummer backed up and then turned westbound onto Coggins Spring Road.

"Well there's something you don't see everyday in Remmelkemp Mill," I said.

"What's that?" asked Richert.

"Three Yakuza—Japanese gangsters. I wonder what they want at the museum."

Five

"Yakuza? You're sure?" asked Sergei.

"Certain enough to be worried about what the tough guy had in his jacket pocket," I said.

"How could you tell who they were?"

"The first *tip-off* was that the bodyguard was missing the first joint from his left pinky finger."

Sergei rolled his eyes and shook his head.

"Why is that important?" Richert asked.

I said, "It's a common injury among Yakuza foot soldiers."

"Why?" Richert asked.

"Because in the Yakuza, giving someone the finger isn't just an expression. If a gangster screws up or embarrasses his organization, he chops off a finger joint and delivers it to his boss as a form of atonement. It's called *yubizume*."

"I'd call it insane." Richert looked a little dazed. "How do you know so much about this?"

"About nine years ago, I worked a murder that was connected with gun-runners who were selling weapons to a Japanese organized crime group. U.S. Customs loaned us one of their experts on the Yakuza and he allowed me to read a bunch of their intel files. They're bad hombres."

Richert noticed Sergei nodding in agreement and asked, "But how do you know about them?"

"Oh, I don't really know anything more about them than what I've seen in the movies," Sergei blandly replied while shooting me a brief knowing look. "If you get the chance, you should rent the DVD of *Black Rain*."

Richert turned to me. "What else made you think they were Yakuza?"

"It's hotter than a freaking sauna outside and the two that came in and the guy outside were all wearing sports jackets. That was probably to conceal their clan badge tattoos—most Yakuza are covered with them."

"What about the matching lapel pins?" Sergei asked.

"Good obs. They're extremely significant," I said walking back to the table and sitting down. "If memory serves, that diamond-shaped pin is the emblem for the *Yamaguchi-gumi*, one of the biggest crime cartels in Japan . . . or at least they were back in the nineties."

"Wait a minute, are you saying that these crooks actually advertise who they are?" Richert's jaw hung half-open in amazement.

"Yeah, they're proud of it. The Yakuza party line is that they are the lineal descendents of the samurai—a bunch of big-hearted Robin Hoods who look out for the little guy, which is complete BS. They aren't called the Japanese Mafia for nothing."

"How so?"

"They're major players in the Asian narcotics trade, world-class extortionists, and also operate prostitution rings that keep the girls in virtual slavery. What would Maid Marian say? However, unlike the Mafia, they are extremely visible in Japanese society."

"So, what are those guys doing here in America?" asked Richert.

"It looks like the *oyabun*—the boss—is on vacation. Although why you'd travel halfway around the globe to visit Remmelkemp Mill is beyond me."

"Actually, I was more interested in *how* they got in. Isn't Customs supposed to stop criminals from entering the country?"

"They are. But if the boss and his entourage don't have criminal records and he's also buds with some high-rollers in the Japanese government, which is probably the case, our Customs people don't really have a choice about letting him in."

"So, what are you going to do with the license number?" Sergei went back behind the counter.

"I'll give the info to Tina after the teddy bear guild meeting. As hard as she works, there's no point in disturbing her. Those guys are suspicious-looking, but they weren't committing a crime."

"And the museum director would have a coronary if he found out you'd prevented three paying customers from visiting," said Sergei.

"Yeah, I imagine it gets a little lonely there, which is a shame, because it's a neat little museum."

Richert grabbed his hat and sunglasses from the table. "Well, thanks for the excitement. But I've got a Summer Bible Camp session to teach, so I guess I'd better be going."

"Before you do, I've got to tell you I'm a little worried about you bringing up those stories about Ash in your sermon. I appreciate your intentions, but it could be that you're just going to give those vicious lies a second life."

"Oh, I wouldn't be too concerned about that." Richert slipped the sunglasses on and gave me a toothy and strangely chilly smile. "You see, up until now these folks have been preached to by Reverend Doctor Jeckyll. Tomorrow morning, they're going to meet Pastor Hyde. Please tell Ashleigh I said hello."

I pushed myself to my feet to shake hands with him. "Thanks, Terry."

"Happy to be of service." Richert put his hat on and went out the door.

After Richert left, I went over to the counter and said, "I like him."

Sergei pulled a fat head of cabbage from the refrigerator and shut the door with his foot. "Me too. So, *that's* what the solemn conversation was about?"

"Yeah. That damn story Poole made up about Ash having the hots for him. Apparently it's still in circulation at the church."

"Really? Nobody had better repeat it in my presence." Sergei slid a small carving knife into the bottom of the cabbage. His wrist flicked and a large chunk of vegetable stalk went flying.

"Anyway, Terry said he's going to bury the story once and for all, tomorrow at church during his sermon."

"Isn't he the optimistic fellow."

"I suspect there's a full supply of old-fashioned fire-and-brimstone behind that affable persona."

"I hope so, for your sake." Sergei discarded the knife, picked up the cleaver, and split the cabbage with a single deft blow. He looked up at me. "But as far as I'm concerned, there's only one thing to be done with people who refuse to keep their mouths shut. It's what we used to do back in Russia."

"What's that?"

"Send them to the Gulag."

I chatted with Sergei for about another hour. The topics shifted from West Coast jazz to handguns and finally to high-speed driving techniques, which led to Sergei telling a funny story about how, back in 1981, he'd driven the 250 miles from a hotel in the center of Paris to Geneva, Switzerland, in less than three hours. I couldn't help but notice that he didn't mention *why* he'd covered that distance at such an insane speed, but I figured it had something to do with the fact he was working as a Soviet spy at the time.

"God, I loved that Mercedes. What an autobahn burner," Sergei said dreamily at the end of the tale. Then his expression became sad. "I was a young daredevil then, and now . . . What business does an old man like me have in even considering courting a woman of Tina's age? Bradley, please tell me the truth. Am I being a fool?"

"Not at all. And what's this crap about being an old man? You look younger than me."

"That's no comfort. Lenin's corpse in Red Square looked younger than you."

"That's true, but look who I get to go to bed with *every* night."

He grunted. "Point taken."

"Look, we're more vain than women about our age, we just keep it a secret. It took me a long time to realize that Ash truly doesn't care how old I look and I can't imagine Tina being worried about that in a man either. My guess is she's looking for someone who first and foremost can be trusted."

"I suppose you're right."

"So, remember you're still the same man who frightened French drivers. Ask her out to dinner. What's the worst she can say?"

"No."

"Or ask whether she'll have to drive or if you'll both ride the assisted living facility's shuttle bus."

"Bradley, you are an unalloyed bastard, but thank you."

The lunch crowd began coming in shortly before 11:30 and the restaurant began to get busy. I said good-bye, grabbed the books, and went out to the Xterra. Sitting behind the wheel, I wondered how I was going to waste the next thirty minutes, because the guild meetings lasted until noon. Then curiosity got the better of me. I started the SUV and a few seconds later was driving southbound on Wheale Road, on my way to the Massanutten Museum of History. All I planned to do was drive by the place and see if the Hummer was still in the parking lot, because I didn't want to waste Tina's time sending her on a wild goose chase on her day off.

Really.

Not buying it, huh? Okay, the truth is, if the Hummer was still there, I planned to go Code Five on it—that is, place it under surveillance—and call Tina on my cell phone to tell her about our intriguing visitors. As a general rule, when Yakuza mobsters come to the United States, they visit places such as Hawaii, California, Las Vegas, New York, and Atlantic City. They gravitate toward casinos, nightclubs, and posh hotels, not insignificant museums in the middle of nowhere in the Shenandoah Valley. The fact is I was dying to know what the three gangsters were doing here.

I was soon driving through lush pastureland. On one side of the road, the field was dotted with grazing black and white Holstein cattle and on the other a tractor chugged along, cutting hay. Off to the southwest and far away, white cumulus clouds were blossoming over the Allegheny Mountains, which meant that before the day was done we might have thunderstorms. The road took me up a gentle hill and through a dense copse of maple, oak, white pine, and scrubby cedar. On the other side of woods, there was a green sign with white lettering by the side of the road. It read, MASSANUTTEN COUNTY MUSEUM OF HISTORY, and there was a white arrow pointing leftward. I turned onto the macadamized driveway and started up the lane toward an old brick mansion, which was about a quarter of a mile away.

I knew from my one previous visit to the museum that the house and its outbuildings were the last vestiges of the sprawling Bromhead Plantation. During the Civil War, the estate had produced wheat, tobacco, and three sons who'd given their lives for the Confederacy. The fortunes of the Bromhead family slowly declined after the war and the farm began to shrink as it was sold parcel by parcel until all that remained was the mansion. After the last Bromhead died in the late 1940s the dilapidated old house sat vacant until 1976, when Massanutten County bought it and began the long task of renovating it and converting it into a museum.

The house was magnificent. Surrounded by majestic oak trees, the large two-storied mansion was constructed in the Federal-style from red brick that had grown darker with the passage of some two hundred years. The front of the building was adorned with four white Doric columns, which supported a protruding gable with an oval window. A large and sun-faded Confederate stars-and-bars flag hung lengthwise from the second-floor porch railing, flapping languidly in the warm breeze above the white double front door. On opposites sides of the house were two brick outbuildings: the stables and the slaves' quarters.

There was no sign of the Hummer. The only car in the gravel parking lot was a salmon-colored Toyota Camry and it was parked in a spot marked with a RESERVED sign, which meant it must belong to the museum director. Unfortunately, I wasn't surprised the lot was empty. From what I'd heard, attendance had been sparse for years and the facility was becoming such a money pit, due to the cost of insurance, employee wages, and maintenance expenses, that a few months earlier the county board of supervisors had been forced to take drastic measures. They'd slashed employee work hours and wages, and reduced the days of operation to just Saturday and Sunday.

I pulled into the handicapped space near the steps leading up to the front door and turned off the engine. The museum was so small that the *oyabun* and his two bodyguards had probably already finished their tour and gotten back on the road. If so, there was a slight chance they might have asked the museum director how to get to their next destination. I decided to go inside and find out.

Grabbing my cane, I climbed from the truck. The air was so hot and muggy and fragrant with newly mown hay it felt as if I were breathing warm vegetable broth. I heard the *prit-tee, prit-tee, prit-tee* call of a cardinal from one of the nearby oak trees and then the sound was drowned out by the grinding whine of the air conditioning unit starting up. Walking up the sidewalk toward the house, I paused to look at the unkempt flowerbeds. There were hollyhocks, coneflowers, and stargazer lilies and all looked wilted and water-stressed, probably because the sprinklers were only turned on once or twice a week. I noticed a fresh white cigarette butt lying on the ground near a parched dianthus plant. Probably one of the Yakuza had discarded it, as it wasn't likely there'd been any other visitors today.

I slowly mounted the steps and went inside the mansion. Despite the air conditioner, it wasn't much cooler indoors.

The museum director probably had orders to set the thermostat at 80 degrees to save on the electrical bill. Once inside, I took my sunglasses off and gave my eyes a few moments to adjust to the dim light. I stood at one end of the main hall, which stretched straight through to the opposite side of the building. The building was equipped with an audio system on which I could hear Stephen Foster's, "Old Dog Tray," being picked mournfully on a banjo.

The door to my right led into a room that housed the admission desk and gift shop. I went inside the gift shop, my footfalls echoing hollowly on the hardwood floor. There was no one inside, yet I paused before pushing further into the house. The souvenirs themselves belonged in a museum rather than as merchandise in a gift shop. There were commemorative ashtrays, Bromhead Plantation whisky shot glasses, coonskin caps, little Confederate uniforms for the kids, complete with the Rebel battle flag on the gray cap, wood and metal toy muskets that looked like real guns, and age-yellowed plastic packages of color photographic slides of the mansion and grounds. It was like stepping back in time about sixty years.

Going back out into the hallway, I called, "Hello! Is there anybody here? Hello?"

There was no response, so I decided to wander through the museum until I found the director. I crossed the corridor and went into a room I knew contained an eclectic collection of household artifacts. There were old quilts hanging from the walls; ceramic clay jugs and kitchenware produced by local artisans in the early nineteenth century; rag dolls; a collection of antique tools on a hand-hewn wooden table; an old Edison gramophone; and my favorite pieces, the two antique teddy bears sitting on the elegant marble mantle above the fireplace. Both were valuable collector's items.

On the left side of the mantle was a slightly frayed and obviously much-loved bear that had been produced by the Bruin Manufacturing Company of New York in about 1907. Bruin bears are very rare, because the company went out of business almost immediately. The bear had distinctively wide shoulders, was made from shaggy golden mohair, had black shoe-button eyes, and a smile embroidered in black thread. I also knew that there was an imported German "growler" inside the stuffed animal, which made a growling sound when the bear was tipped over. Hey, I'm not much at catching felons anymore, but I do know my antique teddy bears. I still haven't decided whether that should make me laugh or cry.

The bear on the opposite side of the mantle was even more amazing and precious. It was an original Michtom, made sometime around 1904. Unless you're an arctophile, which is just a fancy way of saying a teddy bear devotee, the name likely doesn't mean much, but it means a lot to collectors.

Back in 1901, Clifford K. Berryman, an editorial cartoonist for the *Washington Post*, drew a cartoon featuring President Theodore Roosevelt refusing to shoot a captured bear cub. The following year, Rose and Morris Michtom of New York City produced a toy bear inspired by the cartoon. This stuffed animal was known as "Teddy's Bear," which later became simply the Teddy Bear. Michtom bears from the early years are rare and extremely valuable.

The museum's bear was about eleven-inches tall, made from beige mohair plush, with widely spaced ears and the classic triangular face of an initial Michtom effort. It had a frayed nose made from embroidered black thread, a sweet little embroidered smile, elongated and slightly curved arms, and felt paw pads. Unlike many expensive historical teddy bears, this one had a cute face. I'd have liked it even if I didn't know that it was worth thousands and thousands of dollars.

Reluctantly turning from the bears, I resumed my search. There was another doorway leading directly into what looked like a dining room and I headed in that direction. I hoped I'd find the museum director there or in some other first-floor room, because I really didn't want to tackle the stairs with my bum leg. Entering the dining room, I stopped abruptly. Now I knew why my calls had gone unanswered. The museum director was lying flat on the dining room floor, motionless and crushed beneath an enormous oak china cupboard that had fallen on him.

Six

Only the very top of the man's head and his right hand were visible . . . and a fair amount of blood. I hobbled over as quickly as I could to check and see if the guy was still alive, although I didn't think it was very likely. There was broken glass on the floor, which I assumed was from the cupboard's doors, or perhaps glassware that had been stored inside, and I heard and felt it crunching underfoot. I gingerly knelt down and took the limp wrist in my hand. The flesh still felt a little warm, but I couldn't find a pulse. The guy was "sneakers-up," a cheerful cop expression that meant he was dead. I bent my head over to look at the man's face and inhaled sharply. It had been a long time since I'd seen something that bad.

I stood up and backed away from the body. It may sound heartless, but my first thought wasn't to call 911 for the rescue squad and EMTs. The guy was dead and nothing was going to bring him back, but I knew that the rescue squad would feel duty-bound to yank the victim from underneath the cupboard and rush him to Rockingham Memorial Hospital, a well-meaning yet useless gesture, which could also irrevocably contaminate the death scene and perhaps destroy vital evidence. Welcome to the wonderful world of death investigations. True, this appeared to have been an accident, but murder couldn't be ruled out, especially since the Yakuza had said they were coming to the museum.

Looking down at the body, a horrible thought occurred to me: if this was indeed a homicide, could the murder have been prevented if I'd telephoned Tina immediately about the Yakuza? I was deeply ashamed to think that my misjudgment might have cost a man his life.

I pulled the cell phone from my pocket and speed-dialed our home number.

Ash answered, "Hello?"

"Hi honey. Sorry for disturbing your meeting. Is Tina still there?"

"No need to apologize. We wrapped up a little early and everyone's gone but Tina." Hearing my troubled tone, she asked, "Are you okay?"

"I'm fine, but I've stumbled onto a DB." The initials stood for Dead Body.

"What? Where?"

"At the County History Museum on Wheale Road. It looks like a huge china cupboard fell on the museum director."

"What are you doing there?"

"It's kind of a long story and I need Tina out here ASAP. There's a slight chance we're looking at a one-eighty-seven here." I used the California penal code section for murder.

"I'll put her on."

A moment later, Tina got on the phone. "Hey Brad, what's up?"

"Sorry to ruin your Saturday off, but you need to come to the history museum right away. The director is dead."

"Franklin Merrit?"

"Yeah, he's crushed beneath a china cupboard."

"And you don't think it's an accident."

"I'd probably classify it as one if it weren't for the fact that, about ninety minutes ago, three Yakuza came into Sergei's place and asked for directions to the museum."

"*Yakuza?* Are you sure?"

"Almost positive."

"Why didn't you call me?" Tina sounded distraught.

"They weren't breaking any laws, and I figured it could wait until the guild meeting was finished. Turns out I was wrong. Sorry," I said, realizing how lame and inadequate the words sounded.

"If I'm going to be out there in an official capacity for any length of time, I guess I'd better go home and change into uniform."

"And you don't want to be wearing shorts while you do this. There's broken glass all over the place. Besides, our victim isn't going anywhere. I'll secure the scene until you arrive. Can I make a suggestion?"

"Of course."

"Don't put this information out over the radio unless you want reporters from the Harrisonburg newspaper and TV station there."

"Good idea. I'm on my way. Here's Ash."

A second later, Ash was on the line. "Sweetheart, you sound bad. Are you all right?"

I turned away from the body. "No. If this guy was murdered, it's partly my fault. When I was at Sergei's, three Yakuza came in, wanting to know how to get to the museum. I should have called Tina then, but I didn't."

"Brad honey, were these Yakuza committing any crimes?"

"No. They looked like they were on vacation."

"So, how could you have predicted what they were going to do? And for that matter, if they were going to come all the way from Japan to commit a murder, is it logical to think that they would ask local witnesses how to get to the scene of the crime?"

"I hadn't thought of that."

"So, maybe it *was* an accident. Look, hang on and we'll be there in a minute."

"What are you talking about?"

"Sweetheart, my days of sitting at home while you work a homicide case are over. I'm coming to the museum with Tina. Bye, love."

"Hang on. I'm not so certain Tina is going to allow you to come here."

"Why not?"

"Because you don't have any official standing to be at a potential homicide scene."

"Don't worry about that. I'll see you in a little bit."

Ash disconnected from the call and I stood there marveling yet again that I was married to such a magnificent woman. You like mysteries? Try solving this one: We met back in 1977 in Northern Virginia when I was finishing up my enlistment as an army battlefield intelligence specialist at Fort Belvoir and she was an English major at George Mason University. Intelligent, witty, gorgeous, and as sweet as a Honey Crisp apple, Ash could have had almost any man on a campus full of future doctors, lawyers, and business executives. But she picked me, and it still doesn't make any sense. Later, during my career as a cop, Ash chose to be a stay-at-home mom to raise our kids, who are now both successful adults. She'd carried me through the bad days after the shooting and then moved on to create amazing award-winning teddy bears. She's incredible, all right. But who could have predicted that she'd also have a talent for investigating murders?

Yet she does. Sure, we'd discussed my murder cases, back when I still worked for SFPD, but that doesn't explain her amazing natural abilities as an investigator. Since my retirement, we'd found ourselves involved in two different homicide inquiries, and Ash's insights into human nature had played a pivotal role in solving those crimes. So, I didn't object to her assistance; in fact, I welcomed it if she could overcome Tina's objections. My only concern was that she'd never encountered this sort of gruesome death scene, and I wasn't sure how she'd react to the sight.

I decided to wait outside on the porch. It was bloody hot outside, but inside hadn't been much better. Besides, I couldn't run the risk of visitors accidentally coming across the body and contaminating the crime scene by, say, being sick on the floor. I've witnessed that sort of thing happen; talk about tainting a crime scene. So I stood on the porch, leaning against one of the Doric columns and occasionally swatting uselessly at the flies.

Then I heard the crackle of vehicle tires on gravel and a dust-covered blue Isuzu Trooper rolled into the parking lot and parked next to the Toyota. The driver got out, slammed the car door shut, and began walking very quickly toward the house. I reflected on how sad it was that Mr. Merrit wasn't alive to see two groups of tourists coming to his museum in a single day. I vaguely recognized the man as someone I'd seen around town, but I couldn't remember his name.

He was about my height, tan and lean, with a sandy moustache and longish blond hair that hung wispily from beneath a rust-colored Virginia Tech ball cap. He was wearing denim shorts, tennis shoes with white socks, and a baggy canvas-colored sport shirt. Between the cap and the big Oakley sunglasses he wore, you couldn't see much of his face, but I guessed his age as late twenties or early thirties. He also smelled like an ashtray.

As he mounted the steps, I said, "I'm sorry, sir, but you can't go in."

"But I work here."

"Really? And you are?"

"Hey, how about you tell me who you are first." The man put his hands on his hips.

"My name is Bradley Lyon and I'm here as an authorized representative of the Massanutten County Sheriff's Office."

"You don't look like a deputy."

"I'm not. I'm a civilian consultant for the department. Sheriff Barron will be here in a few minutes and then she'll decide whether or not you can go in."

His head dipped for a second and I could tell he was looking at my cane. "Now I know who you are. You're that retired California cop that married Lolly's daughter."

Ash's dad was Laurence Remmelkemp, but he was known universally as Lolly. Lolly and Ash's mom, Irene, live just over the hill from us.

I nodded. "Correct. But I still don't know who you are."

"Neil Gage. I'm the museum's curator, and these days, the janitor, and groundskeeper." He stuck out his hand and I shook it. Gage glanced over at Merrit's Toyota. "Frank's car is here. Is he okay?"

"I'm afraid not."

Gage yanked his sunglasses off. "What's wrong?"

"Mr. Merrit appears to have suffered an accident. I found him."

"Did you call the—oh, my God. Is he dead?"

"I'm sorry to say he is."

"How did it happen?"

"It's still a little early to tell."

"What the hell does *that* mean?"

"That it could have been an accident, but Sheriff Barron has to make sure."

"But I can't even go in and see him?"

"Were you a friend?"

"Yeah. He was a good guy."

"Then, believe me, you don't want to see him the way he is now."

Gage appeared pale beneath his tan. "I can't believe this. He left a message on my answering machine a little while ago. That's why I'm here."

"He asked you to come here?"

"Yeah, he said there was some sort of problem at the museum and that I should get over here right away." He looked down at the floor of the porch. "Nothing else. I was out mowing my yard when the call came in."

"How long ago did he leave the message?"

"I don't know. An hour ago . . . maybe forty-five minutes."

Right about the time the Yakuza would have been here, I thought. "And he wanted you to come right over. Did he sound stressed or upset?"

"Maybe a little annoyed. So I jumped in the truck and came here."

I'd already fumbled the ball big time once this morning, so maybe that made me overly suspicious, but Gage didn't look to me as if he'd just been mowing the lawn in the summer heat. He wasn't sweaty and his socks were pristine white, when his shoes and shins should have been covered with fragments of grass. Then again, he might have gotten cleaned up before responding to Merrit's summons.

"You live far from here?" I asked casually.

"A couple of miles. I live up by Port Republic," Gage replied.

Port Republic was a small community south of the museum, so Gage's use of the word *up* told me he was a Shenandoah Valley native. The valley runs downhill from the southwest to the northeast, so locals refer to any trip southward as going *up*.

"So, did Mr. Merrit have a family?"

"A wife and a son. The kid might miss him, but the only thing she'll be crying about is that there won't be any more paychecks."

"That sounds kind of cold."

"You've obviously never met his wife. Frank was a full-time history professor up at the community college in Waynesboro, but that didn't pay enough as far as she was concerned. That's why he took a second job as the museum director."

"Considering the way the county slashed the museum's funding, it can't have paid much either."

"No, but I guess every penny counted. And it *did* get him away from Marie."

"He told you about all this?"

Gage gave me a sad smile and waved at the almost empty parking lot. "We had plenty of time to talk." There was a long pause and then he shook his head angrily. "Damn. If only I'd gotten that message sooner. Maybe . . ."

"Trust me, it wouldn't have changed anything. But there is a way you might be able to help. You said you're also the groundskeeper here?"

"Yep, which goes to show how valuable a history degree is on the job market these days."

I nodded sympathetically. "So, would you have been responsible for making sure the lawn and flowerbeds were clear of rubbish?"

"Yeah."

"When did you last do that?"

"Last night. Call it five-thirty. It was after I finished my other job."

"Which is?"

"I work part-time at Wal-Mart. It helps pay the bills."

"Working two jobs can be tough. Was there much trash?"

"No. Hardly anyone ever comes here. Still, Frank had a thing about keeping the yard tidy."

"Which means you wouldn't have left any candy wrappers or cigarette butts on the ground, right?"

"Absolutely not." Gage furrowed his brows. "Why do you ask?"

I shrugged. "It's just a routine question. I'm just trying to get some background information on how things operated here."

I heard the low hiss of a car speeding down Wheale Road, coming from town. Seconds later, a Sheriff's patrol car rolled to a stop in the museum parking lot and the vehicle's trunk popped open. They'd made excellent time considering that Tina had stopped at home to change into her brown and tan uniform and put on her gun belt. Ash went to the trunk and retrieved a metal camera case. Then the two women started up the sidewalk to the house. I was relieved to note that Tina didn't look angry, so I assumed Ash had temporarily rescued my reputation by talking to her on the way over. Ash gave me a quick smile, but was obviously trying to remain in the background.

Ordinarily, I call Tina by her first name, but since this was a formal setting, I said, "Sheriff, it's good to see you."

"Has anything else happened since you called?"

"Just the arrival of Mr. Gage here. He said that Mr. Merrit called and left a message on his answering machine about forty-five minutes ago asking him to come to the museum."

Tina looked at Gage. "Did he say why?"

"No, ma'am. I came right over, but he wouldn't let me into the museum." Gage nodded in my direction.

"Which was exactly what I wanted Mr. Lyon to do. I realize that you're concerned, but we need to follow our policies and procedures."

"I just want to know what happened."

"So do we, Mr. Gage. With that in mind, can you please wait outside here for a few minutes until we take a look?"

"I'll be right here." Gage sat down on the steps.

I followed Tina and Ash up the stairs. Once we were inside and the door was shut, Tina said, "The Medical Examiner is en route, ETA maybe thirty minutes. Where's the victim?"

"In there." I hooked a thumb in the direction of the dining room. "But before we go and say howdy, we should do a quick search of the rest of the building."

"For suspects?" Tina cocked an ear toward the ceiling.

"More likely, other victims. I didn't hear anything to make me think that someone else was here. If you want, I can check the kitchen while you clear the second floor."

"Sounds good. I'll meet you back here in a second," said Tina, heading for the staircase.

I gave Ash's hand a squeeze. "Honey, on the off-chance there's a homicidal maniac hiding in the kitchen, why don't you wait here?"

"Okay, but be careful."

"Count on it."

I went down the hallway, slowly pushed the door open, and went into the restored nineteenth-century kitchen, which smelled faintly of cinnamon and cloves. There was a cast-iron stove; a large pinewood table covered with

antique cooking utensils; an authentic butter-churn, and
thankfully, no dead body sprawled on the floor. Upstairs, I
could hear the squeak of wooden floorboards as Tina
moved from room to room. By the time I returned to the
foyer, Tina was coming downstairs, taking the steps two at
a time.

"Nothing suspicious upstairs."

"The kitchen was clear too," I said.

"That's a relief. Oh, and before we get too busy and I
forget to mention it, did you know that your wife is the
most stubborn person in North America?"

"Really? I hadn't noticed."

"Uh-*huh*. I explained that this was potentially an official homicide investigation and that she couldn't come
with me."

Ash smiled serenely. "And I told her that I'm your investigative assistant and that we do everything together."

"True, and I *am* glad you're here, but our partnership
might not be much fun this time, honey. This is a messy
one."

The smile faded a little and Ash shot a nervous glance
down the main hallway. "Not that I don't think I can't handle it, but just how messy are we talking here?"

"The guy's been smashed like a bug and there's quite
a bit of blood."

"I'll be okay."

"I know, but if you do start feeling . . . queasy . . ."

"Don't worry, I'll leave."

I said to Tina: "Before I show you the body, there's
something else I think I should mention. Maybe I'm
overly-suspicious, but Mr. Gage told me that he was mowing his lawn just before rushing over here and there's not
so much as a blade of grass on him."

"Interesting."

"I thought so, but it might not mean anything."

"And he says Merrit called him—what, almost an hour ago now?"

"Yeah, which would have been right about the time the Yakuza were here."

"If this turns out to be a murder, we'll need to get a copy of that message and check the time it was received on his answering machine." Tina grimaced. "In the meantime, I guess we'd better get started."

I led Ash and Tina to the dining room doorway and heard both women inhale sharply. There was a new song playing on the museum's audio system: "The Camptown Races," which added a surreal touch to the scene. Ash looked a little green around the gills, but she didn't turn away, which meant that she was well on her way to handling her first gruesome homicide scene better than I did, twenty-six years ago. I'd lost my breakfast.

Pointing with my cane, I said, "We can't see his face, but it's safe to assume he's sustained major blunt force trauma. I suspect that's where most of the blood came from, although there's the possibility he also got cut by the broken glass."

"Probably abdominal injuries too," said Tina.

"Yeah, that cupboard's made from real wood, so it's damn heavy."

I heard Ash swallowing and saw that her face had grown paler. Touching her hand, I said, "Honey, why don't you move back a little bit and get the camera out."

I could tell she was prepared to rebuff the offer, but she surprised me. "All right. Thanks. It's a little much."

"No, it's freaking awful and you're reacting like any normal person would."

Ash backed away and I heard her put the camera case down on the floor.

Tina shook her head in puzzlement. "I don't understand how this could have happened. What was he doing?"

"And I've got another question," said Ash.

I turned from the body and saw that Ash was near the fireplace mantle. "What's that?"

"Why are these antique teddy bears in the wrong spots?"

Seven

"Haven't they always been up there on the mantle?" I asked.

"Yes, but the placards show that the Michtom teddy is where the Bruin bear should be and vice versa." Ash stood on her tiptoes and squinted at the bears. "And it looks as if they were switched recently. You can still see the marks in the dust."

"I hate to admit it, but I stopped for a second to look at them on the way in and never noticed that."

"So, is the fact the bears have been moved important?" asked Tina.

"Too soon to say. Probably not, even though they are worth thousands."

"You're kidding."

"Oh yeah, together they're probably worth eight—"

"Nine thousand dollars," Ash cut in. "They're both over a hundred years old and extremely rare."

"And they're just sitting on a museum shelf without so much as a DO NOT TOUCH sign to keep people away? That's crazy." Tina shook her head in disbelief.

"Maybe, but from what I've heard, the museum's turned into a money pit and security systems are expensive," I said.

"Besides, I'll bet Mr. Merrit thought they'd be safe. He probably assumed no one would guess that a teddy bear could be so valuable," said Ash. She gave the teddy bears one last admiring look and then knelt down on one knee to open the camera case.

I went over to join Ash. "Still, we'll make a note that the bears were recently moved, although I'd be a lot more concerned if they were gone or . . . destroyed."

Noting my contemplative tone, Tina said, "You don't think this might be connected with the burglary at your house, do you?"

"Unlikely. On the other hand, what are the odds that you're going to find teddy bears at two separate felony crime scenes here in Massanutten County?"

"But these weren't stolen or damaged. I just don't see a connection."

I nodded. "Yeah, you're probably right. And now we really need to get started with the pictures before the ME gets here."

"Sorry about the camera. It's so old it almost belongs here with the other antiques, but it's all we have," Tina said.

Ash handed me a vintage Canon AE-1, 35-millimeter with a 50-millimeter lens and I was pleased to bump into a relic from my early days as a homicide detective. Solid and pretty much foolproof, the AE-1 was the same model camera I'd first used to photograph murder scenes back in the 1980s. Nowadays most big law enforcement agencies employ digital cameras for CSI work, but I'm old-fashioned and favor using film anyway.

"The camera is fine." I popped the back door of the Canon open and said to Ash, "Honey, could you give me one of those rolls of thirty-six exposure ASA two hundred and the flash unit?"

"Coming right up."

"And how would you like to be my scribe?"

"What do I have to do?" Ash cast a quick nervous glance toward the dining room and I could tell she wasn't eager to take a closer look at the crushed man.

"It's easy. All you have to do is stay here and write down what I say as I take each picture."

"Anything else?"

"Sleep with me if you want a good employee evaluation."

"Brad!" Ash's cheeks were pink, but she was smiling.

"Tell me Tina, seeing as I'm a consultant for Massanutten County, under the personnel rules was that just sexual harassment, even if we're married?"

"Don't get me involved in this." Tina held up both hands in surrender.

I snapped the camera shut, manually advanced the film, and handed Ash my cane. "Then I guess it's time for our glamour shoot."

Starting from the doorway, I began snapping a series of orientation photographs and calling out the picture information to Ash. Next, I carefully worked my way into the room, moving crabwise around the dead man and taking shots from a variety of angles. With each step, I felt pieces of broken glass crackling beneath my shoes.

I was taking some photos of the ceiling when Tina said, "Ash, you said the mantle was dusty?"

"You could write your name in the dust. This place is so filthy it's embarrassing."

I turned and saw Tina bent forward at the waist peering down at the body. "Notice something?"

"Maybe. Somebody cleaned some of the dust on the side and back of this cupboard . . . right about at the spot where you'd grab it to pull it over."

Ash said, "Could it be where Merrit grabbed the cupboard?"

I squinted at the wood. "No. This surface has been wiped clean. There aren't any finger marks."

Tina nodded. "And his hands are in the wrong place. Is it possible that someone intentionally tipped this thing over onto him?"

"That's sure how it looks." I leaned forward and took a picture of the wood that had been wiped clean. "But I think we also have to assume Merrit was already unconscious or otherwise incapacitated, because I can't imagine he just stood there and let the suspect send the cupboard crashing down onto him."

"My God, who could have done something so brutal?" Ash asked.

"Jack the Tipper?" Both women groaned and I mimicked the sound of a brief snare drum and cymbal flourish. "Thank you, thank you. I'll be here all weekend. Try the veal."

Although I was trying to be funny, I was anything but lighthearted. The bad pun and third-rate comic shtick was nothing more than camouflage to disguise the fact I was feeling guilty as hell. If I'd called Tina when I'd first seen the Yakuza, Merrit would probably still be alive and maybe even dusting the dirty museum. The only thing I felt I could do to at least partially redeem myself would be to work this case with a laser-like intensity. Which would mean a nonstop commitment to following up all the leads quickly, because it's a fact that most murders are solved in the first seventy-two hours. At the same time, I wondered if I was physically up to the challenge.

"Eh?" Lost in my thoughts, I didn't hear what Tina had just said.

"I said, I guess I'd better get some more deputies out here."

"Sorry, I was gathering wool. Yeah, we'll need a cop for perimeter security and a couple more to search the yard for evidence."

"And maybe one more to start canvassing the farms along this road for witnesses."

"Good idea. We're also going to need crime scene tape, bags and envelopes for evidence packaging, and a latent print kit."

"I've got that equipment in my car."

"Excellent. And at some point we're also going to need a big van or pickup truck."

"Why?"

I jerked my head in the direction of the cupboard. "So far as we know, *this* is the murder weapon and once we've wasted our time dusting it for latent prints, we'll have to collect it as evidence."

Tina's jaw sagged open. "Our evidence storage room isn't big enough to hold that thing. How long do we have to keep it?"

"I don't know how it is in Virginia, but in California you maintain custody of homicide evidence forever."

"Wonderful." Tina jerked a notepad from her breast pocket and made a note.

I tried to push myself to my feet, but found that my crippled left leg wouldn't cooperate. Struggling to keep the annoyance out of my voice, I said, "Honey, I'm kind of stuck. Could you give me a hand getting up?"

"Of course." Looking away from the body, Ash put her arm out for me to pull up on. "Your leg is hurting, isn't it?"

"A little, but I'll be okay."

"And I'm here to help. Remember that."

"I will and thanks. Tina, there's one other thing I need. Does the department have a forensic vacuum cleaner?"

Tina gave a short bitter chuckle. "Not this fiscal year."

"Then we'll have to collect all this broken glass and china the old-fashioned way: with a broom and dustpan." I motioned with the camera at the floor. "Whoever pushed this thing over will have glass and ceramic fragments imbedded in the soles of his shoes. We'll want all the debris for comparison samples."

"I'm assuming we need a brand new broom and dustpan."

"That would be best."

"Well, I think the budget can absorb that. Changing gears, tell me about these Yakuza."

I gave Tina brief descriptions of the trio and pulled the napkin I'd used as notepaper from my pants pocket. "This has got the license plate of their vehicle. It was an orange, newer model Hummer."

Tina took the napkin. "And they wanted directions to the museum?"

"Yeah and they left town westbound on Coggins Spring Road, headed in this general direction."

"But nobody actually saw them here, right?" Ash asked.

"No, but we have to assume they arrived."

Tina said, "You think I should issue an APB on the vehicle?"

"It's your operation, but I wouldn't. Not yet." I noticed that Ash had wandered over to take a closer look at a quilt hanging from the wall near the teddy bears. "We may have damned suspicious circumstances here, but until the

ME confirms that this was a murder, it's not actually a crime."

"I'll go ahead and run the plate now," Tina said. "At least we'll know the owner's name."

"Huh!" said Ash.

"What's wrong, honey?" I asked.

"I don't know if there's anything wrong. It's just this quilt. The sign *says* it came from the collection of Martha Zinzer."

Tina and I went over to the quilt. It was a "Log Cabin" design with a dingy and jarring color mix of calicos and solids that reminded me of a vagrant's mismatched clothing. Think "Joseph's Coat of Murky Colors" and you'll have the general idea. There was a typewritten index card thumb-tacked to the wall saying that the quilt was circa 1875 and had been donated by Martha Zinzer.

"I'm not following," I said.

"Martha lived across the river from us. She had an amazing old quilt collection, but she died about five years ago."

"So, she doesn't need a quilt, especially if she went someplace where it's very warm."

"Don't even think about saying that in front of Mama. She'll beat you like a rug."

Ash wasn't exaggerating. I remembered the first time she'd formally introduced me to her family as her fiancé. Ash's mom, Irene, had waited until we were alone and then quietly promised to skin me alive with a carving knife if I ever hurt her daughter. Don't get me wrong; I love Irene and I think she loves me, but even though she's seventy-one years old, I wouldn't cross her.

I said, "Sorry. You were saying?"

"Mama and Martha were lifelong friends and Mama told me that Martha donated all her antique quilts to the quilt museum over in Harrisonburg."

"Maybe she also donated one to our museum," said Tina.

"Maybe." Ash picked it up by the corner and pinched the fabric between her fingers. "This is supposed to be an antique, but . . . I don't know. I've handled plenty of old quilts—I grew up in a house full of them—and this one just doesn't feel right."

"How so?"

"For starters, the batting is too stiff."

"You think it's counterfeit?" I asked. The growing popularity of antiques had resulted in a flood of bogus artifacts. Many of them quite cunningly wrought and then artificially aged.

Ash flicked the fabric away with her thumb. "I'm no expert, but if this was for sale at an antique shop, I sure wouldn't buy it."

"Even if it is a fake, is it something we want to waste our time on right now?" Tina glanced at her watch. "The ME will be here soon."

"Good point. I'll finish up the orientation photos."

Tina pulled her portable radio from her gun belt. "And I've got to get the extra deputies over here and talk to Mr. Gage before he decides to leave. Ash, could you give me a hand bringing in the rest of the equipment?"

"Of course."

I said, "Oh, and don't forget to tell Gage not to mess with his answering machine. We're going to want to record that message and confirm the time the call came in."

"Got it."

While the women were gone I finished photographing the body and then took overview shots of the other first floor rooms, including what I assumed was Merrit's tiny office cubicle behind the admission desk. There was a guest book on the admission desk and I checked to see if the Yakuza had been thoughtful enough to sign in before offing the museum curator. But I was out of luck. The last entry was from the previous Saturday when a husband and wife from Lizton, Indiana—wherever that was—described the museum as "very fascinating," which told me that Lizton must be a mighty boring place.

Still, I took a photograph of the mostly blank page and made a note to collect the guest book as evidence. Doing that would reduce the chances of the killer's future defense attorney claiming that the "real murderer" had signed the guest book and the lazy, inept, or corrupt investigators had overlooked it. As a defense attorney once reminded me, all he needed to do was convince one credulous juror that the cops had botched the case and he'd win a tactical victory for his client with a hung jury.

The front door opened and Ash came in, a bunch of manila evidence storage envelopes in one hand and the fingerprint kit in the other. "Tina will be here in a second. The Medical Examiner just arrived and they're talking out front."

"Good. I'm done here."

"And I have two bits of bad news. First, Tina ran the plate and the Hummer is registered to Olympus Rent-a-Car."

"Not surprising. What else?"

"Mr. Gage told Tina that he's already deleted the message from Merrit."

"Great. Is Gage still here?"

"No, Tina told him he could go. Why?"

"If his phone is one of the newer models, it'll keep an electronic log of all incoming calls. We may not have the message, but at least we'd know when Merrit made the call." I glanced over my shoulder into Merrit's office. "Then again, we might not have to go to Gage's house to confirm the time. Let's check Merrit's phone."

Setting the camera down, I went into the cubicle and Ash followed. Merrit's cordless telephone had a built-in answering machine, but the LCD display indicated there were no messages. I examined the specialized function buttons and finally found the one I was looking for.

"Can I borrow your pen for a second?"

Ash handed it to me. Even though the chance of recovering a usable latent print from the tiny button was effectively nil, there was no point in giving a defense attorney another area to attack as sloppy crime scene processing. I used the tip of the pen to press the button. The LCD display showed that the last call was made from the phone at 11:14 A.M.

Ash bent over to look and leaned her head against mine. "Four-three-four area code. That's on the eastern side of the Blue Ridge."

"Can I have the notebook, please?" She handed it to me, I wrote down the phone number, and then pressed the button with the pen again. "Eleven-twelve A.M. and five-four-oh area code; a local call."

"I'm pretty certain that's Gage's number. Tina has it in her notepad."

I wrote the number down and pressed the button again. This time the LCD display indicated an outgoing call on Friday night to the same number in the "434" area code.

"So, just two phone calls this morning," said Ash.

"Two minutes apart and about a half hour after the Yakuza left Sergei's. Obviously, something happened here before Merrit bought the farm." I wrote down the second number along with the time of the call.

"I wonder who the other person was he called."

"That's something we'll have to follow up on once the ME finishes with the body."

"Were there any incoming calls?"

I pressed an adjoining button with the pen and the small screen revealed the caller ID information. "This morning at ten-oh-three from . . . Franklin Merrit. Someone must have called from his home."

"Any others?"

"That's the only one for today." From outside, I heard footfalls on the wooden steps and the muted sound of Tina's voice. "And this is something that's going to have to wait for now, because we're going to be needed back at the body."

"Oh, goody." Ash gave me a brave smile.

"Hey, you're doing great. I'm very proud of you." I reached over to squeeze her hand. "But if you'd be more comfortable, you can stay in the other room and I'll tell you when to make notes."

"No, I insisted on coming, so I'm going to tough this out."

"I wouldn't expect anything less from you."

Tina came back into the museum, carrying a plastic fishing tackle box that contained the evidence collection equipment. Behind her was a woman with a briefcase whom I assumed was the commonwealth's regional medical examiner. Through the open door, I could see that Tina had roped off the porch with yellow crime scene tape.

Tina did the introductions. The ME's name was Dolly Grice and she had the sort of pretty face that was as much a reflection of a sweet disposition as it was of physical beauty. As we gave her the basic facts about the discovery of the body, she finished a granola-covered nutrition bar.

"Sorry for inhaling this thing, but I've been on the dead run—literally—since early this morning," Grice explained. "It's a beautiful June day, so everyone is out dying. Once I finish here, I've got a suicide up in Augusta County. A woman threw herself in front of a freight train near Waynesboro."

Ash winced at the image. I said, "She must have had a one-track mind."

"Or was in *training*," Grice added with a small chuckle. Macabre humor is one of the ways that cops and medical examiners deal with the horrors of the job.

"Or had a real loco motive."

"You're a sick puppy, Brad. I like you. Let's see your corpse."

We went into the dining room. Grice pulled a small digital camera from her briefcase and took four photos of the body from different angles. Replacing the camera, she said, "I need this cupboard off him so I can take a better look."

"We're going to need gloves," I said.

"Right here." Tina produced several pairs of latex gloves from the evidence kit and passed them out.

Once we'd pulled the gloves on, Tina took one side of the top of the cupboard and Ash and I grabbed the other. The thing was as heavy as a refrigerator. Grunting with effort, we lifted and I cringed as antique dishes and serving pieces tumbled from the interior, bounced off Merrit's body, and shattered on the floor. We set the cupboard back on its feet and shoved it up against the wall.

Remember the final scenes of *Who Framed Roger Rabbit?* when Christopher Lloyd, as Judge Doom, got flattened by the steamroller? That's pretty much what Merrit looked like, plus a lot of blood. And if the museum director popped back to his feet like Judge Doom did in the movie, I'd be the first one out of the museum, despite my gamy leg. He was somewhat shorter than I'd remembered— maybe five-foot-seven with a medium build. Although his face was battered, Merrit wore that stupefied and sleepy expression so often seen on the faces of those overtaken by sudden death, and by regular viewers of the E! Network.

Grice dropped into a crouch near the body, took another couple of photographs, and then began her preliminary examination. She checked the front pockets of Merrit's Dockers and pulled out a set of Toyota car keys, which she handed to me. Then, shifting the body slightly, she removed the dead man's brown leather wallet, which I also took. Looking inside the billfold, I found Merrit's Virginia driver's license, a miscellaneous assortment of credit cards, and $42 in paper currency. It didn't look as if anything had been taken.

Grice continued her search. She pulled a white business card from the breast pocket of Merrit's pale blue shirt, scrutinized it for a moment, and said, "Here's something odd."

I took it from her and my heart sank. It was a slightly larger than normal business card, made from top quality paper stock, and bore the name "Mitsuru Ota" in English text beneath what was obviously the larger version of his name in Japanese lettering. There was a telephone number at the bottom of the card, but I could tell from the unfamiliar numeric sequence that it was probably to a phone in Japan.

"What is it?" asked Tina.

"Proof that I really screwed up." I handed the card to Tina. "This confirms the Yakuza were here."

"Ota?"

"More than likely it's the boss's name. As far as I understand Yakuza etiquette, he'd be the only one handing out a calling card. You're going to want to contact either the FBI or customs and have them run it."

Ash leaned over to look at the card. "But if they were going to kill him, why would they give him a business card first? That seems kind of stupid."

"You're right, honey, unless they had some sort of business with Merrit that unexpectedly got violent. Otherwise, the boss would never have given him the card."

"And once he was dead, they didn't stop to get the card back. They just made tracks," said Tina.

"Which brings us back to question number one: Why the hell did they come here in the first place?"

As we talked, Grice continued to examine Merrit's injuries. Finally, she said, "Well, he's in no shape for a Christmas card picture, but the major visible injuries appear to have been caused postmortem."

I bent over to look. "I see what you mean. There's almost no bleeding from the facial trauma. So where'd all the blood come from?"

"Can you hold his head up a little, please?"

It was going to be hell getting back up off the floor from my knees, but one look at Ash and Tina told me that the last thing they wanted to do was pick up a dead man's noggin. Once I was on the floor, I carefully lifted Merrit's head and Grice began to run her fingers along the back of the skull.

"J-E-L-L-O," Grice sang the old jingle from the dessert commercial. "Okay, the cause of death is blunt force trauma causing a depressed skull fracture. He was whacked in the back of his head with something generally circular in shape."

"Could it have been caused by his head being slammed against the floor by the cupboard?" I asked.

"No, it's high on the skull—wrong angle and a definite downward impact." She leaned back and began to remove her gloves.

I carefully lowered the head to the floor. "How big an indentation are we talking about?"

"About the size of, say . . . a beer bottle. And it was quite a powerful blow. It killed him instantly."

"So, he was murdered and then the cupboard was dumped on him to disguise the crime."

Grice stood up. "That's how it looks to me."

"Is there anything you can tell us about the suspect?"

"Just two things, right now: The killer was taller than the victim and he *really* wanted Mr. Merrit dead."

Eight

As we went back into the adjoining room, I mentally replayed my brief encounter with the Yakuza. To the best of my recollection, Ota and the posturing thug who'd come into the restaurant had been about the same height as Merrit. However, the bodyguard who'd remained outside with the Hummer had definitely appeared taller than the other two gangsters.

I bumped my fist against my forehead. "My brain just isn't working today."

"What's wrong?" Ash asked.

"There was one Yakuza who was taller than Merrit. He stayed outside, smoking a cigarette, while Ota and the other guy came inside."

"And that's important because?" said Tina.

"When I first came up the walk, I noticed what looked like a fresh cigarette butt in the flower bed out in front. We'll want to collect it as evidence."

"Isn't that kind of a long shot?"

"Yeah, but right now we're clutching at straws and if he did toss that butt we might be able to make him on DNA. That would at least put him as far as the front porch."

"I don't understand why that's important," said Ash.

"We've got three possible suspects, but we don't know who or how many actually entered the museum."

Tina nodded. "And with no other witnesses, they could claim that they met Merrit in the parking lot and gave him the card there."

"Yeah. The cigarette butt might show that at least one of the Yakuza got out of the car."

Grice put her camera into the briefcase. "Sorry, but I've got to run. The transportation crew will be here in a little while and the autopsy will probably be Monday. I'll have someone call to confirm the time."

I said, "Doctor, can you answer a couple of quick questions before you go?"

"As long as they really *are* quick."

"It takes a lot of force and something damn solid to smash in a whole section of skull. Any ideas as to what the suspect might have used besides a beer bottle?" I said. Out of the corner of my eye, I saw that Ash was leaning forward to look at something on the hand-hewn wooden table just to our right.

Grice looked thoughtful. "Assuming it was a weapon of opportunity, I'd say it might have been—"

"A large hammer!" said Ash. "Come and look at this!"

We all gathered around the table, which was being used to display a large collection of nineteenth-century tools. There were old saws, a couple of wood planers, a rust-pitted pry bar, augurs, and about a half-dozen antique hammers all lined up in neat rows. Ash pointed at an oversized hammer with an age-stained wooden handle and a blunt steel head that reminded me of a miniature sledge.

"What do you notice about that?" Ash asked.

I'm a typical guy with the standard myopic male view of just what constitutes tidiness, so it took a couple of seconds for me to figure out what she was talking about. Then I saw, and said, "Every other tool is covered with dust, except the hammer. In fact, it's been wiped completely clean."

"Could it be the murder weapon?" Ash's eyes were bright with excitement.

"Let's have Dr. Grice take a look."

Grice bent low and cocked her head to peer at the hammer. "The striking surface is the right shape and about the same size as the injury. Unofficially, that's probably what killed him, but I can't say for certain until I do some precise measurements at the postmortem."

"When will you know for sure?" Tina asked.

"I'm assuming you'll send it to the state crime lab for processing?"

I said, "Yeah. Even though it's been wiped down, there's still a good chance they can recover some physiological trace evidence."

"The crime lab is just down the hall from our facility. Once they're done with it, I'll take a look and call you with my results." Grice snapped her briefcase shut and headed for the front door. "And now I've really got to go. See you Monday."

Once the ME was gone, Tina said, "Even with the hammer, we don't have probable cause to make an arrest."

"No, but I think we've got enough suspicious circumstances to at least start tracking the Hummer."

"And how are we going to do that?"

"It's a premium GM product and a rental, so you can bet it's equipped with the OnStar tracking system. The problem is that Olympus is probably going to want a search warrant before telling us anything."

"Do we have enough to get one?"

"Yeah, but it'll save us several hours of writing an affidavit if they cooperate."

"I'll give them a call." Tina's portable radio squawked and she answered it. The call was from one of the deputies, advising he'd just arrived at the museum. Slipping the radio back into the holder on her gun belt, she said, "Allsop's here. What should we have him do first?"

"He's CSI-trained, right?" I asked.

"Just back from the school."

"Then have him begin photographing and processing the exterior of the building. Do you need me to come out and show you where the cigarette butt is?"

"No, I'm certain we can find it."

"Good, and tell him to come and get me if he has any questions. Meanwhile, I'm going to finish up with my evidence collection in here before they come for the body. Do we have an ETA on the broom and dustpan?"

"Allsop has them. I'll bring them in. I'm hoping to witness something I've never ever seen."

"What's that?" I asked.

Tina gave me a wicked grin before leaving the room. "A man actually sweeping the floor."

I retrieved the camera and finished photographing the body. Then I inserted a new roll of film and shot a series of pictures of the tool collection and the hammer. As I worked, Ash quietly wandered the museum, pausing at the different displays, and eventually returned to the antique teddy bears.

She said, "Call me crazy, but I think these teddy bears are somehow involved."

"Sweetheart, there's no evidence that you're insane, other than your decision to marry me." I took a final picture of the hammer and lowered the camera. "In fact, this investigation would be dead in the water here if it weren't for you. Tell me what you're thinking."

Ash took a deep breath. "Well, I've checked out all the exhibits in this room and, if we're using dust as an indicator, the only things that were disturbed were the bears and the hammer. Nothing else seems to have been touched."

"The teddy bears are worth a hefty chunk of change, but it's pretty *fur*-fetched to think that three Yakuza would come halfway around the world to steal stuffed animals. Hell, their airline tickets would have cost more than the bears are worth."

"But they didn't steal them, even if they killed Mr. Merrit. I couldn't understand how they might be connected, until I started thinking about that supposed antique quilt."

Suddenly, I understood what she was suggesting. "Do you think these teddy bears are bogus?"

"It's worth looking into. Teddy bear collecting is extremely popular in Japan. There's even a very nice teddy museum near Tokyo."

"Somehow, I don't see those three mobsters as teddy bear collectors." Then a far more obvious theory occurred to me and my jaw sagged. "But, what if some other Japanese collector, who wasn't too particular about legalities, hired the Yakuza to come here to get a Michtom and a Bruin bear—"

"And they stole the originals and replaced them with fakes." Ash cut in. "But Merrit saw them and tried to interfere and they killed him."

"However, that presumes the Yakuza were able to enter the museum carrying two good-sized counterfeit teddy bears without Merrit noticing." I glanced from the body toward the doorway leading to the foyer. "That's possible, but not real probable."

"Okay then, maybe they came here to steal the bears but realized they were phony."

"How could they tell a counterfeit antique teddy bear from the genuine article? I spend more time around teddy bears than most guys and I sure couldn't."

Ash shrugged. "I don't know, but we might learn a little more if I could handle them."

"Let me take some pictures of them and the mantle and then you can examine them." I leaned over to kiss her on the cheek. "Hey beautiful, you're turning into one heck of a homicide detective."

"That's because I have an excellent instructor."

I took some overview photos of the bears and then dragged a Shaker-style wooden chair over to the fireplace, intending to stand on it to snap some overhead shots. Or at least that was my objective, but with my bum leg you'd have thought I was making the final ascent of the Matterhorn while suffering from an acute case of vertigo. I finally had to swallow my pride and ask Ash to climb up on the chair and take the photos, which she did while I held a small flashlight at an oblique angle to bring out the marks in the dust.

Afterwards, she hopped from the chair, handed the camera back to me, and grabbed the Michtom teddy with her gloved hands. I kept quiet as she scrutinized the bear's face and then slowly turned it to examine the seams. Next, she squeezed the teddy's torso fairly hard and lifted the bear to sniff its tummy.

Her nose wrinkled and she said, "This is a first-class re-production. Whoever made this did a great job artificially aging it, but there's something you just can't fake."

"What's that?"

"The smell. Most of the early teddy bears were stuffed with excelsior."

"Sort of a wood fiber, right?"

"Right." She sniffed the bear again. "Old excelsior stuffing gives antique bears a very distinctive aroma and this one doesn't smell as it should."

"Well, of course not. It has an embroidered nose, so it doesn't have any nostrils. It can't smell at all."

"Brad."

"Okay, I'm focusing. That one doesn't smell like an old bear."

"No. As a matter of fact, it doesn't really have an odor at all, which tells me the artist used new excelsior." She handed me the bear. "See?"

I'd just buried my nose in the bear's torso to take a big sniff when Tina came back into the museum, carrying the new broom and dustpan.

Cocking an eyebrow at me, Tina said, "I'm not interrupting anything here, am I?"

"Behave. This may look strange—"

"Just a little."

"But it's actually vital to the investigation."

"If you say so."

"Really, Tina, this is very important." Ash took the Bruin bear down from the mantle and gave it a sniff. "I'm pretty certain both these bears are counterfeit. One of the best ways you can tell is by the smell."

"Counterfeit teddy bears? You're kidding."

I said, "Nope. Antiques are big money and crooks will counterfeit anything these days, including toys."

"But what does this have to do with the murder?"

"Maybe nothing," said Ash. "But somebody did move them recently and a fanatical bear collector would pay a lot of money for these teddies."

"So it's possible the Yakuza were hired to come here to steal them." I added. "Merrit objected and he ended up dead. It isn't a perfect theory, but it's the only motive we've got for now."

"But if the bears are fakes, how'd they end up in the museum?"

"I don't know, and we can't ask him." I glanced over my shoulder at Merrit. "So, that's something we're going to have to look for in the acquisition records when we search Merrit's office, which is our next stop once we finish here."

"Well, I hope you have better luck in there than I just had with the FBI."

"Trouble with the vaunted Bureau? I'm utterly shocked." Like most street cops, I consider the only thing more useless than the FBI is the inflatable life vest tucked beneath a jet airliner's seat. "Did you know the initials stand for Famous But Incompetent?"

"I didn't, but I do now." Tina was simmering. "I spoke with the regional duty agent, who talked to me as if I was retarded and suggested I was overreacting. He told me to call back on Monday."

"Your tax dollars at work. Any luck with customs?"

"I left a message, but haven't heard anything back yet."

"And Olympus?"

"Same thing. I'm waiting for a callback from someone in their legal department."

"You knew that was coming. Has Allsop collected that cigarette butt yet?"

"Just a minute ago."

"Did he notice the brand?"

"Winston. Is that important?"

"It might be, at some point."

Tina held out the broom and dustpan. "You wanted these?"

"Thanks. If you'll help Ash collect these bears and the quilt as evidence, I'll start sweeping up the broken glass and china."

It didn't take long to sweep up most of the debris and pour it into an evidence bag. However, I made no effort to collect the glass shards and pieces of broken dishes that lay scattered on Merrit's body. That stuff would go into the body bag with the corpse. I'd just begun dusting the cupboard for fingerprints when the ME's transportation team arrived with a metal gurney. Five minutes later, they and the body were on their way to Roanoke.

Ash came into the dining room and watched for a moment as I moved the fingerprint brush in a swirling motion. She asked, "Anything?"

"Nah, all I'm doing is making a mess. Between the old furniture oil and dust, you couldn't find King Kong's latents. Where'd Tina go?"

"Out to check on the deputies and to make sure the county is sending out a truck to pick up the cupboard."

"Excellent. By the way, you and I aren't loading this freaking thing into a vehicle. That's why God created young cops."

"Thank goodness. We've got the bears and quilt packaged, but we left the hammer for you to collect. Are you going to try to fingerprint it also?"

"No, there's too great a chance that we'd lose trace evidence such as blood. I'll let the lab process it for prints. And this," I said, tossing the now gummy print brush into the plastic box, "is becoming an exercise in futility. Let me sweep up the rest of the debris and then I'll get the hammer."

Tina came back into the museum as I was sliding the hammer into an evidence sack. She grumbled, "The lawyer from Olympus says that he'd *love* to help, but we need a search warrant before they'll tell us where the Hummer is. That's going to take forever."

"Not necessarily. I've got a boilerplate, fill-in-the-blanks version of that kind of search warrant affidavit on one of my computer discs at home. If Ash doesn't mind, she can go and get it while we go to Merrit's house and make the death notification." I gave Ash a sidelong glance. "That is, unless you want to come with us."

"And witness a wife being told that her husband is dead? No, thanks, but that's just a little too close to home." Ash touched my arm. "I'll get the disc and also let Kitchener out to go to the bathroom."

I stuck the bag containing the hammer into a large cardboard box loaded with the other evidence. "Tina, are you comfortable enough with how Allsop is working to let him finish with photographing the inside of the museum?"

"He seems to be doing a great job."

"Okay, let's do a quick search of the office and go talk to Mrs. Merrit. Maybe she'll be able to tell us something about the bears."

We filed into the small office and I took some photos before we disturbed anything. My leg was aching, so I assigned myself the task of searching Merrit's desk, which meant I could sit down. Ash began searching the four-drawer filing cabinet while Tina checked some document-filled cardboard boxes in the corner of the room.

The computer on the desk looked like it was in "stand by" mode, but I wasn't going to mess with it other than to turn it off. There might be other important information in the computer's files, such as emails or the documents we were seeking, but I'd leave their recovery to the cyber specialists at the crime lab. I opened the top desk drawer, but found nothing of evidentiary value; just pens, paper clips, and a bunch of rolled up little candy wrappers that told me Merrit was addicted to Werther's toffees.

Tina held up a sheet of paper. "Here's something interesting. This form says that Merrit was issued a personal computer so that he could work from home."

"Different from this one here?"

"What brand is that one?"

I bent over to look at the logo on the computer tower. "A Compaq."

"No, this says it was a Gateway. The other one must be at his house."

"We'll want both of them for the crime lab."

Going back to work, I came upon a thick folder labeled "Equipment Inventory Forms" in the bottom drawer. However, the folder was packed with something other than museum documents. There were maybe twenty love letters and romantic cards addressed to Merrit and all were signed, "With All My Love, Linda." I pulled all the amorous correspondence from the file and piled it on the desk.

I said, "We might want to bring these along when we go to make the death notification to Merrit's widow. They might provide her some comfort."

Tina picked up a card, read the sentiment, and looked thoughtful. "Actually, I don't think she'll want them."

"Why not?" Ash asked.

"Because Merrit's wife isn't named Linda. Her name is Marie."

Nine

As far as I'm concerned, one of the most consistently wretched things about investigating a homicide is uncovering the tawdry little secrets of murder victims. However, it's unavoidable. Understanding the victim's background and behavior are vitally important, because that information can tell us much about the killer. So, we peek into the dark recesses of people's lives and often discover unsavory things that may have nothing to do with their murder, but must be explored until they've been eliminated as a causative factor. Sometimes you can mercifully keep the truth from the victim's family and save them some additional pain, but I didn't think that was an option this time. While it was true there was some compelling circumstantial evidence pointing to the Yakuza as Merrit's killers, we could no longer focus solely on them. Marital infidelity was also an excellent and eternally popular motive for murder.

"He was cheating on his wife?" Ash said distastefully. She picked up one of the letters and began to read it.

"That's sure how it looks, but we don't want to jump to conclusions," I said.

Ash's cheeks turned pink and she stared in disbelief at the lilac-colored stationery. "We can go ahead and jump to this conclusion. This Linda is certainly very . . . descriptive."

Tina looked over Ash's shoulder and after a moment inhaled sharply. "Oh my God, I see what you mean."

"And it gets worse," said Ash.

"Really? Let's see." I reached for the letter.

Ash folded the papers and quickly scooped up the rest of the cards and letters. "Honey, I don't think you need to waste your time reading this stuff."

"But it's evidence."

"And mostly pornographic. Tina and I will review the letters while you keep looking for the paperwork on the bears."

I resumed my search for the acquisition documents for the antique bears while Ash and Tina plowed—as it were—through the torrid correspondence. In the end, none of us came up with anything useful. There was no paperwork for the bears and no indication from the letters that Merrit's love affair with Linda was in trouble or had been discovered. Then something else occurred to me. Opening my notebook, I turned to the page where Ash had written down the numbers of the incoming and outgoing calls.

I pulled my cell phone from my pocket and as I pressed the telephone number with the "434" area code, Ash asked, "Who are you calling?"

"Linda, I hope." I punched the button to put the phone on speaker mode.

"While we were in here earlier, we checked the incoming and outgoing phone numbers," Ash explained to Tina.

"There were calls last night and this morning to the same number."

The phone rang three times and then rolled over to the voice mail salutation. It was a woman's voice: "Hello, you've reached the office of Professor Linda Ingersoll of the University of Virginia. I'm not available to take your call, but please leave a message and I'll get back to you as soon as I can."

I disconnected from the call. "We're going to want to talk to her at some point, so I don't think I'll leave a message that her secret lover is now flatter than Kansas."

"A professor? What do you suppose she teaches, Advanced Motel Gymnastics?" Ash rolled her eyes. "So, what now?"

"I think we're done here. Let's take those steamy letters as evidence and tell Allsop that when he finishes up, to seize Merrit's computer too."

"And then I guess it's time to drive over to Merrit's house and make the death notification. I'm not looking forward to that," Tina said.

I heaved a huge sigh. "No, it's never fun . . . unless you tell the family by turning it into a game of charades."

Tina tried not to chuckle as Ash gave me her patented withering I-can't-believe-you-just-said-that look. We went outside where it was still very hot and muggy, but I saw we had weather coming. The western horizon was a solid wall of whitish-gray thunderheads and the freshening breeze told me the front was headed in this direction. It was a good thing that Ash was heading home, because you can add thunderstorms to the long list of things that terrify Kitchener, not that I thought less of him for this particular phobia. Thankfully, we don't often see tornadoes, but Shenandoah Valley thunderstorms are noisier than an artillery barrage, generate lots of lightning, and can pack some pretty powerful winds.

"I'll put lavender oil on Kitch when I get home," said Ash, giving the approaching storm a worried look. It sounds a little weird, but a few drops of lavender oil applied to his head and ears keeps our dog fairly calm during thunderstorms.

I handed Ash the truck keys. "And please unplug the computer, so we don't end up with fried circuits. We'll call you once we're finished at Merrit's place."

"I love you and be careful."

I got into Tina's police car and we drove back toward Remmelkemp Mill and turned west on Coggins Spring Road.

Keeping her eyes on the highway, Tina said, "Since this is our first time working an official investigation together, how do you want to approach this interview?"

"I'm going to keep my mouth shut—don't laugh—while you ask the questions."

"But you've got a lot more experience at this than I do."

"And the best way for you to develop your skills as a tactical interviewer is to do it."

"What if I miss something important?" Tina sounded anxious.

"Relax. I'll say something."

The radio speaker crackled. "Mike Control to Mike One."

Tina grabbed the microphone. "Go ahead."

"Mike One, we're holding a call to the trash transfer station. The supervisor there says that he may have recovered some stolen property."

Tina keyed the microphone. "It will have to wait for now. Tell him to put it in his office and we'll send someone by tomorrow to get it."

"Ten-four."

Replacing the microphone, Tina said, "One other thing:

Do you think I should mention that Merrit was having an affair?"

I pondered that for a moment. "My inclination is to hold off for now. We don't know for a fact that the relationship played any role in Merrit's murder and his wife is going to be upset enough already."

"Okay. Brad, do you think we're going to solve this murder? I don't mean to sound selfish, but I haven't been in office for very long . . ."

"And an awful lot of folks are going to be paying very close attention to how well you handle this."

"Yeah."

"Don't worry. By next week we'll have a suspect in custody and a rock solid case." I only wished that I felt as confident as I sounded.

The Merrits lived northwest of town near the base of Massanutten Mountain. It took about fifteen minutes to get there and the sky overhead was beginning to grow dark and cloudy as we made the turn onto Meacham Lane. The house was a good-sized, single-story brick rancher with black shutters and stood at the base of a low tree-covered hill. We pulled into the driveway and Tina parked behind a red Dodge Durango.

Once upon a time, the house might have been nice, but it was now in the kind of sorry shape that's only achieved by years of neglect. The flower beds were overflowing with weeds, there was a portable basketball backboard and hoop lying on its side in the tall grass and pieces of a radio-controlled toy dune buggy were scattered all over the driveway. There was also a golf club lying nearby and it didn't take enormous deductive skills to figure out what had happened to the toy. One of the windows was spray-painted black and the glass was visibly vibrating from a Goth the-world-sucks-and-I-hate-everything three-chord anthem to the horrors of life in the most affluent country in the history of the world.

We got out of the car and Tina shook her head in annoyance. "My kids aren't saints, but my front yard has never looked like this."

I poked at the dune buggy's broken frame with my cane. "Yeah, but you're part of a vanishing species: a responsible parent."

"And that music."

"Nice, huh? Now you know what hell sounds like."

As we headed for the front door, I saw a jagged shaft of blue white lightning stab the ground off to the south and about seven seconds later there was a low grumble of thunder. Tina knocked hard on the dented steel door with her fist, but there was no answer, which didn't come as any surprise considering how loud the music was. Tina tried again, this time a little harder. There was still no response.

"Can I borrow your nightstick for a second?" I asked.

"Why?"

"I'd like to show you the old-fashioned way to let folks know that you've come about a loud music call, but I don't want to damage my cane." She handed me her black aluminum baton and I began pounding it on the door at about shin level. It sounded like rifle fire and in between the blows, I said, "The secret . . . is to hit the door . . . where nobody . . . is going to . . . notice the fresh dents . . . right away."

The door flew open and I quickly handed the nightstick back to Tina. A tall, dumpy middle-aged woman, dressed in a faded and sleeveless housedress, stood with hands on wide hips, glaring at us. I assumed she was Marie Merrit. She had to shout to be heard over both the music and Gilbert Gottfried's nails-on-chalkboard voice blaring from the big-screen HD television in the living room. "What the hell is going on out here?"

"It's the sheriff, Mrs. Merrit. We need to talk to you," Tina half-yelled, as she put her nightstick back into its ring.

"What about?"

"It's important, so it would probably be best if we go inside."

"Who's he?" Marie reached up with her left hand to massage her right shoulder and then seemed to catch herself and dropped her hand to her side.

"Brad Lyon. He's a consultant for my department."

"You can come in for a second."

We followed her into the house and the moment we crossed the threshold, I was sorry that Tina had insisted on going inside. I hadn't been in a home this filthy since I was a cop. I think the shag carpet in the living room may have once been beige, but now it resembled an oversized Jackson Pollock painting, only this masterpiece was composed of a thousand-or-so food stains and felt as sticky and crunchy underfoot as a movie theater floor. The two armchairs and most of the sofa were piled high with stacks of old newspapers, junk mail, dirty clothing, and a jumbo pack of toilet paper from Costco. Another nice touch was the stylish centerpiece on the coffee table. It was a greasy Domino's Pizza box topped with a bowl containing the dregs of breakfast cereal and milk well on the way to becoming cottage cheese. Making this a full sensory experience, the air stank of rancid cooking oil, cat urine, and burned popcorn, which is a scent combination that you can bet Glade is never going to offer as a room freshener.

Marie walked over to the couch and, using her body to block our view, casually picked something up and tossed it to the floor and out of sight. I couldn't be certain, but I thought it looked like an electric heating pad and I was a little puzzled over the apparent subterfuge.

"Sorry about the mess, but Frank doesn't do a thing to help around the house. You can move that stuff if you want to." Marie motioned vaguely at the junk-filled armchairs as she sat down on the sofa.

"That's okay, I'd rather stand," I said, not adding: *Because God only knows what I'll get on my pants.*

"Any chance we can get the music turned down?" Tina looked in the direction of the bedroom.

"You can try, but Nathaniel keeps his room locked and doesn't answer the door."

A new song had started and it sounded like a punk rock version of an exorcism, complete with howls, screams, and the foulest language.

I asked, "So, how old is Nathaniel?"

"Ten."

"*Ten?* And you're letting him listen to that trash?"

Marie sniffed. "I don't believe in censoring his experiences."

"Then could we at least please put the TV on mute?" Tina asked. By now I could see she'd been watching that masterpiece of modern cinema, *Look Who's Talking Too.* Gottfried was now shouting at a bunch of toddlers while the Elvis Presley song, "All Shook Up" played in the background.

"Sure." Marie pointed the remote at the TV and pressed the mute button. Then she picked up a package of chocolate-dipped Oreos from the end table and fished out a cookie. "So, what do you want?"

Taking a deep breath, Tina said, "We're here about your husband. There's no easy way to say this, but he was found murdered earlier today at the museum."

Marie's eyes widened with shock and she dropped the cookie into her lap. "What?"

"He's dead, Mrs. Merrit. We're very sorry for your loss."

"You're sure?" Marie looked from Tina's face to mine, searching for some sign of hope.

"Yes, ma'am."

"Oh dear God! How did it happen?" she sobbed.

"We're still investigating that."

"Do you know who did it?"

"Not yet, but we're hoping you can help us."

"How would I know who killed him?"

One of the most crucial tasks of a police interviewer is to listen carefully to how a question is answered and Marie's last comment struck me as mighty peculiar. In essence, Marie had replied to Tina's unspecified request for assistance by denying knowing the identity of her husband's killer. I hoped that Tina had noticed the unusual response, but her next question told me she'd missed its significance.

Tina said, "There are other ways you can help us. For instance, did Mr. Merrit have any enemies?"

"He never said anything about any problems with anybody," said Marie, and I noted the second straight passively evasive response.

"We also think there's a possibility that his death might be related to some counterfeit antique items at the museum. Did he ever mention them?"

"No."

"What time did he leave for work this morning?"

Suddenly the television picture vanished and was replaced by a text message saying that the satellite dish wasn't receiving a signal. That meant there was heavy rain falling to the south. Then came a strong gust of wind and the branches of a tall shrub thumped against one of the living room windows. Lightning flared, immediately followed by an ear-splitting blast of thunder. We all jumped.

"I'm sorry, what did you say?" said Marie and I noticed she looked far more frightened than distraught and I had a nagging sense that it wasn't because of the thunderstorm.

"What time did Mr. Merrit leave for work?"

"I assume at about eight. That's the time he normally went to the museum."

"But you don't know for sure?"

"I was asleep. I suffer from severe chronic fatigue syndrome." Marie sounded both whiny and cantankerous.

Glancing at the filth, I thought, *Lady, you aren't sick, just lazy.*

Tina wrote the information down. "Did you talk to him on the phone at any point in the morning?"

"Frank was far too busy to call me."

That was the third devious answer in under a minute. Marie was technically telling the truth, because Merrit *hadn't* called her, but someone in this house had telephoned the museum shortly after ten A.M. However, with as busy as we'd been at the murder scene, I'd forgotten to tell Tina that. Some pieces of the puzzle seemed to be coming together and it was time to jump into the interview.

Clearing my throat, I said, "Ma'am, this is a terrible time for you and that can have a way of scrambling your brain. Are you sure you didn't talk to Frank?"

"Of course, I'm sure." Marie grabbed a wadded-up ball of paper towel and unfolded it to dab at her eyes.

"But somebody called the museum from here earlier today. Could it have been your son?"

Although I knew Tina was surprised, she gave no sign of it. Outside, the rain was beginning to crash in waves against the house. There was another lightning flash and a blast of thunder.

Marie buried her face in the soiled paper towel. "Oh God! I forgot. I was calling a friend and accidentally pressed the speed-dial number for Frank's work."

"Did he answer?"

"No, I hung up before he could. He didn't like to be disturbed at work." Marie's shoulders began to quiver. "And . . . and . . . I missed the chance to tell him one last time that I loved him."

Marie began to wail and I shot a look at Tina that said, *This chick is yanking our chains.* Tina nodded for me to continue, but I had to wait until Marie temporarily stopped crying and blew her nose.

I said, "I know this is hard, but we only have a few more questions. Have you been home all day?"

"Why do you want to know that?"

"Because one of our most important jobs is eliminating innocent people from consideration. Otherwise, some scummy defense attorney can claim that because you can't account for your whereabouts, you might be the killer."

"I didn't kill my husband." Marie was beginning to grow irate.

"No one said you did. We just want to know if you went anyplace today." Tina jumped back in.

"Yes. I went to some yard sales in Elkton."

"Were you alone, or did you go with a friend?"

"Not knowing I was going to need an alibi witness, I went by myself."

"Gee, I'm sorry that you think you need an alibi." I said, giving Marie a bland smile. "Just a couple more quick questions: Did you drive into Remmelkemp Mill or go by the museum?"

"No."

"When did you leave home?"

"Just after ten, and I got back around noon."

I wasn't quite certain what to make of her answer. If she'd murdered her husband, she'd just created major problems for herself by admitting she was away from home within the time frame when Merrit was killed. Although I was convinced she wasn't telling the complete truth, her motive for doing so or what she hoped to conceal was a mystery.

Outside, the rain seemed to be building to a crescendo. I let another roll of thunder pass before saying, "There's paperwork at the museum that says Massanutten County issued your husband a personal computer to do museum work from home. We're going to need that as evidence."

Marie sniffled and hid her eyes behind the paper towel. "The only computer in this house belongs to us."

"Did Frank have an office here at home?" Tina asked.

"Yes, in the garage."

"Could we go out there and maybe look for the computer? It might help us to identify your husband's killer."

"No."

"Would you mind telling us why not?" I kept my tone gentle and nonjudgmental.

"There's no computer out there and I don't want you poking around my house. In fact, I'm getting tired of being grilled and I want you to leave."

Tina said, "But Mrs. Merrit—"

"That's okay, Sheriff," I said. "Mrs. Merrit is overwrought and in pain. In fact, your right shoulder is really hurting, isn't it Marie? How'd that happen?"

"I said, get out!"

"Of course, but in the immortal words of the Governator," I now switched over to my best Arnold Schwarzenegger voice: "We'll be back."

Ten

The rain was pelting down hard and blowing sideways as we went back to the patrol car. However, the storm-line was pushing rapidly eastward and there were already patches of brilliant blue sky to the west. It was perhaps twenty degrees cooler than a half hour earlier, but I knew it would soon grow hot again and be even muggier than it had been before the storm.

Once we were in the car, Tina said, "Did I miss something in there?"

"Sorry for jumping in like that, but that was the most blatant job of stonewalling I've seen in a long time."

As Tina started the car and backed from the driveway, I briefly explained the verbal and visual cues that had told me Marie was concealing information. Tina hit the brakes, stopping the car in the middle of the road, and said, "Do you think that she might actually be the killer?"

"I don't know. She was unequivocal when she denied

killing him, but we know she's a first-rate liar—and also tall enough to fit the suspect profile."

"And she might have injured her shoulder swinging the hammer. God, I'm so stupid for missing that."

"No, you're not. It's just that I've worked about a thousand more murders than you have. Don't worry, you'll learn."

"I hope so."

"And we can't jump to conclusions about Marie. She may be a slob and acting hinky as hell, but she isn't stupid."

"I'm not following."

"She admitted to being alone and away from her house during the time when Merrit was murdered. If she did kill him, that doesn't make any sense."

"Because she'd be implicating herself. I see. So, what do we do?"

The rain abated for a moment and I looked back over my shoulder at the house. "Right now, we've got no leverage to make her tell the truth and there really isn't any physical evidence linking her to the murder."

"Unlike the Yakuza."

"Exactly. So, we need to roll by the museum to make sure they've finished processing the crime scene and then get to work on the search warrant affidavit."

Tina eased up on the brake and let the patrol car start rolling down the road. "Sounds good, but do we have enough time for me to go home and feed my kids some dinner?"

I looked at the dashboard clock and was stunned to see it was nearly five P.M. We'd been so busy, that I'd lost track of time and had assumed the only reason I was feeling hungry was because I'd missed lunch. I said, "Absolutely. We'll eat and meet back at the station."

The rain had stopped and wispy tendrils of steam were

rising from the roadway by the time we arrived at the museum. As we turned into the driveway we saw a remote van from the Harrisonburg television station parked in the lot with its satellite boom elevated into the sky. There were a handful of journalists standing on the lawn and they all noticed our arrival. Obviously, news of the murder had finally leaked out.

"The tragedy mongers have arrived," I said.

"What should I tell them?" Tina sounded glum.

"As little as possible. I'd limit it to saying there was a murder and you're investigating, but nothing else."

"They're going to want more than that."

"And people in hell want ice water. We've got to keep the elements of the crime scene a secret."

Tina got out of the car to talk to the reporters and I limped toward the museum. One of the journalists followed me as far as the crime scene tape, but gave up when I refused to say anything. Inside, I found Allsop and we made one final inspection of the building. He'd done a fine job processing the crime scene and I commended him for his efforts. I looked out the front window and saw that Tina was still talking to the reporters and she looked as tense as a nudist in a cactus garden. Finally, they let her go and she took me home.

Ash was sitting on the porch with Kitchener and they both came out to meet us. "You guys look solemn."

"That's because Mrs. Merrit decided to play truth dodgeball and complicated everything by turning herself into a potential suspect," I said, climbing from the car. "Thanks for the ride, Tina, and we'll meet you at the station at seven-thirty."

"I'll be there."

Tina backed the cruiser down the driveway as I gave Ash a kiss and then limped toward the door. Kitch followed, snuffling at my legs. He seemed to like the scents I'd brought home from Merrit's house, which really wasn't surprising considering that one of Kitch's favorite pastimes is rolling in deer dung.

Ash paused to look at our house. "I noticed that you didn't sound entirely convinced when Tina dismissed the connection between the murder and our burglary."

"I'm not," I said pensively.

"Could the SUV we saw leaving that night have been a Hummer?"

"We can't rule it out, especially since we don't know how long the Yakuza have been in the country and I never got a look at the Hummer's taillights today."

There was a pause before Ash said, "So, they could come back."

"I don't think it's likely. After having been seen in town and then committing a brutal murder like that, they'd be crazy to stay in the area," I said, wondering which of us I was hoping to reassure.

"I suppose you're right." She took my hand. "I'll bet you're hungry."

"Famished and, oh my God, do I smell your famous tequila-lime chicken with pasta?"

"I knew you didn't get any lunch."

I took her hand. "Mark this down as yet another reason why you're the best homicide partner I've ever had."

I made a pot of coffee while Ash scooped the pasta onto plates. As we ate dinner, I told Ash about our visit to the Merrit house and conversation with Marie.

She said, "Maybe Marie found out that Merrit was having an affair. That's a pretty good motive."

"But why would she kill the guy who was holding down two jobs so that she could sit on her fat ass and watch TV?"

"Where else was he working?"

"The museum was only a weekend gig. Gage told me that Merrit's main job was as a professor at some junior college in Waynesboro."

Ash made a sour face. "Maybe Merrit had a girlfriend there too, who found out about Linda the lust monster."

"Murdered by a jealous lover? It's certainly a possibility and something we'll explore in the unlikely event we end up eliminating the Yakuza and Marie as persons of interest."

"So, why was Marie withholding information?"

"I don't know and for the moment we've got to put her on the backburner. She seemed genuinely surprised when Tina made the death notification." I used my fork to scoop up the few droplets of the delicious cilantro, garlic, and tequila pesto on my empty plate. "My compliments to the chef. This was fantastic."

"You're welcome, and there's more for lunch tomorrow."

"Let's hope we're here to have it. Did you have any trouble finding that old computer disc?"

"No. I put it on the coffee table."

I got up to help Ash clear the table. "Thanks. And on a lighter note, do you want to know a juicy little secret that doesn't have anything to do with murder?"

"Of course."

"Sergei is infatuated with Tina and is getting ready to ask her out on a date."

"Well, it's about time."

"You don't seem surprised."

Ash put the pot containing the leftovers into the refrigerator and then turned to give me a pat on the cheek. "Honey, for someone with amazing powers of observation, there are times when you're absolutely clueless."

"It's a guy thing. Since it's obvious you knew, how could you tell?"

"All you have to do is watch Sergei's eyes whenever Tina's around. They kind of remind me of yours when you look at me." She leaned over to give me a kiss.

Breaking for air, I said, "And now I realize why you gave me that amused look this morning when we were talking about the bear I'm making for Sergei. You guessed it was a gift for Tina. By the way, he about had a stroke when he found out that the bear looks like him."

"Tina will love it."

"That's what I told him. So, assuming you've talked to Tina, how does she feel about her secret admirer?"

"There's a reason why she goes to the Brick Pit almost everyday for lunch, and it sure isn't because she loves barbecue."

"So she likes him."

"Of course, but she wishes he'd do something other than gaze at her."

Although I hated doing it, I put Kitch back in his crate and we headed over to the sheriff's department. Tina's patrol car was already in the parking lot and we found her in her office. She looked up from the computer screen as we came in.

"Ready for round two?" I asked.

"Absolutely. Let me close this document out and we can get started with the affidavit."

Tina got up and I sat down in her chair. Slipping the disc into the computer, I accessed the boilerplate *subpoena dueces tecum* warrant for digital information and began filling in the blanks. My typing was a little rusty, so I didn't finish until a few minutes after eight. Then Ash proofread the document for errors, and it's a good thing she did: there were a number of mistakes, the most glaring being that I'd accidentally typed "County of San Francisco" when describing the location of the crime. I corrected the errors, printed the final draft, and Ash read it one more time.

We then drove out to Judge John Skidmore's house to have him read and issue the search warrant that would compel Olympus Rent-a-Car to activate the Hummer's GPS unit and tell us where the vehicle was. Remmelkemp Mill is a tiny place, so I knew Judge Skidmore and liked him both as a person and as a no-nonsense jurist. Skidmore lived in a modest house on the east side of the river, about halfway up the Blue Ridge Mountains foothill the locals call "The Giant's Grave." As we pulled into the driveway, we saw a mama skunk and her brood of youngsters marching Indian-file across the lawn and we made sure they were gone before getting out of the car.

Tina had called in advance and Skidmore met us at the door. We retired to his den where we sat on a leather sofa while he carefully examined the affidavit. About forty-five minutes later, he issued the search warrant and we were on our way back to the sheriff's department to fax the document to the corporate headquarters of Olympus Rent-a-Car in Delaware.

I said, "So, do we have any idea when Olympus is going to tell us where the Hummer is?"

Tina tried to stifle a yawn. "They said that once they received the fax, one of their lawyers was going to have to review it to make sure it was valid before they complied."

"And you can bet that lawyer isn't working at ten o'clock on a Saturday night."

"I know, but they have an on-call attorney and they said they'd forward the warrant to him. Still, we probably won't hear anything until late tomorrow morning."

"It's your call, Tina, but once you've sent that fax, why don't we call it a day? We've done everything we can for now and we'll need a good night's sleep for tomorrow."

"You won't get an argument from me. I'm bushed." Tina pulled into her parking spot at the station. "There's no sense in you guys coming in. Go on home and I'll see you in the morning."

When Ash and I got home, she went upstairs while I took Kitch outside and admired the fireflies as he made his final latrine call of the night. By the time I got upstairs, Ash was in the bathroom and just finishing washing her face.

"Long day," I said.

"I can't wait to get into bed." Ash dabbed at her face with a towel.

I turned on the shower and began stripping off my clothes. Back when I was with SFPD I always took a shower after working at a death scene, and it was a little comforting that I'd slipped back into that old habit. It meant that I'd temporarily recovered my persona as a homicide inspector. Even though I love my new life making teddy bears, there are times when I really miss cop work.

When the water was hot, I got into the shower and pulled the curtain shut. But as I was letting the water splash on my head, I felt Ash's hands on my back as she climbed into the shower behind me.

Turning around, I said, "Hey, I thought you said you were tired."

Ash smiled slyly. "No, what I said was: I can't wait to get into bed."

We slept late. It was almost eight A.M. when the phone rang. I grabbed the receiver and said, "I hope for your sake this is Sheriff Barron."

"Brad! OnStar just called and we know where the Hummer is." Tina was excited.

I quickly sat up. Meanwhile, Ash raised herself onto one elbow and pressed her head against the opposite of the phone receiver so that she could listen too. I said, "Where?"

"At a motel on Steinwehr Avenue in Gettysburg, and Olympus will give us updates if it goes mobile."

"I don't want to keep Kitch in the crate all day. Can your kids watch him?"

"They'd love it."

"Good, then we'll be at your house in about twenty minutes."

Eleven

Actually, it was closer to a half hour. Ash knew we were going to be busy and that I can become a little prickly when I'm hungry, so she made us a quick breakfast of scrambled eggs and soy sausages before we left. Then we drove over to Tina's house and let an overjoyed Kitch out to play with the waiting kids. Tina met us at her police cruiser and handed us each a plastic embossed card.

Ash asked, "What are these?"

"Official ID cards. I thought that as long as we were going to be outside the county, it might be good if you both had some sort of department identification."

My card featured the Massanutten County Sheriff's six-pointed gold star on the left and a small color photo of me on the right. My name was underneath the picture along with the title of "Criminal Investigation Consultant." As I slipped the card into the wallet containing my SFPD retiree badge, I said, "How did you make these things without having our photos?"

"They're your drivers license photos. I had the DMV email me copies last night," said Tina.

Ash was beaming and waved her ID card in the air. "Look, I'm a detective."

"I know, and you did a magnificent job undercover last night," I said in the most earnest tone I could muster.

Tina looked skyward and tried not to giggle. Meanwhile, Ash's cheeks turned pink and she said, "Brad!"

"What? What did I say? All I did was commend my investigator wife on her ability to, um . . . get her man."

"Not another word."

We got into the patrol car and Ash insisted I sit in the front seat, because there was almost no legroom in the back. I didn't argue, because I wanted to be able to walk when we got to Gettysburg. We stopped long enough to pick up cups of coffee, then headed westward toward Interstate 81.

As we drove, I looked at Tina's road atlas. Gettysburg was in southern Pennsylvania and about 160 miles north of Remmelkemp Mill. The town is famous as the site of the climactic battle of the American Civil War, and later, Abraham Lincoln's celebrated speech commemorating the opening of the national cemetery there. It was one of the places that Ash and I had always wanted to visit after moving to the Shenandoah Valley, but between making bears and solving the occasional murder, we'd never made time. The atlas had an insert with a more detailed map of Gettysburg on the next page and I squinted at it.

I said, "It looks like Steinwehr Avenue is the business loop for U.S. Fifteen."

Tina nodded. "I know. I've already talked with Gettysburg PD. The motel is on the south side of town near the National Park headquarters and they're going to have one of their cops meet us there."

"Good idea."

Ash leaned forward to speak through the thick Plexiglas barrier that separated the front and back seats. "What I don't understand is, why did they go to Gettysburg? I mean, if they just committed a murder . . ."

"I know," said Tina. "I would have expected them to be on the next flight back to Japan."

"Maybe Mr. Ota didn't think we'd be able to link him to the Hummer." I took a sip of coffee. "Another possibility is that they aren't running because they have no reason to. Hopefully, we'll find out in a few hours."

Soon we were northbound on Interstate 81 and Tina slowed all the traffic down by only driving five-miles-an-hour over the posted speed limit. It was another hot morning and the air was so hazy with humidity that the mountains looked spectral. After just over an hour, we got off the interstate and took secondary roads that led cross-country toward the town of Harper's Ferry and the Potomac River.

We'd just passed some deliciously kitschy dinosaur statues that stood outside a store and the extinct reptiles reminded me of something important. I said, "Tina, can we talk for a second about how you want to handle this interview?"

"Go ahead."

"The Yakuza is almost exclusively male and like most crooks, they have some pretty old-fashioned attitudes toward women."

"Which means they're Neanderthals. Are you suggesting that you should be the lead interviewer?"

"Ota might be more comfortable talking to a guy, but it's your decision. I'm just offering options."

"Well, I don't really care if they don't like uppity women. I'll be the primary interviewer."

"Good. That's how you learn."

"You'll do great," said Ash.

Tina gave me a nervous smile. "But, I want you there, just in case . . ."

"You need a cavemen interpreter. Don't worry."

We drove past Harpers Ferry and I noticed that the state line separating Virginia and Maryland isn't where you'd logically expect it to be, at mid-channel of the Potomac River. From bank-to-bank, the river is part of Maryland; Virginia stops at water's edge on the southern shoreline. Twenty minutes later, we arrived in Frederick, Maryland, where we got on U.S. Route 15. This was the road north to Gettysburg and a road sign said it was only thirty-five miles away.

As we approached Catoctin Mountain State Park, Tina's mobile phone rang and she asked me to answer it. I said, "This is Sheriff Barron's number, can I help you?"

A man said, "This is Montrel from the OnStar control center and we're notifying you that the Hummer has gone mobile. It's traveling southbound on Steinwehr Avenue."

"Got that. Can you stay on the line and give us regular updates?"

"Yes, sir."

Putting my hand over the phone's mouthpiece, I relayed the news to Tina and Ash.

Montrel said, "The vehicle is continuing southbound from Steinwehr onto Emmitsburg Road now."

Checking the atlas, I said, "All right, I see that on the map."

"Now passing Barlow Road."

"I copy."

There was a long pause and then Montrel said, "Okay . . . the vehicle turned west onto Cunningham Road and has stopped."

"How close is it to Emmitsburg Road?"

"Not far. I can't tell from the computer map, but it looks like they pulled off-road."

"Thanks, Montrel. I need to clear the line so I can call the Gettysburg Police. Please call us if they go mobile again."

"Yes, sir."

Looking up, I saw we were passing Mount Saint Mary University and a sign that said the Pennsylvania state line was only three miles ahead. I also noticed that Tina had now slowly eased the cruiser up to about eighty miles an hour.

I said, "The Hummer has stopped south of town on Cunningham Road. We need to call the Gettysburg cops and give them the new location."

"The number is in that steno pad." Without taking her eyes from the road, she pointed to a notebook that was wedged between her car seat and the center console.

I called Gettysburg PD and was apologetically informed that, since the Hummer was no longer within the borough limits, it was therefore out of their jurisdiction, so they couldn't help. However, they did give me the number for the Cumberland Township Police, which was responsible for the area where Cunningham Road was located. I then spent the next several minutes talking to the Cumberland Township police dispatcher. After convincing her that I represented the Massanutten County Sheriff's Office, I described our situation and also had to explain the difference between Yakuza and ninjas. By the time I finished and she'd agreed to send an officer, we were several miles into Pennsylvania and about to get off on the Emmitsburg Road off-ramp.

Disconnecting from the call, I said, "They've got a cop en route."

"Good, because I think we're almost there," said Tina.

Emmitsburg Road was a winding and tree-lined two-lane highway with a surprising amount of traffic going in both directions. We passed rolling farmland, the occasional home, vacant and boarded-up Civil War artifact shops, and an ever-increasing number of historical markers with information about the Battle of Gettysburg. Then I noticed a blue sign for a tourist attraction up ahead and to our left.

Ash saw it too and said, "You don't think . . ."

"We'll know in a second and, if so, this investigation just got exponentially weirder."

"Cunningham Road," Tina called as she slowed down and made the left turn.

We rolled past a wall of tall evergreens and Tina then pulled over to the side of the road to gape. In the middle of a lush pasture about a quarter-mile away was a red barn with a stone foundation that looked as large as an aircraft carrier. The rectangular building was at least eighty-feet-tall and almost a football field in length. On the end of the structure facing us there was a mural the size of a drive-in movie screen, depicting a huge brown teddy bear leaning on a split rail fence and waving. The words BOYDS BEAR COUNTRY were painted in tall white letters on the wall above the glass entrance doors.

I broke the silence. "So . . . I guess we can safely connect the Yakuza with the teddy bears."

Boyds is one of the premier manufacturers of mass-produced teddy bears in the world and this was their famous flagship store, a place that countless bear collectors all over the globe considered a sneak preview of heaven. We own about a hundred of their sweet teddies and this store was one of the reasons we'd wanted to come to Gettysburg. But who could have guessed that our first visit to the enormous bear emporium would be as part of a homicide investigation?

The parking lot appeared about a third full—I estimated maybe eighty vehicles—but it was filling quickly. Cars, SUVs, minivans, and the occasional tour bus passed us in an almost continuous stream and made the right turn into the bear Mecca. I looked for the Hummer, but couldn't see it.

Tina said, "This place is amazing."

"Yeah, as amazing as the idea that three Japanese mobsters are inside shopping for cute teddy bears," I said. "How do you want to handle this?"

"I think we should wait here until the Cumberland officer arrives."

"Then can I get out and stretch my legs for a minute?" Ash asked.

We got out of the cruiser, and after nearly three hours in air-conditioned comfort, the muggy heat came as an unpleasant surprise. In the distance, I could hear the old Petula Clark song, "Downtown," playing over the store's exterior PA system, but the tune was rendered all but inaudible by the eerie buzzing of the cicadas in the nearby trees.

I said, "I know it's supposed to be here, but I don't see the Hummer."

Tina opened her trunk and removed an oversized pair of OD green military binoculars. She scanned the lot and finally said, "It's over on the far end of the lot. Take a look."

I pushed my sunglasses up on my head and used the binoculars to look where she was pointing. "Okay, I see it now."

Tires crackled on the pavement behind us as a blue and white Cumberland Township patrol car pulled up. Tina quickly briefed the young cop about our mission, stressing that all we wanted to do was talk to the Yakuza. Then we returned to our cars and drove into the parking lot. A minute or so later, we were walking toward the glass entrance doors of the self-described "humongous" store.

I quietly said to Ash, "The Yakuza don't usually fight with cops. But just in case this goes south, I want you to find a safe place and stay there."

"And the same advice applies to you."

"Hey, my nickname is Mr. Prudent."

"Right."

Inside, the store was decorated with a lovely mixture of stonework, polished wood, stained glass, and thousands of teddy bears. Another nice thing was that the ventilation system seemed to be pumping air from Antarctica. There was a tall oak reception desk just inside the door and the two female employees working there eyeballed us a little nervously as we came in. Their expressions didn't grow any more serene when Tina quietly asked if there was a Boyds security officer on duty and, if so, could he meet us immediately.

The guard arrived a minute or so later. Even though he wore a sunshine yellow polo shirt with the Bear Country logo embroidered on the left breast, the young guy might as well have been wearing a nametag that said, "Hi, I'm an off-duty cop." My suspicions were confirmed when the guard and Cumberland officer greeted each other by first names.

When Tina told the guard about our investigation and described the Yakuza, he jerked his head in the direction of a large doorway leading to a salesroom to the left and said, "I just saw them. They're in there."

"Doing what?"

"What everybody else does here. They're shopping for teddy bears."

Tina quickly went over the plan one more time. Our goal was to make contact in a low-key manner and ask Mr. Ota if he'd volunteer to accompany us to the Bear Country security offices where we could interview him and his bodyguards about their visit to the Massanutten History Museum. If they refused, we didn't have any legal right to detain them and they'd be allowed to leave.

Tina stared hard into the faces of the two young cops. "Most importantly, we don't want any violence. Got that?"

"Yes, ma'am," they both replied.

"Okay then, let's do it."

It's never comforting to begin a police tactical operation with Gary Gilmore's last words before he was executed for murder, but I didn't say anything, because I could tell that Tina was very tense. Tina and the cops took the lead, while Ash and I followed. The salesroom was as big as the inside of a good-sized family home and decorated in red, white, and blue for the Fourth of July. There was one tableau of costumed bears marching in a parade, another with teddies posed at the beach, and probably a thousand or so bears for sale.

We found Ota and his two bodyguards standing in front of a display that featured a small Civil War cannon. It was a ludicrous sight. The two young tough guys were carrying fabric mesh bags full of stuffed animals, while Ota scrutinized the face of a teddy bear dressed in a blue Union Army uniform. Still, I found myself lowering the grip on my cane to use it as a bludgeon, just in case things turned ugly.

Flanked by the guard and the cop, Tina walked up and said, "Mr. Ota, I'm Sheriff Barron from the Massanutten County Sheriff's Office. I'd like to talk to you about what happened at the museum yesterday."

Ota put the bear back on the shelf and without looking at Tina said, "I have no desire to speak to the police. Good day."

"But, Mr. Ota . . ."

Tina suddenly knew what it felt like to be a unicorn, because as far as Ota was concerned, she didn't exist. The gangster walked past her, closely followed by his bodyguards. They gave us cold stares that silently dared us to do anything. I saw the security guard flexing his fist and was afraid he was going to accept their nonverbal challenge. The situation had to be defused now, otherwise we'd have a donnybrook on our hands and we'd never get the information we needed.

As the trio walked past, I said, "Mr. Ota, the museum director was murdered and you and your men don't look *gurentai*." Roughly translated, *gurentai* means "hoodlum," something most Yakuza loathe being called.

The gangster noticed me for the first time and stopped. "You were at the restaurant yesterday."

I nodded.

"Why do you think I would know that word, *gurentai*?"

"Because your clan pin tells me you're a member of *Yamaguchi-gumi* and I know that men such as you don't fear identifying yourself to the police."

Ota gave me a stern, searching look. "What do you know about the Yakuza?"

"A little. One of the most important things is that you call yourselves *machi-yakko*—servants of the people. But some say that isn't true anymore."

"Who are you?"

"I'm Bradley Lyon."

"Are you a federal policeman?"

"No, sir, I was a San Francisco Police homicide inspector. Now we live here." I nodded toward Ash. "And we collect teddy bears too."

"Mr. Merrit is truly dead?"

"Yes, sir."

Ota was obviously disturbed. He turned to his body-guards and snapped out a question and I didn't need to understand Japanese to know he was asking: *Did you guys kill the museum director?* The goons' vocal intonations and facial expressions clearly said: *It wasn't us.* Maybe I'm getting more credulous the longer I'm away from cop work, but I believed them.

Pointing at me, Ota told Tina, "I will talk to him."

Twelve

Tina thanked and dismissed the Cumberland Township cop and then we rode a freight elevator up to the administrative offices on the fourth floor. It took some fast-talking on my part, but I finally convinced Ota that Tina could be present during the interview, so long as she remained silent. I knew that Tina was simmering over the snub, but she was far too professional to let it show.

Once on the fourth floor, Tina asked the security guard if he'd babysit the bodyguards in the employee lounge while we questioned Ota in the security office. He agreed and we spent a few moments collecting basic information from the pair. Both men produced their passports. Their names were Ryochei Hikida and Itaru Kawashima and the passports indicated that they'd entered the country on Thursday, which seemed to eliminate them as suspects in the burglary of our home two weeks ago.

We also discovered that there was no point in interviewing them. They didn't speak English and we didn't have any interpreter other than Ota, who wasn't exactly an objective witness. And even if there had been an independent translator, it was crystal clear the guards would have each taken a bullet rather than betray their boss. I grudgingly admired their fierce loyalty, even if it was for a bad cause and stymied our investigation. Thankfully, you don't often see that sort of devotion in American crooks. They're usually discount Judas Iscariots, who will rat out anyone, including their mothers, for a mere two-week reduction in jail time.

Yet we did obtain some evidence from the silent guards. Before going into the security office, I asked Ota if he and his men smoked. All three produced packages of Marlboro cigarettes, which didn't surprise me. A lot of crooks on both sides of the Pacific Ocean consider it a "tough guy" brand of coffin nails.

Tina raised her eyebrows and quietly said, "The cigarette butt we found at the museum was a Winston."

"Which kind of reduces the chances that one of these guys threw it in the flower bed." I turned to Ash. "Honey, I don't know how long we'll be with Mr. Ota and, much as I'd like to have you there, I don't think he's going to allow another woman to sit in on his interview."

Ash glanced uncomfortably at the two glowering gangsters. "I guess I could stay here."

"Or you could wander around the store. You've always wanted to come here."

"You wouldn't mind?"

"I think I'd like that a lot better than you sitting with the Doublemint Twins." I gave her the wireless phone. "We'll call you when we're done."

Once Ash was gone, Tina and I went into the loss prevention unit's office with Ota. It was like almost every other security workplace I've seen over the years. There were a couple desks, a tall metal evidence locker, and a bulletin board packed with pictures of counterfeit money and professional shoplifters. The only thing different was the obviously homemade wooden plaque that hung from the front of one of the desks that read, "Welcome to Boyds Bear County. Thieves will be mauled and eaten."

Instead of sitting behind the desk, I pulled the office chair around to the front to reinforce the appearance that Ota and I were equals. Meanwhile, Tina took a seat at the other desk and out of the Yakuza's line of sight.

Ota initiated the conversation. "I have never met a policeman who collected teddy bears. How many do you own?"

"Just over five hundred. How many do you have?"

"More than three thousand. What kinds do you have?"

I understood that Ota was naturally suspicious of my claim to being a bear collector, which I suspected was the only reason he'd agreed to be interviewed. So, before answering any questions about his visit to the museum, he was going to test me on my knowledge of stuffed animals.

I said, "We have Boyds, of course, and some Steiff, and a couple of Hermann. But most of the bears in our collection are made by individual artists like my wife."

"She makes bears?"

"Wonderful bears. You have some excellent bear artists in Japan. We like Masako Yoshijima's work in particular."

Ota nodded impassively, so I couldn't tell if my flagrant name-dropping had impressed him. He said, "Do you collect antique bears?"

"A few. We had an old Farnell Alpha, but it was stolen last month."

"You have my regrets."

"If you don't mind me asking, how did you start collecting bears?"

"When I was a young child, I received a Kamar bear as a gift. He was a good friend."

"Those were made in Japan, right? They have kind of floppy folded ears and velveteen paw pads? Do you still have him?"

"No, my mother threw him away when she thought I was too old for such things. She said it was unmanly."

"You have *my* regrets."

Ota gave me a bittersweet smile. "Look at us. Two old warriors talking about teddy bears. Many people would think such an interest in toys is childish."

"But not your men." I nodded in the direction of the employee break room.

"I allow my *kobun* to believe I collect the bears as investments."

"But that isn't the main reason, is it?"

"No."

"I feel the same way. And it was your love of bears that brought you to our local museum. Would you like to tell me what happened?"

"We did not kill that man." Ota fixed me with a fierce gaze.

"I believe you, but I need to know what you talked about with Mr. Merrit. I think it's connected with why he was murdered."

Ota took a deep breath and relaxed in his chair a little. "Back in Nippon, I employ an antique expert who searches for rare and old teddy bears. He is very good. Six weeks ago, he told me that he had found a Bruin Manufacturing bear and an early Michtom bear for sale in the United States. You can imagine my joy."

"Yes, I can. How much was the seller asking for the pair?"

"Seven-hundred-and-twelve-thousand yen—six thousand dollars, for the pair."

"That was a bargain." I glanced over at Tina and was relieved to see that she was taking the information down in her notepad.

"I know."

"Did your antique dealer tell you who was offering them for sale?"

"Not at first. I'm a very busy man, so I don't handle minor details. I simply authorized him to pay and to bring me the bears when they arrived."

"But at some point, you learned that the bears were being purchased from the Massanutten Museum."

"Yes. My dealer was informed that the museum was closing and that this was why the bears were for sale."

Suddenly, several pieces of the puzzle fit together and I said, "And when the bears you bought arrived, you were upset, because you realized they were fakes."

"Yes. The workmanship and artificial aging were excellent, but I soon suspected the stuffing was too new. A laboratory confirmed this for me."

"So, you'd been cheated. Were you angry?"

"No, I am a *bakuto*. Do you know what that word means?"

"Gambler." It was one of the two types of original Yakuza, I recalled from my research.

Ota nodded with approval. "Gamblers take risks. This isn't the first time I have bought bears that turned out to be counterfeit. It is a risk of the game. So, no, I wasn't angry at first. But I did want my money back."

"But that didn't happen, did it?"

"No. Up until then, all of the negotiations were conducted by email. But now the seller would no longer answer my dealer's messages."

"But you persisted."

"Yes. My dealer telephoned the museum and could not get satisfaction. Then I telephoned the museum directly to express my displeasure and demand the return of my money."

"When was that?"

"Three weeks ago. I spoke with Mr. Merrit and he told me he did not know what I was talking about. After that, he refused to talk to me."

"So, you came to America to get your money back."

"Or the teddy bears I'd paid for."

The phone on the desk closest to us began to ring and we quit talking until it stopped. Then I said, "And you had to come in person, because your *kobun* aren't teddy bear experts. They wouldn't be able to recognize a fake."

"Correct."

"When did you arrive in the United States?"

"Late on Thursday night. We flew to Dulles and stayed at a hotel near the airport."

"And you came to Remmelkemp Mill on Saturday morning. Was there anybody else at the museum when you got there?"

"No. It was a very lonely place."

"Was Mr. Merrit surprised to see you?"

"Yes, and I think a little frightened at first."

Considering your hoods possess all the charm of attack-trained Rottweilers, he had an awfully good reason to be scared, I thought, but merely nodded for Ota to continue.

"I told him that I wanted my money back. He became annoyed and told me that the bears had never been sold and took me to see them."

"Where were they?"

"On the shelf above the fireplace."

Suspecting what had happened next, I said, "What happened when you told him that those bears were fake too?"

Ota showed a ghost of a smile. "You realized also."

"My wife noticed it. And, you're right. Those bears are first-class fakes."

"At first, Mr. Merrit did not want to believe. But once I convinced him, he became very distressed and angry that his museum was being used to commit crimes."

"So, you decided he wasn't involved in the plan to cheat you?"

"Yes. He impressed me as . . . what is the expression you use for an innocent man who is given the blame?"

"A patsy? A fall guy? A—"

Ota interrupted me before I could go any farther, "Fall guy!"

"Did he ever say who he suspected might have sold you the bears?"

"No."

"What happened after that?"

"Mr. Merrit asked for my card. He said he could not guarantee the return of my money, but would try to find out who was responsible."

"So that you and your *kobun* could get your money or the real bears."

Ota smiled placidly. "Yes. He was eager to help."

"Yeah, I'll bet. Did anything else happen?"

"No. When we left the museum, Mr. Merrit was alive and standing on the porch."

"Can we back up just a little bit? I'm assuming you paid for the bears with an international money order. Who was the check made out to?"

"I have the name here." Ota pulled a palm pilot from his jacket pocket and tapped at the keys. "The seller said he was Adam Mumford, a curator from the Massanutten Museum."

I looked at Tina and she said, "I don't know of anybody by that name working for the county. Probably a false name."

"Which is what Mr. Merrit told me." Ota kept his gaze focused on me, making it clear that he was not conversing with Tina.

I said, "Do you have the address where the check was mailed?"

Ota consulted his computer again. "Post office box number twenty-seven, Shefford Gap, Virginia. That was also the return address on the package."

Shefford Gap was so small, that it made Remmelkemp Mill look like a bustling metropolis. It was about thirty miles away, in western Rockingham County, back in the Allegheny Mountains and almost to the West Virginia state line. The only reason I even knew the tiny settlement existed was because Ash and I had gone there the previous autumn so that she could pick apples that she later converted into the most delicious apple butter I'd ever tasted.

"Did you go to Shefford Gap?" I asked.

"Yes, but by the time we arrived, the post office was closed. I had planned to go back on Monday . . ."

"That's not a good idea. I'm afraid that if you start nosing around up there, someone will begin talking. If the suspect finds out, he'll be in the wind."

"In the wind?"

"Sorry. He'll disappear. Where did you go after that?"

"We drove to Leesburg to visit a teddy bear shop there."

"You went to My Friends and Me?" I knew the shop. Ash and I were addicted customers and, since the store carried bears from local artists, they had several of Ash's bears for sale. "Did you buy anything?"

"A soldier bear by Gary Nett. Do you know his work?"

"Yeah, his costuming is superb." I made a mental note to call the teddy bear shop to confirm the Yakuza had indeed been there. Then I pondered for a second on how best to approach this next portion of the interview. At last, I said, "Mr. Ota, I thank you for telling me what happened and I believe your story. But when we arrest the real killer, his or her lawyer will claim that because you are a Yakuza, you can't be trusted. It would be your word against the murderer's and around here, a jury might not believe you."

Ota's jaw tightened. "Mr. Merrit was alive when we left and I can prove that."

"Really? How?"

"Go out to the parking lot and talk to the undercover policemen. They have been following us since we arrived in your country."

"What?"

"Yes. They are out in the parking lot. The main surveillance vehicle is a white Dodge van with a big window on the side."

I shot a quick glance at Tina, who gaped back at me in astonishment. I said, "And they saw Merrit on the porch?"

Ota replied, "They were in the museum parking lot, so I think perhaps they have videotape of him . . . and us."

Pushing myself to my feet, I extended my hand. "Mr. Ota, I want to thank you for your cooperation. You and your *kobun* are free to go."

Ota shook my hand. "May I ask you a question?"

"If it's about the murder, I can't really share any information."

"No, it is about your wife's bears. Do you have a website?"

I grimaced. "Not yet. We're working on it."

Ota pulled a business card from a gold cardholder and bent over the desk to write his email address on the back. "Would you be so kind as to email me when your site is on the Internet? I am always interested in finding new teddy bear artists."

Thirteen

Once Ota left the office, I said, "I believe him, but even if he wasn't telling the complete truth, talk about an ironclad alibi, especially if there's video. We need to chat with those Keystone Kops out there."

Tina put her notebook in her breast pocket. "Which agency do you think it is?"

"Considering they were burned within minutes by their target, my money is on a FIST."

"A what?"

"A Federal Inept Surveillance Team." I reached for the phone. "I'll call Ash and have her meet us downstairs."

By the time I telephoned and we rode the elevator down to the ground floor, Ash was waiting for us in the lobby. She held a large brown Boyds shopping bag and there was a nutmeg-colored plush bear with a pink gingham bow behind one ear peeking out the top of the sack.

Ash said, "It wasn't them, was it?"

"No, but we learned a lot. Merrit was alive when they

left and the counterfeit bears you spotted are definitely involved," I said.

Tina added, "An unknown suspect pretending to represent the museum was selling them over the Internet. Mr. Ota bought an identical set of fakes and came to get his money back."

"So, how many fake bears are there?" Ash asked.

"Four that we know of right now, but this counterfeiting operation could be a lot bigger than we thought."

"Which probably means they're selling fake antique quilts too. But, it's kind of hard to believe that anyone in town could be involved," said Ash.

"It's possible they aren't. The bears were mailed from Shefford Gap," said Tina.

"But there has to be a connection with the museum, so we're going to have to take a much closer look at Neil Gage and Marie Merrit." I looked at the bear in Ash's shopping bag. "I see that you were successful too."

"I just had to have her. She was too cute," said Ash. "Are we going home now?"

"Right after we finish talking to the rolling surveillance team that's been following the Yakuza since they arrived here."

"You mean there were police at the museum yesterday?"

I held the door open for Ash. "Yeah, and apparently they can confirm that Merrit was alive when the Yakuza left."

We went out to the parking lot, where we found the white Dodge that Ota had described. It was parked about twenty yards from the Hummer. I could tell the engine was running and the air conditioner was on because there was a large puddle of condensed water on the pavement beneath the van. Scanning the parking lot, I noticed several other suspicious parked vehicles, occupied by clean-cut pairs of occupants, all pretending with varying degrees of success to not be paying close attention to the store. There was a young man slouched in the van's driver seat holding up a newspaper as if reading it. I hoped the guy didn't think he was fooling anybody, because a coma victim would have made him as a cop from two hundred yards away.

Tina tapped on the window. "Excuse me, sir. Can we talk to you?"

The driver lowered the window and pulled a small black badge case from his shirt pocket. Lazily waving his FBI identification card in front of Tina's nose, he made no effort to conceal his annoyance. "Hey, County Mountie, we're on the job here. Take off before you burn our operation."

Already irked over Ota's rudeness, Tina was in no mood for this kid's calculated insolence. She snapped, "And I'm on the job too, you little snot. Oh, and don't worry about being burned. That happened on Thursday night when you left the airport."

The agent sat up straight. "How do you know about that?"

"Because we just got done talking to Mr. Ota."

A man's voice came from the van's passenger compartment. "What's going on up there, Wadsworth?"

Wadsworth called over his shoulder, "Uh, sir, we have some local law enforcement here and they've . . . uh, apparently been talking with our . . . um, target."

"What? Tell them to come around to the other side of the van."

As we walked around, we heard the side sliding door open. Inside, there were two men. We didn't get a very good look at one, because he was operating a video camera that was pointed at the front of the barn. The other guy looked tired and wired, like a seven-year-old who'd been Halloween trick-or-treating way past his bedtime but was still riding a major league sugar buzz.

"I'm Special Agent In Charge John Bartle and, pardon my French, but what the hell is going on here?"

"I'm Sheriff Barron and I might ask you the same question," said Tina. "You were operating in my county yesterday and didn't bother to let anybody know."

Bartle tried to suppress a snort of amusement. "Sorry, Sheriff, but we've been through a lot of jurisdictions and it's been our experience that . . . well, don't take this wrong, but the locals sometimes get in the way."

Tina put a hand out to lean casually on the side of the van. "Well, then I reckon this time the locals are *really* going to get in the way. We had a murder at our museum, right about the time it was surrounded by FBI agents."

"What?"

Before she could continue, Tina's mobile phone trilled. Pulling it from her belt, she looked at the screen, and frowned. "It's the chairman of the county board of supervisors and it says nine-one-one. I've got to take this call. Brad, can you carry on until I finish?"

"My pleasure."

"And who are you two?" Bartle asked.

I flipped my badge case open. "Bradley and Ashleigh Lyon. We're investigative consultants for Massanutten County."

Bartle looked from my ID card to my cane and then to Ash's new teddy bear. "And precisely what qualifications do you need for *that* job?"

"Check the badge out, G-man." I love using that expression because most feds hate it. "I'm a retired San Francisco PD homicide inspector and I'd also advise you to stop looking down your nose at my wife, because she's got more natural investigative ability than a dozen FBI agents. Not that that's anything to brag about."

"Hey, I didn't mean anything."

"Of course not. Look, I'll keep this short and sweet. The museum director was found murdered not long after the Yakuza and your road show left there. Mr. Ota says that you can confirm our victim was alive when he and his *kobun* left the museum. Is that true?"

"Mr. Lyon, I'm sorry, but this is a confidential investigation and I'm not prepared to be interrogated over what we might or might not have seen." Bartle folded his arms, a nonverbal cue that he considered our conversation finished.

"Fair enough. Ash, could I borrow the phone for a second?" She handed it to me and I pressed the long-distance directory assistance number for New York City. When the operator answered the phone and asked whose number I wanted, I said, "The Columbia Broadcasting System."

Bartle's face went white. "Who are you calling?"

I held my hand for silence, covered the phone's mouthpiece with my thumb, and whispered, "*Sixty Minutes*. I'll be with you in a minute."

"Who do you think you're kidding? It's Sunday. There's nobody there."

"Yeah, but when I leave a message offering to share the unsavory story about how the FBI sat outside a museum while a murder went down and then told the investigating cops to pound sand, I'll bet I hear back from them."

"You're a devious son of a bitch."

"Ouch. Nobody's ever called me that before. So, will you talk to me or Lesley Stahl?"

"Hang up and I'll tell you what you want to know."

I disconnected from the call. "What time did you guys arrive at the museum?"

Bartle grabbed a clipboard and flipped through a couple of pages. "It was ten-fifty-seven."

"Was there anybody else there?"

"No. There was only one car in the lot: a Toyota registered to a Franklin Merrit. Was he the victim?"

"Yep. How long did the Yakuza stay there?"

Tina snapped her cell phone shut and rejoined us.

Bartle said, "They left the museum at eleven-eleven hours. When the Yakuza came out, there was a Caucasian male following them. He stayed on the porch and waited until the Hummer was gone."

I said, "Lucky for the FBI, that means the victim was alive when your surveillance targets left. Did any of your people go inside the museum to find out why Ota went there?"

"No, we figured we'd follow up on that later."

Tina nodded in the direction of the video camera. "I'm assuming all of this was videotaped."

"Yeah."

"We'll be sending you a formal request for a copy. During the time you were there, did anyone else come to the museum?" asked Tina.

"Not to the museum, but a truck pulled into the driveway and then did a turnaround and left."

"What kind of truck?"

Bartle looked at the clipboard again. "A beat-to-crap older model Ford pickup, green in color. It looked like a decommissioned army truck and it was occupied by a white male adult."

"Did you get the license plate?" I asked.

"There wasn't one. It had 'Farm Use' placards. We figured some local farmer used the driveway instead of making a U-turn on the road."

It was getting hotter and hotter as we stood there on the

asphalt. Wiping some sweat from my upper lip, I said, "After the Yakuza finished at the museum, Mr. Ota said they went out to Shefford Gap. Is that correct?"

"Yeah, and then they went to a teddy bear shop in Leesburg." Bartle rubbed his eyes wearily. "Now we're here. It's the damnedest rolling stakeout I've ever seen. What's with the friggin' bears?"

"Mr. Ota collects them."

"How about a little more information sharing? Can you tell me anything about the murder?"

I looked at Tina, who gave the agent an icy smile and said, "I'd really like to, but . . . well, don't take this wrong, sometimes the FBI gets in the way. We'll be in touch."

As we walked across the parking lot to Tina's patrol car, I said, "That's going to leave a mark. Where did you learn to be so sarcastic?"

"Oh, I wonder," said Tina with a humorless chuckle.

Ash took my hand. "She's been hanging around you too much."

"So, what did Captain Queeg want?" I asked, using our private nickname for County Board of Supervisor Chairman and resident megalomaniac, Kelvin Stieg.

Tina unlocked the doors to the cruiser. "It seems that Marie Merrit has been calling members of the county board of supervisors all morning. She wants to know when she'll receive the payout on Frank's county employee life insurance policy."

Ash narrowed her eyes. "My God, what kind of wife would do that? Her husband has been dead for less than twenty-four hours."

Getting into the car, I said, "If she knew about those steamy letters in Merrit's desk, maybe she's the kind of wife that figured she'd better get the money now, before Linda Ingersoll makes a claim."

Tina said, "Or maybe she found out about the affair and killed him. In light of this news and the fact that she's deliberately withholding information, I think we have to strongly focus on her as a possible suspect."

"Absolutely. But before we approach the grieving widow again, we need to learn more about Merrit's relationship with Ingersoll."

"And find out whether she has a husband who might have objected to her teaching Sex Ed classes in local motels," Ash said.

"Or if she killed him because he wouldn't leave Marie," said Tina.

"Both excellent points. So, let's head back. We're back to square one and we've got a lot of work to do."

As we headed southward, I telephoned OnStar to advise them that they no longer needed to track the Hummer. It took about three hours to get back to Remmelkemp Mill. Along the way, I finally convinced Ash that it was necessary for me to read the love letters before we contacted Linda Ingersoll, which we planned to do on Monday.

As we came into town, Tina said, "Is it okay if we stop at the station for a moment, before we go home? I'm briefing Supervisor Stieg a little later and I need to pick up some paperwork."

"No problem," I said.

We went into the station and as we filed along the hallway behind Tina, she stopped suddenly and darted into the tiny report writing room. When I got to the doorway, I understood why. The battered remains of a personal computer and monitor stood on the table and it looked as if the machine had been used for batting practice. The metal body of the CPU had more dents than a bumper car and there was a large jagged hole in the glass monitor screen. A deputy sat next to the computer, filling out a crime report.

"A Gateway?" I asked.

Tina tilted the CPU to look at the back. "Yes, and it has Massanutten County identification stickers."

"Is that the computer that was supposed to be at Merrit's house?" said Ash.

"I'd be willing to bet a year's worth of retirement checks it is. Isn't it interesting how it looks like someone worked it over with a hammer . . . just like its former owner?"

Tina turned to the deputy. "Where did this come from?"

"The trash transfer station. It was one of the calls holding from yesterday," the cop said.

Tina massaged her forehead. "Jeez, that was the call I told dispatch to hold yesterday afternoon."

"Hey, you had no way of knowing," I said.

"I don't understand, Sheriff. This is just an unlawful dumping case," said the deputy.

"No, Tommy, that may be homicide evidence," said Tina. "What happened at the trash station?"

The deputy stared at the broken computer in awe and then replied, "Yesterday morning, the guy running the trash compressor saw a man dumping this stuff in the big trailer they have for metal items."

"And that isn't an authorized dump site for electronic equipment like this."

"That's what the sanitation supervisor told me. By the time the worker got free, the guy had already driven off."

"What time did this happen?"

"Sometime around nine-thirty."

"Did you get a description of the man and the vehicle?"

"Not a very good one." The deputy sounded sheepish and I suspected it was because he'd done a slapdash job on what he'd considered an inconsequential report.

Tina impatiently waved for him to continue.

The deputy said, "He was a white male adult driving a full-sized green pickup truck, unknown make, with a black spot on the driver's door. Oh, and it had 'Farm Use' placards."

Fourteen

"The same truck the FBI saw at the museum?" Ash asked.

"So, whoever this guy was, he wasn't just doing a turn-around in the driveway," said Tina.

I said, "No, he went there to see Merrit, but was scared off when he saw there were other people at the museum."

"Which means he didn't want any witnesses when he met Merrit."

"You usually *don't* want folks watching when you're planning to turn someone's skull into a scale model of that meteor crater in Arizona."

Ash winced at the imagery. "Do you think he went back later?"

"Until we know more, we have to assume he did."

Tina turned to the deputy. "I want you to put this stuff with the other homicide evidence and write a *full* report. Understood?"

"Yes, ma'am."

Ash pointed at the wrecked equipment. "Is this the

personal computer issued to Merrit that Marie Merrit said she didn't have?"

"Yep," I said.

"So, if the man in the pickup truck was seen at the dump throwing this away and then later at the museum, there's a good chance he's connected with Marie."

"Probably. But, until we identify the guy and establish a relationship, Marie will claim she doesn't know him and we can't prove otherwise," I said to Tina. "What are the chances we can ID the vehicle?"

Tina frowned. "Not good. We've got hundreds of farms and probably just as many unlicensed farm vehicles in this county alone."

"And with the hue and cry over the murder, that truck will stay hidden. So nothing has really changed. We have to interview Linda Ingersoll tomorrow."

Ash said, "And while you're in Charlottesville, it occurred to me that there is something else I could do to help."

"What's that?"

"I really want to examine those counterfeit teddies before you send them to the crime lab. Correct me if I'm wrong, but at best, all they'll be able to establish is who manufactured the mohair and stuffing and confirm whether it's new."

"And maybe identify what was used to artificially age the bears." Suddenly, I understood what Ash was about to suggest. "But a teddy bear expert could potentially tell us a lot more."

"I'm not an expert," Ash said hurriedly.

"As far as a judge would be concerned, you are. The legal definition of an expert is simply an individual who knows more about a certain subject than the average person. That qualifies you as a bona fide *fur*-ensic expert."

"I knew that was coming," groaned Tina. "What do you think you could find out from examining the bears?"

Ash said, "The needlework, fabric piecing, and how the eyes are attached all might give me an idea of who made them. Bear artists usually have a distinctive sewing style. I know most of the teddy bear makers around here and I'm pretty good at recognizing their work."

"Even if the bears are supposed to look like someone else made them?" Tina asked.

"Hopefully, that's only on the outside. The artist—and whoever it was *is* an artist—might not have been so careful with what he or she did on the inside."

"It's hard to imagine that someone from around here made those bears."

I said, "I know, but the suspect's mailing address is in Shefford Gap. So, the counterfeiter has to live close enough to mail packages from the post office there and pick up the incoming checks."

Tina took her key ring from the clip on her gun belt. "Okay, you've convinced me. Before we leave, I'll get the bears out of evidence and you can sign for them."

"But I want you to understand that all I'd be offering is an opinion as to who made them." Ash looked a little apprehensive.

I patted her on the shoulder. "Anything you can tell us will help, because we're pretty much dead in the water right now, love."

Tina said, "And as far as talking to Ingersoll tomorrow is concerned, I just thought of something: It's summer. She's probably not going to be at the university."

"But the fact Merrit called her yesterday shows that she's still in Charlottesville. We'll have to call her. I know you've been busy, but did you run a driver's license check on her?"

"It's in my office."

We followed Tina down the hallway to her office. After a few seconds sorting through the stack of papers on her desk, she produced a sheet with Ingersoll's driver's license information and a small digital photo. The face in the picture didn't fit my image of a sexually adventuress homewrecker. Curiously, although Ingersoll looked to only be in her midthirties, she wore the oversized eyeglasses with rectangular frames that were popular in the 1970s and a hairstyle that was vaguely reminiscent of the Princess-Leia-dual-mounted-cinnamon-bun look. Then again, she was a history professor and perhaps her area of specialization was the wonderful decade that gave us Watergate, disco, and that modern "Chariot of Fire," the famously flammable Ford Pinto.

"She looks basically harmless," I observed.

"And she's going to look basically *armless* if she offers you some private tutoring," warned Ash.

Meanwhile, Tina pulled a Charlottesville phone book from her desk drawer. After a few moments of flipping pages, she looked up from the book and said, "Believe it or not, we finally caught a break. She's got a listed number and a husband. His name is Jeffrey."

I perched myself on the desk to give my leg a rest. "Not good. If we call and he's there, she's going to deny knowing anything."

"I know, so I guess I'll call her office number at UVA and hope she's checking voice mail for a message from Merrit."

"That sounds best."

Tina made the call, left a brief message requesting a callback on her cell number, and then retrieved the two counterfeit bears from the evidence room. Then she took us to her house, where we picked up the Xterra and Kitch.

It was after six P.M. when we finally got home. I fed Kitch and then made a gin and tonic for Ash, while she sautéed some hamburger and salsa to make tacos. I'd just opened a cold bottle of Indian Pale Ale and was grating the Monterey pepper jack cheese when the phone rang.

It was Tina, who said, "I just talked to Ingersoll, and we're scheduled to meet her tomorrow at nine A.M. in her office at UVA."

"Did you tell her that Merrit is dead?"

"Yeah, and she didn't take the news very well. She broke down completely."

"Did she say why he called her yesterday morning?"

"I asked, but she was crying so hard, she couldn't answer."

I took a sip of beer. "Do you think it was genuine or was she blowing smoke?"

Tina was silent for a second and then said, "Maybe I'm easily fooled, but if that was a performance, she's the greatest actress of our time."

"Anything else?"

"She asked if we could keep a low profile, so I agreed to come in plainclothes."

"And your patrol car would stick out like someone with a life at a Trekkie convention. You want me to drive?"

"Yes, please. Oh, and I've got some other news. I ran Adam Mumford's name through the DMV computer."

"The guy Ota sent the check to, right? I'll bet it's a fake name."

"Nope. Mumford is real and he lives in Richmond, but his file is red-flagged. His wallet and driver's license were stolen last August."

"We only have his word for that."

"I know, so I called him. He sounded about eight hundred years old and I almost gave him a heart attack when I told him that his name had come up in a murder investigation," Tina said with a nervous chuckle. "Then I got his daughter on the phone. She told me her dad has cataracts and could no more drive to Shefford Gap than the moon."

"Then our counterfeiter is using Mumford's ID."

"Yeah, and I've sent out a statewide bulletin to see if the name has come up in any other criminal investigations."

"Excellent work. I'll see you tomorrow morning around eight."

"Better make it seven-thirty. These days, there's some real gridlock getting into Charlottesville."

I hung up and brought Ash up-to-date. Less than ten minutes later, just as we were sitting down to eat, the phone rang once more.

It was Tina and she sounded flustered. "Sorry to bother you again, Brad, but I just got off the phone with the medical examiner's office. They told me Merrit's autopsy is scheduled for tomorrow morning at nine-thirty and as the primary investigator, I have to be there."

"And that's in Roanoke?"

"Yeah, two hours from here."

"Then go. I can handle the interview with Ingersoll."

"Should I call and tell her that it will just be you there?"

"No, let's not give her an opportunity to change her mind. I'll touch base with you after I talk to her."

I could hear the rustle of pages over the line as Tina consulted some notes. She said, "Okay, you're going to meet her at Stoller Hall, room number two-oh-seven. If you go to the UVA website you can print out a map."

"Sounds good. Oh, and have fun at the autopsy. Those MEs can be real cutups."

"Good night, Brad."

I hung up the phone and, between bites of wonderful guacamole-laden taco, told Ash about the change in plans.

She took a sip of her drink and said, "How would you like me to come with you?"

"To interview Ingersoll? I don't know if that's such a good idea."

"Why not?"

"Tell me, are women more perceptive than men about how other people are feeling?"

"Most women."

"I agree. So, how long do you think it would take for Ingersoll to figure out you think she's lower than pond scum? My guess is we're only going to get one chance to question her and she'll be more inclined to talk if she doesn't feel as if she's being judged."

Ash smiled ruefully. "I guess I shouldn't play poker, should I?"

I reached out to take her hand. "Just strip poker with me. Besides, we need you to examine those bears. It might turn out that they're our only tangible lead."

"You're right. I thought I'd get started on that after dinner."

"There's no point in jumping into it tonight. It's been a long two days and being tired only leads to mistakes. So, once we finish dinner, why don't we go outside and watch the sunset and not talk about murder for the rest of the evening."

Ash smiled. "I'd like that."

"And you can tell me where you're going to put our newest teddy bear."

As I left town the following morning, I saw Sergei and Terry Richert standing near the minister's mailbox by the road. Sergei was grinning and eagerly signaled me to stop. I pulled over and lowered the passenger window.

Sergei said, "I thought you might want to hear this. I was just giving Terry an after-action report on his sermon from yesterday morning. Some of his flock were still punch-drunk when they arrived at the restaurant after the service."

Richert gave an embarrassed smile. "All I did was remind them that it was wrong to bear false witness against their neighbors."

"In a voice audible from outside the church and forty yards away in my parking lot," Sergei said gleefully. "Then he told the gossipers that they were tin-plated frauds and said that if they wanted to use a church as a place to gossip, they'd better find a different one because he wasn't going to tolerate it any longer."

"I wanted to get their attention."

"Take my word for it, my friend, you did." Sergei slapped Terry on the back.

I leaned over and extended my hand to the pastor. "Thanks, Terry. I wish I had time to talk, but I've got to get to Charlottesville."

Terry shook my hand. "I heard you and Ashleigh were helping the sheriff. Is this connected with the tragedy at the museum on Saturday?"

"Yeah, unfortunately I'm the lucky stiff that discovered the unlucky stiff."

"Did those Yakuza kill him?" Sergei asked.

"Unlikely, but it's looking as if their visit to the museum might have somehow led to Merrit's murder." I glanced at my watch. "There's more, but it'll have to wait. I've got to interview someone in Charlottesville and if I don't leave now, I'll be late."

Shouting a final good-bye, I started down the road again. I drove eastward over the Blue Ridge Mountains through Swift Run Gap and then headed south along U.S.

Route 29. The highway is known as Seminole Trail, but with all the new commercial construction lining the road, I think Strip Mall Trail might be a more accurate name. Charlottesville is an attractive and upscale university town, but it's growing faster than the national debt.

As Tina had predicted, the traffic was heavy. It wasn't bad by California standards, but that's like comparing a hot summer day to the temperature of hell. It was 8:40 A.M. when I turned on to Ivy Road and entered the campus. Time was growing short. I had only a general idea of where Stoller Hall was, and I didn't know how far I was going to have to walk once I did find it. Still, I slowed down to admire the scenery. With Thomas Jefferson as an original architect and nestled at the base of the Blue Ridge Mountains, the University of Virginia is one of the loveliest campuses in North America. I passed the white-domed, brick Rotunda and saw a road sign pointing in the direction of Stoller Hall, a three-story Romanesque building that was mostly concealed by tall maple trees.

Few summer students meant plenty of parking, and I easily found a handicapped space near the rear entrance of the hall. There were only a few other cars in the parking lot and the nearest was a cobalt blue Chrysler 300C. I automatically jotted down the license plate, just in case it belonged to Ingersoll. One of the things about working a homicide investigation is that you never have the luxury of knowing what might be a clue, so you have to collect all the information.

I got out of the truck and limped toward the building. It was already hot and muggy, so I was sweating by the time I made it inside. Fortunately, the air conditioning was on. A couple of minutes later, I tapped on a wooden door with a frosted glass window. It had old-fashioned black painted lettering that read, PROF. L. INGERSOLL.

Linda jerked the door open. Not having paid attention to her height on the driver's license printout, I was surprised at how tiny she was. I mean, we're talking the Munchkin Lullaby League here, because she couldn't have been more than four-foot-eleven. The other thing I noticed immediately was that she was an emotional wreck. She wore a pink sweat suit that looked as if there were chocolate ice cream stains on the chest, her hair was unwashed and uncombed, and her eyes puffy and red.

She glared up at me and said, "Who are you?"

"I'm Bradley Lyon and I handle special investigations for the Massanutten County Sheriff's Office. Sheriff Barron sent me. She was called away."

"I'm not talking to you."

Something told me that offering words of comfort would be perceived as being patronizing, so I said, "Professor Ingersoll, I realize you're very upset and with good reason. The man you loved is dead, but I'm going to need you to behave like a grown-up for a little while."

Her jaw jutted out a little. "Who do you think you are?"

"I think I'm one of the people trying to figure out who killed Frank. Look, I know this sucks and the last thing you want to do is tell some stranger about your adulterous affair with a married man. But lady, we're running out of leads and I need your help."

Linda stood frozen for a moment and then swiped at her nose with the back of her hand. Pulling the door open, she said, "Come in."

Fifteen

I went inside and pushed the door shut behind me. Looking around, I saw that Ingersoll had obviously spent the night in her office. A small black suitcase lay on the floor and there was a wadded-up jade-colored blanket on the arm-chair near the window. Despite the air conditioning, there was the faint yet wonderfully pungent scent of curry in the air. That, combined with the Indian restaurant carryout containers in the trashcan, told me what she'd had for dinner last night. The rubbish also contained an empty pint carton of Ben & Jerry's Chocolate Peanut Butter Swirl ice cream, which probably accounted for the stains on Linda's sweatshirt.

Linda slumped into the chair behind a large cherrywood desk and, looking upward at the ceiling, sluggishly waved at a chair on the opposite side. "Sit down and let's get this over with. I know you're here because you found those letters. I'll bet you and all the cops had a great big laugh. Look at me, the porn queen professor of UVA."

"There's a big difference between smut and genuine passion between a man and woman. What I saw wasn't porn, and the only ones who read the letters besides me were my partner and the sheriff." I eased myself into the chair.

"Does her indolent majesty know about them?"

"Marie Merrit? No, we didn't tell her."

"Why not?"

"At this point, there's nothing to show they're connected with the murder. Besides, Marie ended our interview kind of abruptly." Ordinarily, I wouldn't share information about another witness interview, but I decided to subtly exploit Linda's contempt for Marie as a goad to induce her to speak further. Does that sound callous and manipulative? Welcome to Club Homicide. Check your compassion at the door.

Linda asked, "Tell me, how did she react when you told her that Frank was dead?"

"Surprised and upset, but not nearly as distraught as you are."

"That's because the only thing Marie will miss is being able to sit on her fat ass while Frank works two jobs."

"But you're going to miss him for a lot more than that, aren't you?"

Linda turned to look at me and swallowed hard. "No one had ever loved him like I did. I was more of a wife to him than she ever was."

"Marie didn't say much about Frank. Could you tell me about him?"

"He was kind and intelligent and had a way of looking at things that made me laugh. And he was one of those rare scholars who could fire his students with a passion for history. Did you know he was a writer?"

"No. What sort of stuff did he write?"

"He'd had articles published in *Civil War Times* and he was about three-quarters finished writing a nonfiction book about Sheridan's burning of the Shenandoah Valley." Although I'm not a history fanatic, you can't live in the Valley and not know about how the Union Army put most of the farms to the torch. It may have happened back in 1864, but there are local folks who are still angry about it.

I said, "I'm assuming you read it. Was it good?"

"Extremely. It was our secret, but he already had an editor at the University of North Carolina Press interested in it."

"Wow. So, how long had you known Frank?"

"Just since last November. We met at an academic conference at William and Mary. Do you believe in love at first sight, Mr. Lyon?"

"Yeah, as a matter of fact I do."

"It wasn't as if he was this Greek god or something, but after we'd spent three hours together, I just knew he was the man I'd waited for my entire life."

"Believe me, I understand. Did he feel the same way about you?"

"He used to tell me that he was in love with me before he ever met me, because I was the woman he'd always been looking for."

"So, why didn't you guys get divorces and start a new life together?"

Linda sighed. "I wanted to, but in the beginning Frank was incapable of it. He was like . . . How much do you know about World War Two?"

Uncertain of what direction the interview was now headed, I said, "The basics."

"In the final days of the Third Reich, the SS guards abandoned the concentration camps, leaving the prisoners unsupervised. Most of the inmates were still in the camps when the Allied forces arrived. They made no attempt to escape, because they'd been conditioned to accept their captivity. That was Frank, at first."

"Being sent to a concentration camp isn't quite the same thing as an unfulfilling marriage."

"Isn't it, detective?" Linda fixed me with a challenging gaze. "Despite what was in those letters, Frank and I talked a lot more than we . . . did those other things. He'd been raised by an abusive and domineering mother and, like so many men, he married her spitting image."

"Trying to earn the love he never got from mom."

"Exactly. He'd been trained to be a servant and a victim for thirty-six years, but that was changing."

"How so?"

"The longer he was with me, the more he saw and understood how wrong his life was with that bitch."

"And he began to tell you he was planning to leave her, right?"

Linda's eyes narrowed. "I know what you're thinking: He was just saying that in order to keep our sexual relationship."

I shrugged. "Sorry if that hurts, but it wouldn't be the first time a guy did that."

"That's true, but you didn't know Frank. He was going to leave her and soon."

"I'll take your word for it." I leaned back in the chair and folded my hands across my chest. "So, if you don't mind me asking, who did *you* marry?"

"My control-freak father, squared." Linda closed her eyes and shook her head. "Jeff is a miniature Darth Vader, but without the charm."

"What does he do for a living?"

"He's a real estate developer, one of the biggest in the mid-Atlantic."

"Did he know about your relationship with Frank?"

"He suspected something."

"And what would your husband have done if he knew you were going to drop him like the payload from the *Enola Gay*, once Frank got up the gumption to tell Marie *hasta la vista*?"

Linda put a hand to her forehead in such a way that it briefly and seemingly accidentally covered her eyes. "I don't know."

She was lying and I realized I might be on the verge of developing a new and strong lead. I said, "You just called him Darth Vader and yet you don't know how he'd react to some other guy stealing his wife?" When she didn't respond, I continued in a voice I hoped sounded like James Earl Jones as the cinema's most identifiable villain, "Linda, your sudden lack of candor is disturbing."

She dropped the hand and glared at me. "I'll tell you this just once: Don't badger me."

"Then don't lie to me, because you aren't very good at it. I'll ask the question a different way: Has Jeff ever shown the potential for violence?"

"Sometimes."

"Has he ever assaulted you?"

"No, just . . . well, we had a cat once . . . but . . . he said it was an accident." Her brow wrinkled as she recalled the incident.

"So, along with despoiling the countryside, he abuses animals. Was he home on Saturday morning?"

"No."

"Do you know where he was?"

There was a long pause before she answered, "He left at about eight and said he was going over to Waynesboro to look at some property for a housing development."

"And as we both know, Waynesboro is in the Shenandoah Valley and less than thirty miles from the museum. Don't tell me you haven't wondered about that. Do you think Jeff might have killed Frank?"

"I don't know." She wiped at a tear in the corner of her eye.

"What time did he get home on Saturday?"

"Around one."

"And when he got home, was there anything about his behavior or attitude that, in retrospect, strikes you as odd or suspicious?"

"No."

"Which doesn't change the fact that you think Jeff is capable of murder. It's got to be scary as hell living with someone like that. Is that why you're staying in your office?"

"Yes."

"How does Jeff feel about that?"

"He alternates between begging me to come home and then yelling at me to pull my head out of my ass."

"Well, isn't he a silver-tongued devil? You did the right thing, but you need to find someplace to stay where he can't find you."

"I know. Please tell me something. How did Frank die?"

"All I can say is that it happened very fast and he probably didn't feel any pain. Trust me, you don't want to know any more."

Linda pressed her lips together to stifle a sob. "Thank you. When is his funeral?"

"I don't know yet. Would you like me to call you when I find out?"

"Please. I'll give you my cell phone number. Is that all you needed?" Tears were running down her cheeks, but she kept a stoic face.

"No, unfortunately I have a few more questions. Did Frank ever mention any problems at the museum?"

"Just that he thought he was going to have to quit because of the budget cuts."

"Did he ever talk about being physically abused at home?"

"By Marie?"

"Men are victims of domestic violence far more frequently than most people guess."

Her reddened eyes widened with sudden fury. "Oh my God, could she have killed him?"

"There's absolutely no evidence she was at the museum." I raised my index finger in warning. "And I'd strongly advise you to both stay away from her and not call her."

"Why?"

"Because you'll make it that much harder to catch Frank's killer. Is that what you want?"

"No," she grumbled.

"Besides that, we're following up on other leads that aren't connected to Marie. Which brings me to his phone call to you on Saturday morning at . . ." I flipped the notebook open. "Eleven-fourteen. Why did he call you at the office on a Saturday?"

"I told him to. The spring term just ended and I was cleaning out some things. Besides, it was safer," said Linda.

"Because Merrit's number wouldn't show up on your home phone."

Linda nodded.

"So, what did you and Frank talk about?" I asked.

"He called to cancel our . . . time together. He'd planned to close the museum at about noon and we were going to meet for a few hours."

"At a motel?"

"No, on the front lawn of Monticello," she said wearily. "Of course, at a motel."

Knowing the sarcasm was merely to camouflage her grief and anger, I ignored the jibe. "What did Frank say?"

"That there was a major problem at the museum and that he wouldn't be able to make it."

"Did he tell you what sort of problem it was?"

"Something about finding counterfeit artifacts at the museum. The fact is, I didn't believe him. I thought Marie was having one of her regular migraines and he'd been roped into doing the grocery shopping or something. That happened sometimes."

"Actually, he was telling the truth. Did Frank say anything else?"

Linda wore a haunted look. "Two other things. The first was that he'd already talked to the curator, who was on his way to the museum."

"Neil Gage?"

"I think that was his name. Anyway, Frank said it was a huge mess and he didn't know how long it was going to take to straighten it all out."

"And what was the other thing?"

"That he'd finally decided to leave Marie and that we could begin looking for a home of our own. And do you know what I told him?"

"What's that?"

"That he was just saying that to placate me and that I was tired of all his empty promises. I was mad. I didn't mean it." She looked disconsolate. "Those are the last words he heard me say and I'll never forgive myself for that."

"Look, I hate to ask this, but if I don't a defense attorney will: Where were you the rest of that morning?"

"After hanging up on Frank, I went home."

"Can anyone confirm that?"

"The Charlottesville police."

"Interesting. How'd they get involved?"

"After about forty-five minutes, I realized there wasn't any point in sitting at home stewing, so I decided to go shopping. I went out to my car and found that some creep had poured acid all over the hood," Linda was fuming. "The paint job was completely ruined."

"That Chrysler out there?" I nodded in the direction of the parking lot.

"It's a loaner. My car is a PT Cruiser and I took it to the dealership after the police left."

"So, you called the cops and they came to your house to take a report? Were there any witnesses to the vandalism?"

"No, but I knew—"

She didn't get a chance to finish the thought, because the door flew open with a bang and a man swaggered into the office like a bad guy entering a saloon in a Grade B Hollywood western. He was short and stocky, with a Mussolini set of the jaw and the sort of bright and malignant eyes you'd expect to find on a wild boar. It was a speak-of-the-devil moment, because you didn't need a triple-digit IQ to know this was Jeffrey Ingersoll and he'd come for his truant wife.

Ingersoll snarled, "All right, you adulterous bitch, I've had enough of your shit. Get your stuff. You're coming home."

Linda was breathing raggedly through her mouth. "Jeff, I told you that—"

"Shut your frigging mouth, or you're going to be picking up broken teeth with broken hands." He held up a fist. "Now, let's go."

I stood up and adjusted my grip on my cane just in case I wanted to use it like an oversized nightstick. "Linda, do you want to go with him?"

"No."

Ingersoll seemed to notice me for the first time. "I don't know who the hell you are, but stay out of this, unless you want to find out what ICU is like."

"Mr. Ingersoll, I'm Brad Lyon from the—"

He shouted me down. "Oh, don't tell me! Are you some other guy that's been screwing her? *An old cripple*? Jeezus, she'll do anybody, except her husband."

My first inclination was to blurt, *Yeah, and I can understand why*. Instead, I kept my voice calm and firm, saying, "Look, I understand you're upset, but the bottom line is that I'm not going to let you kidnap your wife."

Ingersoll showed an ugly smile, shook his head as if amused, and reached into the back pocket of his pants. A second later, a small blue steel auto pistol was pointed at my nose. "Oh, I'd really like it if you tried to stop me."

Sixteen

The gun was only inches from my face, unpleasantly close enough for me to see two things: that it was an older model Browning .380 caliber and, more importantly, that Jeff needed some remedial classes in felony gunslinging. Although the hammer was cocked, the pistol's safety switch was still on, which meant he couldn't shoot. However, it would only take a quick flick of his thumb to release the safety, so if I was going to do anything stupid, it was now or never.

Twisting my upper body so that I was momentarily out of the line of fire, I quickly raised my cane and chopped downward on Jeff's right wrist. There was a metallic snap as he pulled the trigger and the gun's hammer hit the safety mechanism. Less than a second later, there was another and slightly louder snapping sound as my cane struck bone. The pistol popped from his hand and fell to the carpeted floor. Jeff clutched at his wrist and howled with pain, while frantically scanning the floor for his gun. But before he could make a move for it, I grabbed him by a handful of pink Izod shirt and tucked the knobby handle of my cane under his chin.

Pushing his head upward so that he could look into my eyes, I said, "Hey, did you ever see *2001: A Space Odyssey*?"

Jeff's pupils were constricting with fear. "Yes."

"Remember the scene near the beginning of the movie when one ape beats another with a big bone like he was a piñata?"

"Yes."

"Well, if you so much as look at that gun again, that's exactly what I'm going to do to you. Understand?"

"Yes."

"Good. Sit down." I shoved him into the armchair.

Jeff watched as I edged over and scooped up the Browning. He whined, "You bastard. You broke my goddamn wrist."

"Considering you tried to kill me, you're lucky I stopped there."

"I knew the safety was on. I was just trying to scare you."

"Nice spin. You should be working in Washington." Turning to Linda, I said, "Call the campus police and tell them there was just an attempted murder here."

Jeff peered imploringly at Linda with golden retriever puppy eyes. "Linda, please don't. You know that I love you."

"Have you been smoking crack?" Linda lifted the phone from the cradle. "You killed the man I love and then tried to shoot a cop, and I'm supposed to save you? Go to hell, Jeff, and when you get there, say hi to my dad."

"He's a cop?" Jeff blinked at me. "And what do you mean that I killed someone?"

"We'll get to that in a minute," I said.

I removed the ammo magazine from the pistol and ejected a live bullet from the chamber. The gun was loaded with nasty-looking hollow-point rounds, the same kind of ammunition cops carry for its knockdown power. As I handled the piece, I noticed that my hands were still a little jittery from adrenaline palsy.

Putting the unloaded gun on the desk, I said, "Okay, Jeffy, let's talk."

Jeff tried to look imperious. "I've got nothing to say to you. I want my lawyer."

"Good. That means you can take the fall for Frank Merrit's murder."

"But I didn't kill anybody!"

"Maybe that's true. But you just tried to execute one of the people investigating the murder of your wife's lover." I leaned against the desk and folded my arms. "A skilled prosecutor can connect the dots for a jury. It might not be the *right* dot-to-dot picture, but hell, it's not as if we'd be sending the Dalai Lama to prison. Nobody's gonna miss *you*."

"The guy she was screwing from the museum is really dead?" Jeff bit down on his lower lip.

"Let me commend you on the earnest-and-puzzled expression. It's the best I've seen in a long time. But you're going to have to do much better than that to convince me you didn't kill him."

"The police are on the way," Linda said, hanging up the phone.

"I *am* friggin' puzzled!" Jeff was beginning to sound a little panicked. "What makes you think I did it?"

"Because you knew about your wife's relationship with Merrit, you're a violent asshole, and you were in the Shenandoah Valley on Saturday morning."

"No, I wasn't."

"You damn liar, you said you were going to Waynes-boro!" Linda shouted.

"Yeah, what she said," I added serenely.

"Well, I didn't go to Waynesboro!" Jeff yelled back at his wife.

I held my hand up to silence Linda and asked, "How about Remmelkemp Mill? Did you go there?"

"No. I never went into the Valley."

"So, where *did* you go?"

From somewhere in the distance a police siren began to wail. It was joined a second later by two more, a synthe-sized and dissonant Greek chorus singing the keening theme song of modern human tragedy. The cops would arrive soon, so I had to finish the interview quickly.

Jeff looked down at his wrist, which was beginning to swell and turn red. "I was up in Burnley."

"Where is that?"

"North of here, almost up to Orange County."

"What kind of vehicle were you driving?"

"My Mustang Shelby Cobra."

I wanted to say: *Why is it that it's almost always the lit-tle dorks that drive muscle cars?* But time was short and I couldn't waste any smoothing Jeff's ruffled feelings. So I said, "Can someone confirm you were there?"

"Yes . . . her name is Jeanette Sleeman."

Linda's eyes bulged. "That skank with the fake boobs from your office?"

Jeff's jaw tightened and he looked out the window.

I said, "I think we can take that as a big yes. What's her address?"

"One-nineteen Beck Road."

"How long were you there?"

"From around nine until eleven-thirty."

"And once you were finished, what did you do the other two hours and twenty-five minutes?" Linda snapped.

Although it was fun watching Jeff squirm, I held up my hand for silence again. "Sorry, Jeffy, but a girlfriend isn't much of an alibi witness. Did anybody else see you there?"

"No. Her ex-husband had the kids this weekend."

"Then you've still got problems."

Jeff looked back from the window at me. "What if someone could confirm that they saw me at eleven-forty-five?"

"Can somebody?"

"The maitre d' at the restaurant at the Barboursville Winery. We went there for lunch."

"That's a pretty busy place. Will he remember you?"

"He should. We're sort of . . . regular customers."

The sirens were growing very loud now and I heard a cruiser skid to a stop outside Stoller Hall. I said, "Linda, will you go open the door and wait there so the officers can see we don't have a hostage situation here?"

"And you had the gall to call *me* an adulterer. I'll be gone by the time you post bond. Don't come looking for me," Linda said, glaring at Jeff as she went to the office door.

I said, "I have just a few more questions. Do you smoke?"

"No."

"How about Jeanette?"

"What does that have to do with anything?"

"I'll assume the answer to that one is, yes. Okay Jeff, you say you didn't kill Merrit, which might technically be the truth. But do you know who did?"

Jeff looked dumbstruck. "You mean, did I pay to have him murdered?"

"Stranger things have happened."

"Hell, no. I just figured she was having a fling. But if I'd known how she really felt about the guy, I . . . I suppose I should stop talking now."

"It's the first bright thing you've done since we met."

A pair of UVA cops and a Charlottesville officer came into the office and they eyed us warily. I showed them my identification and handed them the gun. While I told the cops what had happened, Jeff tried to shout over me. He called me a liar, claimed I'd been the aggressor and offered his broken wrist as evidence, and when that didn't seem to make the cops any more chummy, he began naming all the local politicians who were his friends. The sad thing was, the "servants of the people" probably *would* try to pull some strings for the developer, but I couldn't let that concern me now. Then Linda corroborated my story and Jeff was arrested, but the officers couldn't handcuff him because his right wrist was now about the diameter of a large coffee mug and just about as flexible. As they led him from the office, Jeff began moaning about the excruciating pain and the cops assured him that they were going to take him to the hospital before booking him into jail.

After that, Linda and I followed the police car in our own vehicles to the campus police station to make written statements. We were allowed to use one of the department's report writing computers, so I had my account typed up in less than thirty minutes. Meanwhile, Linda sat at another workstation, staring as if hypnotized at the winged toasters flying across the computer screen.

Getting up to collect my papers from the laser printer, I paused to put a hand on her shoulder. "Are you all right?"

She tensed her shoulder and I thought she was going to jerk away from my touch. Then she relaxed slightly and said, "I'm just numb."

"That's understandable. Can you help me with one other thing? Are Jeff's offices here in Charlottesville?"

"Yes. They're at the corner of Pantops Drive and Ringwood. It's the ugly cement building with a sign that says JRI Homes." She looked up at me. "Do you promise you'll call and tell me when Frank's funeral is?"

"The moment I find out. But—"

"I don't give a damn whether Marie will like it or not. I'm going. It's what a wife would do."

"I agree. Take care of yourself, Linda."

It was almost noon by the time I left the campus police station and the sudden transition in temperature from the air-conditioned atmosphere inside to the tropical environment outside was like a physical blow. I moved into the shade of a huge oak tree and called home on my cell phone. As the phone rang, I frantically tried to think of some innocuous way to break the news that I'd nearly been shot that wouldn't give my wife a bad case of déjà vu.

Ash picked up, and seeing my name on the caller ID screen, said, "Hi honey. How did it go?"

"Everything went really well. She confirmed the relationship and said something interesting: When Merrit called her on Saturday, he was doing it to break a date, because he'd just spoken with Gage and told him to get over to the museum ASAP."

"But Gage said Merrit just left a message on his answering machine."

"Which was conveniently erased, so we only have his word the message ever existed."

"But why would he lie?"

"I don't know, but I think we'll have a better idea once we take a look at the museum's acquisition policy. How are you coming along with the bears?"

"I'm trying to be very careful, so it's going slowly. I've

taken the Bruin teddy apart and I was right. It's new excelsior and the growler is made out of plastic."

"Which proves it wasn't made in 1907. Has the workmanship given you any ideas as to who might have made it?"

"Actually, yes." Ash sounded uneasy. "But I want to take a look at that counterfeit antique quilt we took from the museum before I make a final decision."

"Do you think it's the same artist?"

"Possibly. The quilt is in the evidence room and I haven't heard back from the message I left on Tina's voice mail. She's got to authorize a deputy to release it to me."

"Tina's probably still in the autopsy."

"That's what I thought. So, where are you now? Are you coming home soon?"

"I'm just leaving the UVA police station and now I've got to run up to Barboursville to follow-up on a couple more leads. I'll head home after that."

"Why did you have to go to the police station?"

"Um . . ."

"Brad, I thought you said everything went *really well.* Those were your exact words."

"Well, I was getting to that, and it did go really well . . . from a certain point of view. Ingersoll's husband didn't shoot me and I *did* get the gun away from him." Meanwhile, I was thinking: *Congratulations, Lyon. That was about as smooth as a gravel road.*

"What?"

"I'm okay. There are no holes and I'm still full of O positive."

"That's not funny."

"I know and I'm sorry. But I didn't have any control over this. Linda's husband, Jeff, came crashing into her office and pointed a gun at me. It was a real been-there-done-that moment, so I smacked him with my cane and now he's in custody. That's why I'm here at the police station."

Thankfully, Ash sounded a little less annoyed. "But why did he attack you?"

"Linda moved out last night because she half suspected that her husband killed Merrit. Jeff came looking for her and apparently thought I was one of her lovers."

"It's a natural mistake, but *could* he have killed Merrit?"

Deciding that this wasn't the best time to try and defend Linda's honor, I said, "He says no, but I have to check out his alibi. Jeff claims he was in bed with one of his employees at her house at about the same time the murder went down."

"These people are amazing. And so you get to talk to *another* bimbo?"

"And then go up to that winery in Barboursville to check out the other part of his story. After that, I'll head right home. Promise."

"Okay and, Brad honey, you *know* why I get so upset. Bad things just seem to happen to you."

"Good things too. You happened to me. I'll see you in a couple of hours, my love."

I went to the SUV, checked the map book for Pantops Drive, and then drove eastward across town. The headquarters for JRI Homes was located in a large business park and Linda was correct; the building was ugly. With its slanted, gray cement walls and narrow, mirrored windows that were evocative of machine-gun slits, the place looked like a bunker. If this was any evidence of JRI's architectural designs, I wondered if their housing developments looked like the Maginot Line. I parked the truck and went inside.

I asked for Jeanette Sleeman at the reception desk and was told she worked as a clerk in the legal department. It was lunchtime, but the receptionist said that she'd check to see if Jeannette was still in the building. A few minutes later, Jeanette came into the lobby. She was a thirty-something redhead with a gravity-defying bust, too much makeup, and a smudge of what looked like peanut butter in the corner of her mouth. I told her that Jeff had asked me to talk to her, but neglected to mention that he was currently in jail. She agreed and we went outside.

It wasn't a long chat and I tried not to focus on the bobbing dab of peanut butter as she spoke. Jeanette confirmed that Jeff had been at her house on Saturday morning and that they'd had lunch at the Barboursville Winery. Upon further questioning, she told me she smoked Salem cigarettes and backed up Jeff's statement that he didn't smoke. When we finished I told her about the peanut butter and suggested that the JRI legal department might want to get to work on posting Jeff's bond.

Although I dislike fast food, there wasn't time to stop for a proper lunch, so I hit a drive-through to pick up a box of chicken fingers and a soda. I ate as I drove up to the small town of Barboursville. The winery and restaurant were closed on Mondays, but I was in luck. Several members of the staff, including the maitre d', were in the restaurant for a meeting to plan menus for the next week. The maitre d' verified that Jeff and Jeanette had been at the restaurant on Saturday. So, what had originally seemed a promising lead had petered out faster than the Teddy Ruxpin robotic teddy bear craze of the mid-eighties. It was time to go home.

I was westbound on U.S. Route 33 and had just crossed over the Blue Ridge Mountains, when I passed a green pickup truck coming in the opposite direction. Hunting is a popular pastime around here, and there are lots of green trucks in the Shenandoah Valley, so the odds against me spotting the suspect vehicle were probably a thousand to one. But, Ash is right. Things do just happen to me. The truck was a decommissioned military pickup—you could see where the U.S. Army stencil and numbers had been covered with black spray paint—and the driver was a white guy wearing a baseball cap. There was no time to drive to one of the turnarounds, so I hit the brakes and made a U-turn across the grass median. By the time I was headed eastbound, the truck was turning left onto Callison Lane. I accelerated and fumbled with my phone to call Ash. But again, things happen to me. There was no cell service because I was too close to the mountains. Prudence said to go and get some backup, but we might never find the truck again in the wilderness that bordered Shenandoah National Park. So I turned left too, and followed the truck while trying to figure out how I was going to explain *this* to Ash.

Seventeen

The lonely two-lane road followed a lazy and meandering course northward through dense forest along the base of the Blue Ridge Mountains. It was beautiful country, wild yet mellow, verdant, and basically unchanged from the time when the Shawnee lived here. However, I really wasn't in the proper frame of mind to appreciate the scenery, because there was no sign of the Ford. I sped up, but couldn't go too fast, in case the truck had turned on to one of the unpaved driveways that occasionally intersected with the highway. Glancing at my cell phone, I saw that I still didn't have any service.

I drove across a creek on a narrow bridge and soon came to a fork in the road. On the left side, the trees gave way to a dead cornfield and this gave me an unobstructed view of the lane for a couple of hundred yards to the west. The truck wasn't visible, so I had to assume the man had turned right and followed the road farther back into the hills. I swung the Xterra to the east and slammed my foot down on the accelerator, choosing speed over caution.

The road became increasingly serpentine and I couldn't always see very far ahead. I was traveling way too fast and this fact was driven home a second later when, while rounding a tight curve, I almost smashed into the rear of the Ford as it poked along the road. I slammed on the brakes and slued to a stop, while the guy in the pickup truck looked at me in his rearview mirror. Unfortunately, I couldn't get a good look at him due to the GUN CONTROL MEANS HITTING WHAT YOU AIM AT and PETA—PEOPLE EATING TASTY ANIMALS bumper stickers on the truck's back window. Talk about botching a rolling stakeout. I could have given the FBI lessons.

The standard operating procedure for a mobile surveillance is that if your target has burned you, you're supposed to go past him and pretend he doesn't exist. That tactic might work well in an urban setting with a full surveillance team, but it's pretty much useless on narrow roads in a rural environment and when you're working solo. My options were limited, so I remained behind the Ford as it made its leisurely way down the road. Then, after about three hundred yards with the right turn indicator on, the truck turned east onto a rutted dirt track that led up a hill.

I drove past the turnoff and made a big production out of stomping on the gas, in the hope I'd convince the truck driver that I'd been frustrated by the delay. Continuing about a quarter-mile farther down the road, I made a U-turn and went back to where the Ford had gone up the hill. I pulled over to the side of the road and checked the phone again, but it still couldn't find a cell signal. The smart thing would have been to withdraw and return with Tina, some deputies, and maybe even Sergeant Preston of the Royal

Canadian Mounted Police and his dog, Yukon King, because the terrain looked pretty damn rugged. But there was no guarantee that this was a driveway and if it was an old road, it might come out anywhere. The bottom line was that being cautious could mean losing a potential investigation lead. I slipped the Xterra's transmission into four-wheel drive mode and slowly drove up the hill.

Pine trees and fallen logs hemmed the road. It looped around the hill and started upwards at a more acute angle and I wondered if I wasn't already inside the National Park. I crested the steep ridge and had to stop. The Ford was parked directly in my path and there was no way around it, due to the boulders and dense foliage. Furthermore, there was no safe way to back down the hill. Then the driver stepped out from behind a pine tree and I saw he was brandishing an old baseball bat. Can anybody say, "Ambush?" And I'd driven right into it.

Now that he was no longer in the vehicle, I could see the man was in his late fifties and big and burly—like a Coke machine with arms. He had thick salt-and-pepper hair with a curly mullet, a bushy gray moustache stained yellow in places from cigarette tar, and he wore a blue ball cap with a Colt Firearms logo above the black silhouette of an M-16 rifle. Approaching the driver's side of the SUV, he casually swung the bat and smashed out my left headlight. It was a big bat, and I suddenly wondered if we'd jumped the gun in identifying the hammer as the weapon that had killed Merrit.

He yelled, "You been following me since the highway and I want to know why."

I realized that if I tried to back up and escape, he'd simply pulverize the driver window and I'd probably lose control of the vehicle and hit a tree. Then the real fun would begin. I was frantically trying to assess the situation and realized that something just didn't make any sense. If this were the man who'd killed Merrit, the most natural course for him to follow now would be to kill me. After all, we were in the middle of nowhere, there were no witnesses, he had to know that I couldn't call for help, and it might be months or even years before anyone found my body or the truck.

Yet, it was clear he wanted to interrogate me and I hoped that meant I could talk my way out of this situation. There was no point in denying I'd been tailing him and it didn't seem likely that admitting I worked for the sheriff was going to impress him. But, I suddenly thought of something that might. Ash's ancestors helped settle the Shenandoah Valley and the Remmelkemp clan was large and enormously respected among the local population, so I decided to employ some emergency name-dropping.

So, I lowered the window, shut the engine off, and called out the window, "Now, do you *really* want to start a feud with the Remmelkemps?"

"What about the Remmelkemps?" The man squinted at me, slightly uncertain now. He was close enough for me to see the bat was a "Harmon Killebrew" autographed model. Imagine a caveman's club and you'll have the general idea.

"Do you know them?"

"I do and you ain't one of them."

"But I'm married to one."

"Who?"

"Ashleigh Remmelkemp. Her dad is Lolly and her mom is Irene."

"You're married to Josh's sister? I went to school with him." The man lowered the bat perhaps an inch.

Ash's younger brother had just turned thirty-seven two months ago, so the news that this powerful yet aging hulk of a mountain man had been Josh's schoolmate was a shock. Usually, I'm pretty good at estimating ages, but this guy was twenty years younger than he looked.

Trying to keep the conversation flowing in a direction that didn't involve blunt force trauma, I said, "Josh is a good man. He and his wife and kids were over at our house last weekend. When was the last time you saw him?"

"Been a while. You still ain't told me why you're following me."

I decided it was better to share the truth now rather than later. "Because I'm helping the sheriff with a murder investigation."

"Is this Frank Merrit's killing you're looking into?"

"Yeah, did you know him?"

"Uh-huh. The no-good little snake was married to my sister and dyin' was the best thing he could have done by her."

"You're Marie's brother?" I feigned nonchalance, but was instantly on guard again.

"Yep. I'm Sheldon Shaw." He didn't offer his right hand, keeping it gripped on the baseball bat.

"And my name is Brad Lyon."

"You got a gun?"

"If I did, don't you think I'd have been busting some caps at you?"

Sheldon thought about that for a second and then gave a humorless chuckle. "I reckon. So, what's Frank's murder got to do with me?"

"Can I get out of the truck so we can talk?"

"Sure, but do it slow, cause I still don't know if I trust you."

"No problem, because I couldn't get out of this thing quickly if my life depended on it." I slowly climbed from the SUV and held my cane up. "I hope I can keep this."

"Something wrong with your legs?"

"I got shot in the left shin when I was a cop in California." Somewhere off in the distance and to the left I heard the maniacal laugh of a pileated woodpecker, sometimes known as the "Oh, my God" bird due to its impressive size. Sheldon and I both turned to look for it. When the sound died, I said, "Mr. Shaw, I'm not sure I can trust you either, but I'm going to be up front with you. Your truck is pretty distinctive and it was seen at the museum on the morning that Frank was murdered. That's one of the reasons why I need to talk to you."

"So, you was shadowing me because you done thought I killed him, right?" There was a flinty tone to his voice.

"I'd have been a moron if I'd ignored the possibility."

"It ain't right to judge a man before you speak to him."

"Or smash his headlight out with a ball bat."

Sheldon looked a little sheepish. "I reckon. You said that me being at the museum was *one* of the reasons. What's the other?"

I leaned against the Xterra. "You were also seen dumping Frank's smashed-up computer at the trash transfer station in Elkton."

"Since when is it against the law to throw away garbage?"

"Well, I think the issue is how the computer, which belonged to Massanutten County and was issued to Frank, by the way, *became* garbage. It looked like somebody beat it with a hammer."

"I didn't see how that happened."

I thought: *That may technically be the truth, but I'll bet you know* how *it happened.* I said, "And then there's the problem of Marie lying to the sheriff and me about the computer. When we went to her house on Saturday afternoon to make the death notification and talk to her, she told us that Frank never had a county computer at home. Unfortunately, we knew otherwise."

Sheldon studied the barrel of the baseball bat. "Which means you'd like to know where I got it. That's easy. I found it."

I sighed. "Sheldon, you seem like a decent guy and I'd hate to see you do something for family and end up getting yourself in a world of hurt. Can I share some information and then offer you some advice?"

"I reckon."

"Almost nobody knows this, but Frank was beat to death with a hammer. It might even have been the same hammer used to smash the computer that you *found*. Then there are the FBI agents who are prepared to testify they saw you drive up to the museum and do a turnaround."

"FBI?" Sheldon involuntarily looked down the rutted track for Jimmy Stewart and Efrem Zimbalist Jr. Then he gave me a cagey look. "You had me going there for a moment. Now, why would the FBI be in Remmelkemp Mill?"

"I know it's hard to believe, but they were there tailing that orange Hummer you saw."

"Oh Lord."

"So, you were at the museum. Add that to the fact that Frank and Marie were having marital problems and that you probably made no secret of how much you disliked your brother-in-law. Now what do you think a jury would make of all that?"

Sheldon propped the bat between his legs and dug a package of Camel nonfilters and a disposable lighter from his shirt pocket. Lighting up a cigarette, he said, "I didn't kill Frank."

"I believe you; but it looks as if you've been left holding the bag."

It took a second or two for him to understand what I was inferring. "By Marie?"

"Sorry, but that's sure how it appears to me."

"But she's my sister."

"And family has screwed-over family ever since Adam ate the apple and blamed Eve."

"Did Marie tell you about me? Is that how you found me?"

"No, but she sure didn't go out of her way to protect you either. Why did you go to the museum?"

"I was going to kick Frank's ass, but I wasn't going to kill him." Sheldon sucked deeply on the cancer stick and blew out a furious stream of smoke. "Marie done called me on Saturday morning all crying and mad. She said that Frank just told her he was moving out that day after he finished up at the museum."

"Do you know if there was any advance warning that this was going to happen?"

"Back in the winter, Marie told me that she thought Frank was stepping out on her. But she didn't think he had the guts to leave."

"But when he decided to, you were furious."

"Nobody does that to my sister."

"Did she say anything else?"

"She needed my help. Marie told me Frank was writing a book on that computer and she'd be damned if he sold it and spent the money on his girlfriend."

I swatted at a big horsefly that was buzzing around my face. "And so she took a hammer to the machine."

"I don't know what she hit it with."

"But she hoped that smashing it would destroy the computer file for the manuscript? That's stupid. Even if she'd somehow ruined the hard drive, didn't she figure that Frank would have saved a backup copy of his work someplace else?"

"I don't know nothing about computers and I didn't have to ask Marie why she done it. That was obvious. She was madder than hell."

"And you agreed to dispose of the computer."

"Yeah, she asked me to get rid of it."

"Which wasn't bright, and not only because it was a county computer. Besides, Marie probably would've been entitled to half of whatever Frank made if he sold the book."

Sheldon tossed the cigarette butt to the ground and crushed it beneath his boot heel. "Maybe so, but all my sister was thinking about was how bad Frank would feel when he found out that his book was gone for good."

"So, why didn't *she* take it to the dump?"

"She was worried that someone would get the license number of her truck."

"Yet you ran the risk of being identified as an accessory to felony vandalism by taking it to the trash station. That doesn't make any sense. Why not just dump it by the side of the road or bring it up here?"

Sheldon gave me an aggrieved look. "I'd never do that. There's all sorts of stuff in those computers that'll ruin the land and get into the water. Ain't there already enough rubbish been dumped in the Valley?"

"I agree," I said, wondering if Sheldon was even marginally aware that he'd littered only a few seconds earlier, when he'd thrown his cigarette on the ground.

"And besides, I really didn't know how the computer got broken, so I wasn't breaking any laws." Sheldon might have been the quintessential uneducated country boy, but he wasn't a fool.

"Did Marie ask you to go to the museum and talk to Frank?"

"Not directly, but I think she knew what I was going to do."

"And what were you going to do?"

"Like I said before, I was going to give Frank a righteous ass-whipping. So, I drove over to the museum, but there was cars and people there."

"Do you remember what kind of vehicles?"

Sheldon stuck another cigarette in his mouth and looked skyward. "I saw a white van—it was on the road—Frank's Toyota, and an orange Hummer in the lot. Frank was out in front talking to the three Oriental guys."

"So, what did you do?"

"You already know what I did. I turned around in the driveway and left. Usually there ain't a damn soul at that museum."

"Did you go back later?"

"Yeah, but you already knew that too." He lit the cigarette.

I nodded sagely, deciding it wouldn't be wise to tell Sheldon that this was news, and that nobody had seen him the second time. I said, "Obviously, the FBI saw you, but I'd like to hear your version of what happened."

"Okay, but there ain't much to tell. When I got to the museum, this time there was a couple of SUVs there: a blue one and a black one."

"Could the blue one have been a Isuzu Trooper?"

"Maybe. But to tell the truth, all them import trucks look alike to me."

"How about the black one?"

Sheldon looked thoughtful as he let some smoke leak from his nostrils. "A Ford Explorer, I think. Not a new one, though."

"Did you see anybody outside?"

"No, and that was when I said, 'Shel, you've got things to do. Give it up for another day.' "

"Where'd you go after that?"

"Back home to wrap hay bales."

"And home is?"

"Over near Furnace." He pointed downhill, presumably in the direction of the tiny community.

"So, if you didn't do anything wrong, why in the hell were you so paranoid about me following you?"

"Mister, I'm sorry about your headlight, but the mountains here are changing." He made a sour face. "We've got crank cookers using abandoned houses and other riffraff up here now. You weren't in a police car, so I thought you were one of them."

"If it's that bad, why haven't you spoken to the sheriff?"

"Because it's our way to take care of things ourselves. And if you're married to a Remmelkemp, I reckon you know what I'm trying to say. Nobody pushes mountain folk."

For a moment we were silent and listened to the rustling leaves. Then I said, "We don't know where Marie was when Frank was killed. She told us that she was at yard sales in Elkton, but I don't believe her."

"Mister, even if my sister did set me up, I won't turn on family." Sheldon turned and went to the Ford. Tossing the bat inside, he said, "I'll move my truck, so that you can turn around. Oh, and don't call your insurance about the headlight. I'll mail the money to Lolly."

Eighteen

"I can explain" is one of the most unnecessary phrases in the English language. Inevitably, the situation is such that the person being offered the explanation already has a pretty clear picture of what happened and isn't going to be soothed by verbal damage control, no matter how skillfully or penitently it's delivered. So, as I drove down the mountain, I tried to figure out how I was going to tell Ash that, despite her all but begging me to be careful, I'd nearly gotten myself killed for the second time in less than four hours.

I turned into our driveway and saw that Tina had returned from the autopsy in Roanoke. Her patrol car was parked in front of the house and she and Ash were sitting on the porch drinking lemonade. Ash's warm smile turned into an expression of distress when she saw the smashed headlight. The women rushed from the porch, followed by Kitch.

Ash was standing at the driver's door as I pushed it open. "My God, what happened?"

"I can explain."

"Oh, Brad honey, you promised me you'd be careful."

"I was. I'm sorry. I can explain."

Tina bent to look at the damage. "This wasn't caused by a traffic collision."

"No, a baseball bat."

"You were attacked with a baseball bat? Are you all right?" Ash began scanning me for injuries.

"I'm fine. The only thing he hit was the Xterra."

"Why?"

"Because he thought I was a crook."

"Do you think you could identify him if you saw him again?" Tina asked.

"ID'ing him isn't a problem. His name is Sheldon Shaw and it might interest you to know that he's Marie Merrit's brother and also the owner of that green Ford pickup truck we've been looking for."

"The one seen at the museum and the trash station?" Ash asked.

"Yep. I was driving home and had just come over the mountain when I saw the truck going in the opposite direction. I tried to call for backup, but couldn't get a signal. He turned on to Callison Road and I decided to take a calculated risk and follow him."

Tina squinted at me as if I'd just announced that I thought I looked like Leonardo DiCaprio. "A calculated risk? You went up into the mountains after a possible murder suspect by yourself, unarmed, and without communications? Are you nuts?"

"Oh, like you wouldn't have done it?"

"No, I wouldn't." Tina looked away, unwilling to meet my gaze.

"Give me a break. As long you're telling fairy tales, can I have *Little Red Riding Hood* next?"

Ash said, "But honey, what you did was reckless."

I touched her cheek. "Look, I'm not going to pretend it worked out perfectly, but it was worth a broken headlight. Once we started talking, and Sheldon found out I was married to Ashleigh Remmelkemp, he gave me some very valuable information."

"Such as?"

"For starters, Marie knew that Frank was having an affair, and on Saturday morning he'd broken the news to her that he was leaving."

Tina arched her eyebrows. "Funny, she didn't mention that."

"And Sheldon also told me that she smashed the county computer with a hammer or something and then asked him to get rid of it."

"And she flat out lied about that. Why'd she destroy the computer?"

"Frank was writing a book about the Civil War and Marie was in scorched-earth mode." Kitch shoved his head under my right hand and I began to scratch him.

"Did Sheldon tell you whether he thought his sister was involved in the murder?" Ash said.

I said, "He refused to say anything about that. But at the same time, he didn't offer to be her alibi when I mentioned we didn't know where she was when Frank was killed."

"So, is she our primary suspect?" Tina asked.

"One of them; maybe the best one. The way she wrecked the computer tells us that she has a capacity to become unhinged."

"True."

"However, we can't overlook something else Sheldon said about going to the museum. By the way, his mission was to PR Frank."

"Public Relations?" Tina was clearly puzzled.

"Nope. Pound and Release. When Marie called and told him that Frank was leaving, Shel was determined to defend his sister's honor." I switched to a Groucho Marx voice and waggled an invisible cigar. "Which is more than she ever did."

"But he didn't go into the museum when he saw there would be witnesses," said Ash.

"Exactly, but what we didn't know was that Sheldon went back a second time and had to postpone Frank's ass-whipping again, because now there were two SUVs in the museum lot. He thought that one may have been a black Explorer and the other was a blue import SUV."

"Gage's Trooper?" asked Tina.

"There's no proof of it. But if so, then he lied to us about Merrit leaving him a phone message as well as leaving out the little detail that he'd already been there that morning."

"But if Gage was at the museum when Merrit was killed, why would he come back?"

"Maybe to pretend he'd discovered the murder. Possibly trying to throw suspicion elsewhere. Maybe he thought that if he raised the hue and cry, nobody would suspect him."

"Ash told me what happened in Charlottesville. Are you absolutely convinced it wasn't Ingersoll's husband?"

"Unfortunately, yes. His girlfriend confirms that he was at her place in Burnley until eleven-thirty or so and she didn't impress me as being bright enough to lie. Then another witness places them at the Barboursville Winery about fifteen minutes later."

Ash said, "Well, we have some other news, so why don't we get in out of the heat and I'll pour you some lemonade?"

A minute later, we were seated in the living room. Kitch lay sprawled at my feet and I was in the process of giving myself a headache from drinking the iced lemonade too quickly.

Tina said, "There were no big surprises at the autopsy. Dr. Grice did some measurements and confirmed that the hammer is the murder weapon."

Massaging my brow, I replied, "A weapon of opportunity. That might signify that whoever went there didn't intend to kill him."

"And then there's this." Ash held up the limp mohair body of the fake Bruin Manufacturing bear. "Once I removed the excelsior, I went over to the sheriff's department to compare it with the quilt we seized from the museum. Then I drove over to the fabric store in Dayton, just to be sure."

"You've lost me."

"The style of hand-stitching on the bear is almost identical to that on the quilt and I was certain I'd seen it before. I didn't want to believe it, but I was almost one-hundred percent certain it was Holly Reuss's work."

"Holly? The same woman who's a member of the teddy bear guild?"

"Yes, and also a quilter. The last time we were at the fabric shop, I noticed that one of her quilts was for sale and hanging from the wall. I didn't have any other samples of Holly's work, so I went over to compare it with the sewing inside the bear." Ash looked both incensed and sad. "And I'd be willing to testify in a court of law that all three items were made by the same person . . . that is, if I don't break Holly's neck first."

"What do we know about her . . . other than the fact that we've been allowing a crook into our house for months?"

Tina said, "Widowed—her husband died in an industrial accident—and she has two kids at the middle school. She works at some veterinary office in Harrisonburg and supplements her income by making quilts, or at least that's what she says. No criminal record."

"And there's one other thing we know about her." Ash threw the teddy bear down. "She used the guild classes to learn how to make counterfeit teddy bears. I can't believe she sat here, week after week, Little-Miss-Meek-and-Mild-oh-Ashleigh-thank-you-for-being-my-friend, and all the while she was conning us."

"Where does she live?" I asked.

Tina said, "Across the river, at that little trailer park on Rocky Bar Road."

Ash punched her open hand. "And I can't wait to talk to her. When do we go?"

"I hate to disappoint you, honey, but she's probably still at work, so it'll have to be later. What's our next move, Tina?"

"Why not go over to the vet's office and question her right now?"

"Talking to her is important, but we also want to schmooze our way into her house to see if there are any signs of the counterfeiting operation in plain sight."

Tina nodded. "And if we make contact with Holly at work, she'll deny knowing anything. Then, once we're gone, she could call and have her partner-in-crime, or maybe even her kids, go and remove the evidence."

"Precisely. So, what's our next move, Tina?"

"I really think we need to talk to Marie."

"I agree. Holly may be producing fake antiques, but there's nothing to connect her with the murder . . . yet."

"So, do we go back out to her house?" The look of dismay Tina wore told me that she wasn't looking forward to another visit to the pigpen.

"No, she probably wouldn't let us in. Besides, we need to lure her out of her safety zone."

"But how? I don't think she'll come to the station voluntarily."

"No, but what if the county risk management supervisor called the grieving widow and said he was going to recommend the insurance company pay off on Frank's policy and asked her to come to his office and sign some forms?"

"But the board of supervisors hasn't made a decision on that yet."

"Never let the facts interfere with a useful story. You know she'll break a land speed record getting to his office and we'll be there, waiting for her."

"But . . ."

"What's the problem?"

Tina looked uncomfortable. "This may sound ridiculous, but we'd be lying. I don't know if I want to do that, considering how corrupt the sheriff's department was before I took office."

From my point of view, it *did* sound ridiculous; I wasn't suggesting anything illegal or even that uncommon in law enforcement practice. But I didn't say so, because I also understood what was troubling her. Tina was acutely aware that she represented law and order in a county where, until recently, the cops had been as crooked as a mountain switchback road.

Still, I said, "Tina, it's your investigation, and I'll abide by your instructions. But as your consultant, I have to tell you that making a decoy call like that is perfectly lawful. Every court in the land has ruled that it's okay to use a ruse to catch a crook."

"I suppose." Tina heaved a huge sigh. "But I don't like doing it."

"Well, God help me, I do. But then again, you're a much better person than I am. You want me to call risk management?"

"No, I'll do it. Can I borrow your phone?"

While Tina made the call, I took some ibuprofen for my leg and assured Ash that Sheldon Shaw was going to pay for the damage to the Xterra.

Tina hung up the phone. "He agreed to do it. He'll call Marie now and ask her to come to his office at four. If she falls for it, he'll call us right back."

"Then I guess we'd better put Kitch in his crate and turn the TV on," I said.

"Does that mean I'm coming along?" Ash had been looking downcast until that moment.

I caressed her chin. "Hey, you're my partner. Let's get ready to roll."

The phone rang and Tina answered it. After a few moments of conversation, she hung up and said, "She bought it. She'll be at the office in a half hour."

"That's a good sign. It probably means Sheldon hasn't called to warn her that we're looking at her as a suspect. But before we go, where is Saturday's newspaper?"

"Out in the recycling box in the shed," said Ash as she ushered Kitch into his crate.

"Can you grab it for me?"

"Sure, but why?"

"It might be useful when Marie starts lying to us."

Ash got the paper and then we all got into Tina's patrol car and sped into town. Tina parked the car in the sheriff's station's parking lot, where it wouldn't be noticed, and we walked over to the old brick courthouse, which also housed the county's administrative headquarters. The risk manager's office was on the second floor. His name was Wilfred Hughes and he surrendered his gloomy wood-paneled office while repeatedly telling Tina that he hoped she understood that *he* wasn't responsible if anything went wrong. Bureaucrats . . . it's a shame there isn't an official season to hunt them.

Tina sat down behind Hughes's desk, while I took the other office chair and Ash remained standing, leaning against a filing cabinet.

"If you think I've missed something, please jump in," said Tina.

"I won't have to, if you get a twist on her and don't let go."

"But . . . I'm not . . ."

"A cruel and manipulative ogre like me?"

"That's not what I meant."

"But it's true. Despite appearances, I'm probably more of a grizzly than a teddy bear, which works out fine for cop work. You want me to give her a taste of the wild kingdom?"

Before Tina could answer, there were two tiny raps on the door and it slowly swung open. It was Marie Merrit and she was dressed in what I guess was intended to be a casual mourning ensemble of baggy black pants, a black pullover T-shirt, and ugly black shoes. Still, she didn't look sad so much as anxious and fatigued.

When she saw who was waiting for her, Marie said, "What the hell is going on here?"

"We really need to talk to you again, Mrs. Merrit," said Tina.

"I can't believe you tricked me into coming here. Don't you people have any compassion? I just lost my husband."

"And we need to talk about that. Please, sit down."

"So you can try to twist my words around again? I'm going home."

Tina shot me a look that said: *You can let that grizzly out of his cage any time now.*

"Oh, spare us the moral outrage. It's like a slaughter-house worker complaining about his steak." I stood up and shoved the chair over. "Have a seat."

"Are you deaf? I've got nothing to say."

"Wrong. You're going to tell us the truth and you know why? You want the money, but you've screwed yourself."

"What are you talking about?" There was a flicker of uncertainty in Marie's eyes.

"I'm happy to explain. Life insurance companies live for the opportunity to deny a payoff on a policy and you've provided them with the best excuse in the world."

"Really? What's that?"

"You've given us deliberately false statements and we can prove it. Once the insurance investigator reads that in the crime report, he'll tell his company that you might very well be the primary suspect in Frank's murder. You can kiss the money good-bye."

"I didn't kill him!"

"Maybe, but you did lie to us. Was that to protect the real killer?"

Marie's chin fell. "I didn't know it was going to happen."

I gently tapped the side of the chair with my cane. "Sit down, Marie. You and I both know you want the money, and for people like you, betrayal never tastes as bad as you think it will."

Nineteen

Marie stood in the doorway, white-faced with anger. Based on everything I'd observed and what Linda Ingersoll had told me, Marie was an archetypal bully and Frank had been the classic wishy-washy enabler. Therefore, it wasn't likely she was accustomed to direct confrontation and my aggressive stance was intended to exploit that potential weakness. But the longer she stood there, with an invisible comic-strip thought-bubble above her head that clearly said, "Pound it up your ass," the more I worried that I'd miscalculated. She wasn't under arrest, so we couldn't stop her from leaving, yet I knew our only chance to get the truth was by surreptitiously bullying the bully, so I continued to look at her with an expression of bored contempt. Finally, Marie closed the office door and sat down stiffly in the chair.

I folded my arms. "Okay, let's establish the ground rules right now. You lied to us during the first interview and you aren't going to waste our time again. You'll answer all my questions honestly and completely. If you get stupid and start to lie, the interview is over and you don't get the money. Understood?"

"Are you enjoying this?"

"As a matter of fact, I am. Do you understand?"

"Yes." Marie spat the word out and then noticed Ash. "Who is she?"

"That's my wife, and she's played a major role in helping us investigate your husband's murder." I perched myself on the edge of the desk so that she would have to look up at me. "And now that we've all been properly introduced, who killed Frank?"

She devoted almost three seconds to pondering the ethics of shivving a family member in the back before saying, "I don't know for certain, but I think it was my brother, Sheldon."

Not wanting her to know that I'd already spoken with Sheldon, I asked, "What's his last name?"

"Shaw."

"And where does he live?"

"On Old Forge Road in Furnace."

"Do you know if he has a history of physical violence?"

"He's never been arrested for anything like that . . . that I know of."

Talk about damning with faint praise, I thought, while trying to look thoughtful. "And why do you think he did it?"

"I love Shel, but he has a hair-trigger temper and he was madder than a hornet at Frank."

"Over?"

"On account of Frank leaving me for another woman. On Saturday morning, Frank told me he was moving out and wanted a divorce. He said he'd be back for his things after work." Marie looked at the floor. "I was so hurt. I couldn't understand what I'd done."

"Hurt, or upset the gravy train was pulling out and you weren't on board?"

"What the hell do you mean by that?"

I shrugged. "Just that Frank was working two jobs, while you played couch potato, shoveled down cookies, and let your house turn into the residential equivalent of a landfill. When he said adios, that was all going to change."

"I'm not lazy. I told you that I suffer from severe chronic fatigue syndrome."

"Yeah, but the strange thing about *your* illness is that it's conveniently selective. You're too fatigued to do housework, but you weren't too tired to go to yard sales or rush over here to collect a life insurance check."

Marie bristled. "Oh, so just because I wasn't chained to a vacuum cleaner, that gave him the right to abandon me?"

"Abandon? It looks to me like you drove him out," Tina interjected.

"That isn't true. I loved him."

I said, "Well, you've got a damn funny way of showing it. Why didn't you tell us about Frank saying he was moving out, when we were there on Saturday afternoon?"

"Because . . ."

"You would have had to tell the rest of the story and implicate your brother, right?"

She looked up at me searching for some sign of empathy. "Yes."

I kept my face stern. "That's understandable and maybe even admirable, but we've got to have the entire truth now."

"I know."

"So, let's begin with the other woman. Do you know who she was?"

She folded her arms. "No."

The body language told me she was lying, so I made a game show buzzer sound and stood up. "You lose. I told you what would happen if you lied to me. What, did you think I was kidding?"

"But—"

Turning to Tina, I said, "Come on, let's go."

"All right, I knew about her!"

"Too late. Oh, and by the way, do you want to know how I know you're lying? I talked to Sheldon just a little while ago."

Marie looked panicked. "Please! Give me one more chance."

"Why? So you can ask for *another* chance the next time I catch you lying?" I leaned close to her. "Here's a major news alert: I'm not flexible and forgiving Frank. I'm Attila the freaking Hun. Maybe all the men in your life have been spineless wonders, but you're not going to manipulate me like you did them. Try it again and the least of your concerns will be losing out on the money."

"If you've already talked to Sheldon, why are you bothering me? Why didn't you just put him in jail?" Marie grumbled.

"Because I don't think he killed Frank and, just for the record, he was a hell of a lot more forthcoming than you are." I settled back on to the desk again. "Tell me about the other woman."

"Her name is Linda Ingersoll and she's a professor at UVA. Frank started acting sneaky back in November, right after coming home from a conference at William and Mary. I assume that's when he met her."

"How do you know who she is?"

"I followed Frank one day when he said he was going to the UVA library to do some research. Instead, he went to a motel in Ruckersville. A woman showed up a little later and went into the room." Marie looked at Tina. "I got the license plate of her car and had one of your deputies check it through the DMV for me."

It was one of those intellectual long-expired-date-on-the-milk-carton moments. You know it's going to smell awful, but you still open it and take a whiff. I said, "Accessing a law enforcement database for personal use is against the law. Why would a deputy do that for you?"

"Because we're very close old friends." Marie tried to sound innocently kittenish, but the statement came out as a smirk.

I glanced at Ash, who gave me a cross-eyed look of disgust.

Meanwhile, Tina was tight-jawed. "Which one of my deputies?"

Marie said, "Ron Mooney. Gee, I hope I haven't gotten him into trouble."

Clearing my throat, I said, "Getting back to Linda, the DMV paperwork would only have given her name and address. How did you find out she worked at UVA?"

Marie took a deep breath. "I, uh . . . Sheldon told you about the computer, didn't he?"

"You mean the computer that you claimed was never in Frank's office in the garage? As a matter of fact he did, and coincidentally, we've been holding it as evidence since Sunday morning."

"How?"

"Sheldon took it to the trash transfer station and a witness saw him dump it."

"What an idiot."

"No, just environmentally conscious. What was it about the computer that told you Linda worked at UVA?"

Marie gave me a challenging look. "I installed surveillance software on his computer at home. It allowed me to read his emails and everything else he typed."

"Whoa. That's more than a little intrusive."

"I had a right. He was being unfaithful to me."

"Maybe so, but you could have taken the direct approach and talked to him about the state of your marriage."

"Why was it my responsibility? I was happy and he decided to have an affair with that slut. I had to protect myself."

"So that if it did come down to divorce, you'd have some damaging material from the emails, right?"

She broke eye contact. "You don't understand."

"Fortunately, I don't have to. Did you destroy the computer because you were afraid that Frank would discover that spyware?"

"No, he'd never have found it."

"So why *did* you destroy the computer?"

"He was writing a book about the Civil War. Apparently it was good. He had a couple of hundred pages written and I knew that there was a publisher already interested."

"Because you were eavesdropping on the email?"

Marie flared. "Hey, don't sit in judgment of me. I wasn't the only sneaky one. I wasn't the one that had the affair or wrote to my sleazy girlfriend that I'd hold off on selling the book until I'd separated from 'Jabba the Gut.' "

"For someone utterly convinced about how right you are, you seem mighty touchy. But hey, no more talk about flagrant invasions of privacy," I said in an artificially cheery tone. "Back to the computer: You were going to tell me your reason for smashing it."

"I was angry and hurt and there was no way in the world that I was going to let him profit from something that he'd worked on while we were married."

"I think you want to believe that, but it doesn't make any sense."

"What do you mean?"

"Unfortunately, most people would rather read about Britney Spears forgetting to put on underpants than American history, so the publisher couldn't have been offering much money for Frank's manuscript."

"It was four thousand dollars."

"And you'd have been entitled to half of that. You aren't stupid; you had to have known the manuscript would have been declared community property in a divorce agreement."

"But you weren't worried about the money," Ash said meditatively. "You just wanted to hurt him."

"What if I did?" Marie shot a glowering look at Ash. "He'd hurt me."

I said, "And just so that we're clear on this, you did know that the computer actually belonged to Massanutten County, right?"

I could tell Marie was calculating the odds on slipping a lie past me. Then she noticed I was grinning at her and she said, "I suppose."

"Good girl. Just what did you use to smash it?"

"A piece of two-by-four."

"And I imagine that's how you injured your shoulder."

"Yes."

"Was your son aware of what you were doing?"

"No, he was still asleep in his room."

"So, what did you do after you finished whacking the hell out of the computer?"

"I called Sheldon and told him what happened."

"What time was that?"

"Sometime around nine."

"And how did Sheldon react?"

"He was furious and said that he was going to go over to the museum and give Frank the beating of his life." Although she was trying to sound distressed, there was an underlying trace of gleeful vindication in her voice. "He said that he wasn't going to sit there and do nothing while I was being dishonored."

"Knowing how much you loved Frank, did you say anything to dissuade your brother or otherwise prevent the assault?"

"Don't you sneer at me. I loved my husband but I had no control over Sheldon."

"Really?" I asked with a bitter chuckle. "Did you love him enough to call him and warn him that he had an ass-whipping inbound?"

"I called him."

"Yeah, at ten-oh-three. That's about an hour after you'd fired Sheldon up. Was that call to ask Frank how it felt to be in the same sort of pain you were?"

"If he got beat up, it wasn't my fault." Marie sounded slightly coy. "It's not like I *told* Sheldon to go over and attack him."

"Not directly, but you did a superb job of pushing his buttons to nudge him in that direction. What happened when you spoke to Frank?"

"Nothing. He hung up on me."

"And you assumed he'd done that because it was hard for him to talk with broken teeth and that he'd put two and two together and come up with you having sent Sheldon over there."

"I don't know what he was thinking."

"Right. This may come as a disappointment, but he hadn't been beaten up. He just didn't want to talk to you. Fortunately for Sheldon, he didn't get the opportunity to thump Frank. Did you know that?"

"No. I haven't heard from Sheldon since Saturday."

"Do you know why he's been incommunicado?"

"No. I thought maybe he'd accidentally killed Frank and was hiding out."

"No, it's probably because he thinks *you* might have killed Frank."

"What?"

"He didn't say it directly. In fact, he refused to roll on you. But, just like us, he knew you went someplace by yourself on Saturday morning. And I imagine he wonders if it was the museum."

"This is getting crazy. I told you I didn't go there."

"That's right. You told us that you'd gone to yard sales in Elkton." I pulled the classified section from the newspaper and held it out for her. "There's a listing of all the yard sales in Elkton. Would you please take a look and tell us which ones you went to?"

Marie looked away from the newspaper and began tapping her foot.

"All you have to do is pick one of those addresses out. We'll go over there with your driver's license picture, they'll say, 'Oh yeah, she was here and bought the old Village People LPs,' and you're in the clear."

I moved the classified section another couple of inches closer to her face and Marie suddenly slapped it from my hand. "All right, goddamn it, I didn't go to garage sales."

"Oh dear! That means you don't have an alibi witness for your husband's murder." Then, I sang to the tune that signaled the end of the original Mickey Mouse Club TV show: "Now it's time to say good-bye to all that blood money."

Marie gave me a venomous look, huffed, and said nothing.

"Sorry, that was unnecessary, *but fun*." I leaned closer to Marie, daring her to slap my face as she had the newspaper. Suddenly, I knew exactly where she'd been and I knew it was time to nail her inside the coffin. I continued, "I'll bet I know where you were and if I'm right, you have a decision to make. Keeping your mouth shut about where you were means the insurance company will deny your claim.

But if you cop to the malicious mischief, you've got a rock-solid alibi and it's payday, right?"

Marie's lips were compressed and white with anger, yet she still said nothing. Meanwhile, Ash looked a little perplexed. With everything else we'd discussed about what had happened in Charlottesville and later, on the mountain, I'd forgotten to mention that Linda's car had been vandalized on Saturday morning.

After another couple of seconds of silence, I said, "Come on, Marie, you went to Linda Ingersoll's house in Charlottesville, didn't you? You had her address."

Finally, she nodded and said through gritted teeth, "I gave that little slut a taste of the misery she's given me."

"Go on."

She slapped her thigh. "You already know what I did, so why are you making me say it?"

"Because you're playing passive-aggressive word games—phrasing things so that you can deny them later. What precisely did you do?"

"Fine. I poured acid all over the hood of her PT Cruiser and I'm not the least bit sorry. Are you happy, now?"

"Ecstatic, because that proves you couldn't have been at the museum when Frank was murdered. You've chosen wisely, Grasshopper." I stood up, just in case she changed her mind about slapping me after what I had to say next. "But I wouldn't spend that insurance money too fast."

"Why?"

"Well, when we're finished with this murder investigation, I'd be betting that Sheriff Barron is going to charge you with felony vandalism for destroying the computer, as well as with providing false information to the cops."

We both looked at Tina, who flashed a cold smile and nodded.

I continued, "Then the Charlottesville police are going to charge you with another count of felony vandalism. Add up all your lawyer's fees, penalties, and the financial restitution you'll have to pay to Massanutten County and Linda Ingersoll, and by the time it's all played out, I doubt you'll have enough money left over to buy a package of chocolate-covered Oreos."

Twenty

Marie stalked from the office and slammed the door.

Tina said, "How did you know she vandalized Linda Ingersoll's car with acid?"

"Linda told me about the damage, but it wasn't until a minute ago that I connected that event with Marie being away from home. Sorry, but between being threatened with guns and baseball bats, I forgot," I said. "The weird thing is that Merrit's wife and lover have mutually supporting alibis."

"And she doesn't seem to miss him. All she cares about is the insurance money." Ash was still looking at the door.

"And herself. But Merrit deserves some of the blame too. He helped create that cookie monster by rewarding her dysfunctional behavior."

Tina's jaw tightened. "Speaking of rewards, once we're finished with *this* investigation, I'll have to start another one on Deputy Mooney."

"What will you do if you find out he misused the computer system?" Ash asked.

"Fire him and file felony charges."

"Good for you," I said.

Tina glanced at her watch. "It's pushing five now. Give me ten minutes to brief the county legal counsel and then we'll head over and talk to Holly Reuss."

"Oh yeah, I can hardly wait for that," Ash said with unsavory relish as she interlaced her fingers and pushed her palms outward.

I touched her shoulder. "Sweetheart, I hope you understand that 'grilling a suspect' is just an expression."

Not surprisingly, Tina spent triple the time she expected talking to the county attorney, so it was nearly five-thirty by the time we left the office. It was hot and oppressively humid outside and the air was as unpleasantly stagnant as the debate on congressional ethics. We got into her patrol car and headed eastward on Coggins Spring Road, leaving town and crossing the Shenandoah River. As we approached the Blue Ridge Mountains, Tina turned south onto U.S. Route 340, otherwise known as the Stonewall Jackson Highway.

As we drove through a combination of pastureland and forest, I said, "Just so I have my facts straight, Holly was at the teddy bear guild meeting on Saturday morning, right?"

"Yes. She got there about ten and was one of the last ones to leave our house," said Ash.

"Probably not more than five minutes before you called," added Tina.

"So, we know she wasn't present when Merrit was killed. Did either of you guys notice anything different or strange about her demeanor?"

Ash thought for a second. "No, she was her usual self."

"I agree," said Tina.

"And based on the times I've talked with her at meetings, wouldn't you say that her usual self is pretty . . . I don't know . . . let's say, naïve?"

"Yes, but it had to have been an act," Ash said.

"You're probably right. It's just a little hard for me to imagine that someone who blushes and hides her eyes when we kiss, also possesses the ice-cold self-presence to sit and scam us for months while making counterfeit teddy bears."

"That doesn't mean anything. The way you guys kiss, sometimes *I* blush," said Tina.

After another few miles, we saw an old wooden billboard ahead on the left side of the road that read, ROCKY MOUNT COVE MOBILE HOME PARK. The trailer park was surrounded by a white-painted brick wall and looked to be about the size of a normal city block. Two Bradford pear trees flanked the entrance and, inside, there were three rows of single and doublewide mobile homes, separated by narrow asphalt lanes. The prefab houses were old, but most looked well-maintained with tidy little yards. There was a small manager's office just inside the entrance and beside it was a grassy playground with a metal jungle gym, swings, and a teeter-totter. It wasn't the exclusive Seacliff district of San Francisco, but at the same time it wasn't a slum.

Which brings me to something I've wondered about ever since moving to the South. In this era of social sensitivity and political correctness, why is it still considered perfectly acceptable to call the residents of mobile home communities "trailer park trash?" It seems to me that making cruel jokes about folks because they live in low-income housing is just a form of bigotry. What's more, I've met plenty of "trash" that lived in bayside condos and million-dollar mansions. It isn't where you live that's important, but how.

Holly Reuss and her kids lived in space number twenty-two, on the third tier of homes. The house was a white doublewide with a pair of ceramic gnomes on the tiny front

lawn and a brightly colored windsock dangling from a
window awning support. An older model Honda Civic was
in the carport, which seemed to indicate that Holly was
home. Tina parked the patrol car in front of the house and
we got out. There were birds chirping and the faint grinding
hum of an overworked air conditioner could be heard from
the back of the house. Otherwise it was quiet and peaceful.

We went up onto the claustrophobically small screened-
in porch and Tina rapped on the aluminum door. The door
opened a second later and Holly Reuss blinked at us in surprise, brushed away a stray strand of black hair, and then
her moon-shaped face broke into an expression of wary de-
light. She was still wearing her work uniform: A dowdy
calf-length gray corduroy skirt that accentuated her pear-
shaped figure and a pale blue linen blouse that bore cartoon
images of cats and dogs dressed as doctors and nurses.

"Hi, you guys! What brings y'all over here?"

It was a cheerful greeting, but I noticed that Holly remained in the doorway.

Tina looked nonplussed and I think she was expecting a
more furtive greeting. She said, "Holly, I'm sorry but this
is more of a business call than social."

Holly's face froze. "Oh my God, is there something
wrong with my kids? They—"

"No, your kids are fine. We need to talk to you about
something else. Can we come inside?"

Rubbing her upper lip, she said, "Oh, I don't know, the
house is such a mess. Can we talk out here?"

Tina shook her head. "This is kind of a sensitive issue
and it's hot out here."

"But I'm getting supper ready."

"I guess I'm not making myself very clear. This is a
criminal matter, Holly." There was just a touch of iciness in
Tina's voice now. "We have reason to believe that you're

making counterfeit antique teddy bears. It's also possible the bears could be connected with a murder. *Now*, can we come in?"

"Murder? Oh Lord, yes! Come in!" Holly threw the door open.

Going inside, we stopped and stared in astonishment at what had once been a living room, but was now a minia-ture assembly plant for teddy bears and quilts. There was a large unfinished wooden worktable in the corner of the room. On it was a Bernina sewing machine, piles of folded fabric, and dozens of neatly stacked unassembled quilt squares. Suspended from the wall above the table, was an antique Log Cabin–design quilt that Holly was obviously using as the model for her efforts. It was iden-tical to the bogus quilt we'd recovered from the museum.

In the other corner of the room was a smaller table that was serving as a teddy bear tanning gallery. A sturdy metal frame straddled the tabletop and there were three sunlamps attached to it. The bright lights shone down, baking a pair of bogus Michtom teddies that were just beginning to have their mohair fur artificially aged and faded. Seen in their pristine state, I wasn't as impressed with their quality as the bears we'd found at the museum. I realized that the weathering process also served to camouflage the unre-markable workmanship.

Beside the table was a workbench laden with an assort-ment of metal files, pet grooming brushes and combs, tweezers, sandpaper, and emery boards. It was pretty much everything needed to give a counterfeit antique teddy bear the authentic scuffs and wear marks that an experienced collector would expect to find on a century-old stuffed animal.

Standing against the opposite wall was a modular metal shelf unit and it was neatly loaded with teddy bears, attesting to the fact that Holly had been busy. Six or seven sham Michtoms were on the top shelf and there were maybe ten bogus Bruin Manufacturing bears sitting on the shelf below that. But when I realized what was on the bottom shelf, my amazement gave way to simmering rage. There sat two counterfeit Farnell Alpha bears identical to the one stolen from our home two weeks earlier. I tapped Ash gently on the arm and nodded in the direction of the Farnell bears. She stifled a gasp and turned to look accusingly at Holly, who wore an expression that said she was dimly aware that our visit was about to suddenly turn nasty, yet seemed to have no idea why.

The smart thing would have been to let Tina handle the interrogation. But the memory of our home being violated and my brush with death was too fresh, so I was mad and unwilling to wait for answers. I bent over to grab one of the Farnell bears and then held it up in front of Holly. "Pardon me if this sounds just a little abrupt, but where the hell did you get the original to make this fake?"

Holly shrank from me. "It's not a fake, it's a replica."

"Oh, don't play word games with me."

"But I'm not, Brad—Mr. Lyon," she corrected herself when she saw from my expression that we were no longer on a first name basis. "I don't understand why you're so upset."

"Okay, let's pretend you don't know. Two weeks ago, some crook broke into our home in the middle of the night, took a shot at me, and stole the original."

"What! I don't know anything about that!"

"As if your partner in crime didn't tell you about it when he delivered the bear."

"I don't have a partner in crime!" Holly wailed.

"Stick with that story and you'll be doing as much prison time as he will."

"But Mr. Lyon, we're friends. I'd never do anything to hurt you or Ashleigh." Holly began to cry.

"That's the bear taken from your house?" asked Tina.

"A first-rate copy, right down to the little bald spot on the left side of his muzzle." I handed the teddy to her.

Ash touched my arm and I saw that she looked concerned rather than angry, which wasn't really a surprise. My wife's anger is like a Fourth of July skyrocket: quick to explode and then burn out. Also, she's more kindly than I am. She's inclined to believe the best about people and give them the benefit of the doubt, which was obviously the case now. Ash murmured, "Brad, I'm as mad as you are, but I think she's telling the truth."

"Why?"

"Because she's scared to death of you hating her; not of being arrested. Also, I can't imagine she'd have let us in if she'd known where the bear came from."

I reined in my anger a little, recognizing Ash's observations were valid. "That may be. But if she's innocent, how do you explain the fact that she'd been to our house all those times for guild meetings, yet didn't recognize the Farnell as one of the bears on display in our living room?"

Ash gave me a quizzical look. "Honey, do I have to remind you that we own over five hundred teddy bears? Sometimes even I don't remember them all. Besides, we never took the Farnell out of the curio cabinet. Holly could have easily missed it."

"I never saw that bear at your house. And if I'd known what happened, I'd have given it back to you." Holly wiped her nose on her arm.

I was beginning to believe her too, but I still had questions. In a gentler voice I said to Ash, "Okay, then what about this counterfeiting operation?"

"Tina and I will ask her."

I was bright enough to understand that Ash was discreetly advising me that she thought it best if I didn't ask Holly any further questions, and I knew she was right. In my anger, I'd jumped to conclusions, terrified Holly, and might well have ruined our chances to learn what she knew. So, I shut my mouth and let the women take over.

Tina said, "Holly, we're sorry if you're upset, but we need to know about these bears and quilts because they might be connected with Frank Merrit's murder."

"Mr. Merrit is dead? Oh, God have mercy on his soul. I liked him."

"You didn't know? It was in today's newspaper and on the news."

"Between work and taking care of the kids, I almost never follow the news." Holly was recovering her composure as fear gave way to curiosity. "Did someone rob the gift shop and kill him?"

"We're not quite certain how it happened, but while we were investigating, Ashleigh noticed a couple of your bears on display in the museum."

"In the gift shop, you mean."

"No, they were up on a mantle and identified as real antiques."

Holly looked confused. "But he said the bears were for the museum gift shop."

"*Who* said that?"

"My boyfriend, Neil."

"Neil Gage?" Tina and Ash asked simultaneously.

"Yes."

I bit my lower lip to prevent myself from jumping in.

Ash said, "How long have you known Neil?"

"I met him at a quilt show in February and we began dating a little while after that."

"And was he the one that got you started with all of this?" Ash pointed at the sewing table.

Holly nodded. "Back in March he told me about how his museum job was in trouble and how he'd come up with an idea to save it."

"How was that?" Tina asked.

"He said that they were going to offer nice replicas of antiques at the museum gift shop. It'd be just like the stuff they sell from the Franklin Mint. Neil was even talking about them starting up a museum shop website."

"And he wanted you to make replica quilts and teddy bears, right?"

"Neil said my needlework was so good and I was such an artist, that he didn't believe there was anybody around here that could do a better job," Holly said, with a trace of pride. "It seemed like a great opportunity to make a little extra money. Being a single mom, it isn't always easy to make ends meet."

Tina and Ash both looked a little sad and I'm certain it was for the same reason that I felt a pang of empathy. Although Holly was indeed a superb quilter and an increasingly skilled bear artist, it was obvious to the three of us that Gage had romanced her for the sole purpose of duping her into participating in the counterfeiting operation. It was nothing more than a slight variation on the age-old "lonely heart" embezzlement scam. No doubt the cold-hearted bastard had also hinted at matrimony, but I hoped the women wouldn't ask her about that. Holly would learn the full extent of Gage's deceit soon enough.

Tina said, "So Neil brought you the antique bears to use as models . . ."

"And the fabric, accessories, and equipment and I started in to work."

"But you never told any of us at the teddy bear guild about it. Why did you keep it a secret?" Ash asked.

Holly turned her gaze to the floor. "Because I needed the money and Neil said he'd broken a rule because he loved me."

"And what rule was that?" Tina asked.

"He said that other people should have been allowed to bid on the contract to make things for the gift shop. It was some sort of county law and if anyone found out about how he bent the rules, he'd be fired and I'd lose the extra money."

"So, you do have a contract?"

"Not a written one. Neil said that we had an oral agreement, which was safer because if there were no papers, nobody could prove I had a contract with the museum."

Or that you had any sort of business relationship whatsoever with Gage that could later implicate him. Talk about being left holding the ball, I thought.

Ash asked, "How much money were you paid for this stuff?"

"Three hundred dollars for each quilt—we don't sell so many of those—and one hundred and fifty dollars for each teddy bear." Holly shot a grateful glance at the sun-tanning teddies. "That money sure came in handy when the dentist told me that my daughter, Beth, needed braces."

I only had a vague idea of what a genuine antique quilt would cost, but I knew the bears were being sold for three thousand bucks a piece, which meant that Holly's cut from the action was chump change.

"Did Mr. Merrit know about this arrangement?" Tina asked.

"Neil said he knew, but I never talked to Mr. Merrit about it. Neil said it was best if I stayed away from the museum, so that people wouldn't be suspicious."

It took some real self-control not to add: *And also so that you wouldn't see your bears weren't in the gift shop and start asking unwelcome questions.*

"Did Neil have any other associates? You mentioned something about "them" starting a website."

"There was a man I saw once. He showed up at the house one time when Neil came over to pick up some bears. But I never actually met him. He stayed outside in his truck."

Tina did her best not to sound too eager. "Can you describe him?"

"Just a guy in his forties with a big beard. He didn't seem real friendly."

"When was this?"

"Back in April, I think."

"And what kind of truck was he driving?"

"A black SUV. I think it was a Ford Explorer, but I wasn't really paying much attention."

Tina, Ash, and I exchanged glances. Tina said, "Did Neil ever talk about him?"

"Just that he was supposed to be starting a website to sell the bears on the Internet."

"Do you know the web address?"

Holly shook her head. "No. Come to think of it, Neil never gave it to me—not that I had any time to play around on the computer."

"When was the last time you saw Neil?"

"On Friday night. He took the girls and me to the movies in Harrisonburg."

"And you haven't heard anything from him since?"

"No." Holly then saw something in our faces that alarmed her. "Is Neil in trouble?"

"He might be." Tina paused for a second and then

sighed. "There's no nice way to break this news, but Neil was lying to you. Your bears and quilts aren't at the museum gift shop and never were. It looks like he and the other man have been selling your work to collectors as original antiques."

"Neil wouldn't do that." Holly flashed a nervous and rigid smile.

"I can prove it. We already know of one instance where two of your 'replica' bears were sold to a Japanese buyer for six-thousand-dollars."

"Six thousand . . . and I got three hundred?"

Ash said, "And I imagine it's a similar percentage for your quilts. You've been cheated on so many levels, it breaks my heart."

"No. This is all a mistake."

"No, Holly." Ash slipped an arm over Holly's shoulder. "Neil took advantage of your loneliness and used you. Denying it will only make it harder for you in the long run."

"But why would he do that to me—to us? My kids really like him." Holly was blinking back tears.

"Because he's a conman and you're a mark. And here's the scary thing: He also lied to us about Frank Merrit's murder."

"Oh God, this is like a nightmare."

Tina said, "I know and that's why we need your help. Where are the first two bears he brought you to copy?"

"He said he took them back to the museum. That was back in April. I'd gotten so good at making them, I didn't need the originals anymore."

"And how about the quilt?"

"I finished the first replica in May and he took it back." Holly searched Tina's eyes. "But the things on display in the museum are mine, aren't they?"

"Yes. Neil probably sold the real antiques to some other collector."

"Oh Lord, am I going to be arrested?"

"No, you weren't aware that you were breaking the law."

"But what about the money? I don't have it to give back."

"I don't think that's going to be a problem. Let's not worry about it now," said Tina.

Ash patted Holly's shoulder. "What about our bear? Do you still have it?"

"Yes! I have it in my bedroom closet. Neil wanted it back, but I still needed to use it for making the replicas." Holly nodded in the direction of the bear Tina was holding. "Those are the only two copies of yours I'd ever made. Can I get it for you?"

"Please."

We filed down the hallway into Holly's tiny and cramped bedroom. She slid the mirrored closet door open, pulled the Farnell Alpha bear from the top shelf, and handed it to Ash.

As my wife hugged the bear that represented twenty years of happy marriage, I said, "Holly, I'm truly sorry for snarling at you. I jumped the gun and hurt a friend. I'll understand if you don't want anything more to do with me, but I want you to know that you're always welcome in our home."

Holly looked at Ash and said, "That's all right. I can see why you were so upset and I'd really like to stay a member of the teddy bear guild."

I reached out to shake her hand. "I'm glad to hear you say that. Can you answer just one more question for me?"

"I'll try."

"What brand of cigarettes does Neil smoke?"

"Winston Lights."

"They're the kind with the white filter tip, right?"

Holly's eyes shifted upward as she tried to recall. "I can't remember, but—oh, I know! Come with me."

We went outside and walked around the side of the trailer.

As she stooped to pick up a white cigarette butt, she said, "He isn't allowed to smoke in the house, but sometimes he does out here."

The filter had WINSTON inscribed on it in miniscule letters and was identical to the one we'd recovered from the museum.

Twenty-one

Five minutes later, we were driving southbound on U.S. 340 through the verdant farmland again. This time our destination was the village of Port Republic and Neil Gage's house. At first glance, Port Republic has a strange name, when you consider that it's a stone's throw from the Blue Ridge Mountains and a couple of hundred miles from the Atlantic Ocean. But it derives from the town's origins as a Shenandoah River anchorage during the pioneer era.

The museum curator was now a "person of interest" in a homicide investigation, so Tina radioed for a backup unit. However, the dispatcher told her that both on-duty deputies were tied up with other calls and there was no idea of when they'd be available.

"Tell them to clear ASAP and start rolling in our direction," said Tina, giving the dispatcher Gage's address. Slipping the microphone into the metal dashboard clip, she said to us, "I don't like waiting."

"Me either," I said. "Because you know sooner or later he's going to call Holly and, even though she promised not to, she's going to give him an earful. Then he'll be in the wind."

"But if he is a possible murder suspect, I don't want to expose you guys to danger."

I turned around to look at Ash in the back seat. "Hey honey, you want to chicken out and let Tina go there alone?"

"Not happening," said Ash.

"Agreed. Besides, if he's there, it means he hasn't tumbled to the fact he's in trouble. He'll probably assume we're just collecting more background information on Merrit."

"I hope you're right," said Tina. "So, could the suspect vehicle from your burglary have been a Trooper?"

"Like Gage's? I can't say for sure. For that matter, it might even have been the Explorer driven by the bearded guy. It was dark and a long way off."

"But remember, you said the left taillight had a hole in it," said Ash, from the back seat.

I shifted in my seat to look back at her. "You're right. We can check that out when we get to his house."

"But what I don't understand is how Gage could have known about that Farnell bear. He's never been inside our house."

"Which is something else we'll have to ask him. Oh, and thanks to both of you for saving the day back there. I almost screwed the pooch."

"Brad! You know how I hate that expression," said Ash.

"Sorry, *made love* to the pooch."

Tina rolled her eyes. "Getting back to police work, any thoughts on how to handle the interview with Gage?"

"Depends. How quickly do you want to arrest him?"

"I'd like to see what he has to say first."

"Then I'd start by talking about the counterfeit bears, but do it in such a way that he can blame any crimes on Merrit."

"And then I ram the lies down his throat and get the real truth."

"Gosh, that sounds kind of harsh. Who are you and what have you done with nice Sheriff Tina?"

Keeping her eyes on the road, Tina said, "Sheriff Tina has just been paying attention to how her consultant legally intimidates people to get the truth."

"Gee, you make me sound like a bully. I won't sleep a wink tonight."

Tina turned west onto Port Republic Road and followed a curving course through the small community. After another mile or so, she turned right onto Carrsbrook Dairy Road, a narrow lane that took us through a small grove and around the base of a gentle grassy hill. A tidy white Cape Cod–style house stood near the top of the hill and there was a blue Isuzu Trooper parked outside with its back snug against an aluminum shed. Tina drove up the gravel driveway to the house.

As we approached the home, Tina observed, "Well, he *did* mow recently. You can see the lines of dead grass."

"But not necessarily on Saturday morning. Otherwise, he'd have had grass all over his legs," I said.

Neil Gage emerged from the house and stood on the sidewalk leading to the driveway. He wasn't wearing his ball cap and I saw that he'd grown his hair long in the back and on the sides to compensate for the lack of it on the top of his head. He was wearing denim shorts and a lime green T-shirt with a breast pocket that was puffed out in the rectangular shape of a cigarette package. We'd obviously caught Neil at suppertime. He had a can of Coors Lite beer in one hand and a fried chicken leg wrapped in a greasy paper towel in the other.

We got out of the cruiser and Tina said, "Hi, Mr. Gage. How are you this afternoon?"

"Fine, I guess. Have you caught Frank's killer yet?" He took a swallow of Colorado Kool-Aid.

"We think we're making progress. I wondered if you could help us by answering a few questions?"

Gage wiped his lips with his fingers. "I don't know how I can help, but I'll try."

"That'd be great," said Tina, and I was impressed with how utterly clueless she sounded. "Now, I'm going to tell you something that no one else knows but us, but I need your promise not to say anything to anybody, okay?"

"Of course."

"We discovered something pretty shocking at the museum. It looks like someone has sold some of the display pieces, like the teddy bears and a quilt, and replaced them with top-quality fakes. Did you notice anything suspicious like that while you were working there?"

Gage took a bite from the chicken leg. "Nope, I don't know anything about that."

"That's interesting. I would have thought that with you and Frank working so closely together, you might have some idea of how that fraud happened."

"Sorry, I can't help, Sheriff."

Obviously, Gage wasn't going to take the bait to implicate Merrit, so Tina casually said, "I'm kind of surprised to hear you say that, considering we just came from Holly Reuss's house."

"Is that so?" Gage bent his head back to take a gulp of beer.

"Yeah, that's so. How would you like to tell us about the counterfeit bears?"

Suddenly, Gage tossed the can and the chicken leg aside as he spun around and began to run down the hill. Tina took off after him and, before I could say otherwise, Ash was also sprinting after the fleeing felon. Meanwhile, I stumped along in slow motion pursuit like a golf cart in a NASCAR race. Tina overtook Gage after about thirty yards and delivered a violent forearm blow to his back, knocking the man to the lawn. Then she and Ash jumped on the guy and started wrestling with him. By the time I got there, Gage was in handcuffs and being pulled to his feet. I was also relieved to see that Ash looked no worse for the wear and, indeed, was wearing a huge smile of triumph.

Spitting out dried grass, Gage shouted, "What am I under arrest for?"

"Grand larceny, fraud, impeding a police investigation, and maybe murder before we're done," said Tina as she pulled him up the hill toward the patrol car.

"You're breaking my frigging arm!"

"Then stop struggling, you moron."

I said, "So, *now* would you like to tell us about those counterfeit bears? And while you're at it, you can also explain why you were at the museum on the morning Merrit was killed."

"Screw you! I want my lawyer!" Gage gave me a poisonous glare.

"Lawyers are good. But shifting the blame for a murder onto your partner in the black Explorer is better," I said, hoping to tempt him into changing his mind about answering our questions. "Why should you be the only one to take the fall?"

"I've got nothing to say. I want my lawyer. These handcuffs are too tight!"

"I guess that also means you won't give us permission to search your house, property, and vehicle, right?"

"No, you can't search and I want my lawyer."

"That's fine. It won't be any problem getting a search warrant." I reached into his shirt pocket and pulled out a half-crushed package of Winston Lights. "Fortunately, we don't need a warrant to collect these."

"My cigarettes? What, are you too cheap to buy your own?"

"No, these are evidence. You see, you've got a nasty habit of tossing butts and we recovered one of them from the flowerbed at the museum on Saturday morning."

"Lots of people smoke that brand."

"Yeah, but lots of people won't have your DNA signature. That cigarette filter will have your saliva on it."

"So what? I work there. I might have tossed it on the ground any time."

"Maybe. But do you remember telling me that you went to the museum on Friday night to pick up trash?" I took my sunglasses off so that I could lock eyes with him. "If Frank Merrit paid as close attention to the yard as you said, I can't imagine you left a cigarette butt in the flowerbed that night."

"I never said that."

"Considering we can prove you're a world-class liar, I think a jury will buy my version of our conversation."

"I want my lawyer."

"The best defense attorney in the universe can't change your genetic fingerprint on that cigarette butt."

"You've got nothing on me." Gage jutted his chin out defiantly and barked an unsavory laugh. "Just wait 'til court. My lawyer will make that fat loser Holly look so stupid, nobody will ever believe her."

"Hey, you do realize you have the right to remain silent?" I placed myself directly in Gage's path, so that Tina and Ash had to stop.

"Yeah."

Tossing my cane on the ground, I chucked him gently under the chin. "Then I'd begin exercising that right immediately. Otherwise I'll have Sheriff Barron take your handcuffs off, so that it's a fair fight, and I'll cheerfully do the jail time for smacking the living crap out of you."

"He's threatening me!"

"Oh, shut up and get in the car." Tina pulled the cruiser's back door open and pushed Gage inside. Slamming the door closed, she turned to exchange a high five with Ash. "Thanks for the backup. You can come and be one of my deputies any day."

"Thanks, but I think I'm a little old for that," said Ash.

"Not from what I just saw, and heck, you aren't *that* much older than me."

"Well . . . I still have to give it a lot of thought." Ash gave me a nervous look.

Tina saw the stunned expression on my face and said, "Haven't you talked to him about it?"

"No, we've been so busy, I haven't had the chance," said Ash.

I was shocked and—I'll admit it—a little stung to learn of my wife's secret interest in law enforcement this way. She'd never given me so much as a hint that she wanted to be a cop and, trying to be rational, I understood why. Ash knew how much I missed police work and was concerned that I'd be miserable in the role of bystander. At the same time, I wanted her to be fulfilled and happy, particularly since she'd chosen to turn her back on a professional career when she became my wife. Ash was intelligent, brave, honest, had a sense of humor, and was level-headed, all the ingredients for a successful cop. So, although I was frightened at the thought of losing her to someone who might shoot straighter than the guy who'd popped me, I had no right to stand in the way of something she might want to do.

Stooping to pick up my cane, I said, "Honey, if it's what you want, I'll do everything in my power to help you."

"I just want to explore my options. Maybe I could become an auxiliary deputy."

I put on a brave face and took her hand. "Whatever you want, we'll make it happen. It's a fun job and if you decide to do it, you'll be great. But right now, I think Tina needs to check Gage's house for other suspects."

Tina said, "But he told us we couldn't search his house."

"Yeah! Stay out of my house!" Gage's voice was muffled as he screamed from inside the cruiser.

I said, "But we have a right to make a quick cursory search for officer safety to ensure there aren't any other suspects in there. Remember, we still have one crook and at least one gun outstanding." I reminded them, thinking of the break-in at our house and the shot fired at me.

"That's true."

"And when you're done, you can get a deputy out here to freeze the scene, and we'll get a search warrant."

"Can you watch this idiot while I check the house?" Tina jerked her head in Gage's direction.

"We'd be happy to keep him company."

Tina opted on the side of caution and pulled her pistol as she mounted the porch steps. Opening the door, she shouted, "Sheriff's Office! If there's anybody inside, come out now!"

Receiving no answer, she slipped inside, holding her gun in a two-handed grip. Ash and I watched the silent house, our anxiety building with every passing minute. It was a small home and it seemed to be taking her far too long to complete the search. I was on the verge of grabbing the 12-gauge shotgun from the cruiser and going inside to check on her, when Tina came out the front door with her gun holstered. She looked pleased.

She said, "The house is clear of other suspects, but not teddy bears. There were two of them on the table. Talk about careless."

"Maybe they were his escape claws," I suggested in an innocent tone. Both women groaned and I said, "Before we forget, we need to check the taillights of idiot's SUV."

"I heard that! I'm not an idiot!" shouted Neil.

I turned to yell, "You're right, because freaking Knucklehead Smith had more brains than you."

"Who's Knucklehead Smith?" asked Tina.

"He was one of Paul Winchell's ventriloquist dummies from back in the sixties . . . and I just really dated myself."

Ash went to check the back of the Trooper. "Both taillights are fine."

"I realize it might be hard to tell, but does the lamp cover on the left look like it might be new?"

"No, it's kind of scratched and it matches the one on the right side."

"So, it must have been the guy in the Explorer who took the shot at you," Tina said.

"If so, let's hope he hasn't gotten the damn thing fixed in the meantime," I said.

A deputy arrived a few minutes later and after a short briefing from Tina, he assumed control of the scene until we could return with a search warrant. However, the first order of business was taking Gage to jail. Getting into the car, Ash and I switched places. She sat in the front seat while I rode in back with the sullen prisoner.

I said, "Hi, Neil. Let's be earth friendly and carpool to the county slammer."

"I asked for a lawyer. That means you can't talk to me."

"Actually, that isn't true. But rather than get into a boring discussion about the nuances of Miranda versus Arizona, let me offer you some advice."

"I don't need your friggin' advice."

"I'm just as happy calling it a warning. When you're booked into jail, you're going to be allowed to make two telephone calls. Now, there are two people I'd strongly suggest you don't try to communicate with."

Gage turned to look out the window, ignoring me.

"First, don't call Holly and don't think you're being clever by having somebody else call to threaten her. You've already done enough harm there," I said. "Besides, intimidating a witness is a felony and judges generally like to make an example of people who do it."

"Fine. I've got nothing to say to that backstabbing cow anyway." Gage kept his eyes on the passing scenery.

"Yeah, she's a real Lucretia Borgia, that one. Now, the other person you shouldn't call is your partner with the ZZ Top beard."

Gage turned to give me a contemptuous look. "Oh yeah? Why?"

"Because the minute he learns you're in jail, he'll sky out of here so fast we'll all be able to hear the sonic boom. And you know what that means, don't you?"

"You have all the answers. You tell me."

"Jesus, are you *that* stupid?" I gave him a wintry smile. "If he escapes, you get charged as the primary player in Merrit's murder. Silence isn't just golden for you; it'll keep you off death row."

Twenty-two

Gage swallowed nervously and turned his head away from me. I knew I'd scared him, because he didn't say anything else during the rest of our journey to Remmelkemp Mill and the county detention facility. There was no way of being absolutely certain he wouldn't warn his partner, but I didn't think it likely now that he realized he'd be cutting his own throat.

We arrived at the sheriff's department and parked outside the prisoner's entrance to the jail. As Tina assisted Gage from the police cruiser, I said, "Don't forget to grab his felony flyers as evidence."

"His what?"

"Tennis shoes. We'll have the crime lab check them for fragments of broken glass and ceramics."

"I'll take care of it. See you in a minute."

As Tina took Gage into the jail, Ash and I remained outside. The summer solstice was just a few weeks away, so although it was nearly seven P.M., the sun was still fairly high in the western sky. It was the first time we'd been alone together since I'd returned from Charlottesville and there was a moment of strained silence.

Ash came over and put her palms on my chest. "Honey, I know you're upset, but I didn't know how to tell you."

"Not upset, so much as . . . I don't know. It just kind of blindsided me." I looked at the mountains. "Are you going to give up making your teddy bears?"

"No, of course not. I'm not looking for a career and this isn't because I'm dissatisfied with my life." Ash grabbed my chin and pushed it so that my eyes met hers. "And you're partly to blame, because you've infected me with your love of police work. So, I'd really like to become an auxiliary deputy sheriff. That way I can spend most of my time with you and the bears, yet still work a few patrol shifts every month."

"Like I said before, if you want it, then you have my complete support. But it's only fair to tell you that I have an ulterior motive for agreeing so readily."

"What's that?" She gave me a mischievous smile as she read my thoughts.

"I've always had this thing for a woman in a police uniform." I leaned over to give her a long slow kiss.

We were still at it when Tina emerged from the jail a few seconds later. She sighed and said, "Jeez, you guys! Why don't you get a motel room?"

"Okay," I said breathlessly.

"*After* we finish with the search warrant." She held up a grocery bag. "And I wonder if this guy ever heard about Odor-Eaters? His shoes smell worse than the morgue."

As we walked up the sidewalk to the main entrance of the sheriff's department, I asked, "What's Gage's bail?"

"I didn't think I had enough probable cause to charge him with the homicide—"

"You don't."

"So, it's twenty-five-thousand dollars."

As we filed into Tina's office, I made a sour face. "That's not enough. I know we're already jammed with paperwork, but we need to get a bail enhancement on that little creep. Between all the bears and quilts he's sold, there's no telling how much money he's squirreled away. Once he posts bond, he'll vanish."

"How do we get a bail enhancement?" Tina sat down behind her desk and began rubbing her forehead as if it ached.

"It's a simple judicial request form and as long as we're going to Judge Skidmore's house to have him sign the search warrant affidavit, he can approve the bail increase too. Let's ask for a million."

"Whatever you think is best," she said with a frown.

Ash said, "Tina, are you all right?"

"Yeah. Sorry, it's just been a long day. I missed lunch and I get a nasty headache if I don't eat."

"Well, how about while you guys do the paperwork, I'll go across the street and get some barbecue from Sergei?"

"God, that would be wonderful."

Ash went to get our supper and I logged the cigarette package into evidence and then started typing up the request for a bail increase. Meanwhile, Tina completed Gage's booking sheet and went to drop it off at the jail. She was still gone by the time Ash returned with a brown bag filled with food.

Looking up from the computer screen, I said, "That smells great."

"I got pulled pork sandwiches and fries for everyone." Ash put the bag on the desk and began unloading it. "Since we're doing paperwork, I figured that would be neater than ribs or chicken."

"Good thinking. How was Sergei?"

"Curious because he hasn't seen us. He might stop by here later this evening when we get back from serving the search warrant," she added in an innocent tone.

"And was that his idea or yours?"

"Mine." She grinned as she handed me a sandwich.

I began humming the tune to "Matchmaker" from *Fiddler on the Roof* but had to stop as Tina came back into the office. She said, "Oh thank God, food. Hey, I checked the phone numbers that Gage called from the jail and it looks like he took your advice. He called some defense attorney's office in Harrisonburg and then his mommy."

"And probably asked her to post his bond, which means the clock is ticking on this bail enhancement. Tina, once you've got some food in you, you might want to call Judge Skidmore and give him a heads-up on why we want to boost Gage's bail into the stratosphere." I took a big bite from the sandwich, wiped my hands on a paper napkin, and resumed typing.

Tina wolfed down her supper and called the judge while I completed the document. Hanging up the phone, she said, "He's on board to increase the bail to a million."

"Excellent." I clicked on the PRINT icon and the printer started to whine. "Why don't you guys run that over to Hizzonor's house right now and get it signed? We've got to get it filed at the jail before Gage posts bond."

"On our way," said Tina, snatching the sheets from the printer.

"And I'll finish eating and then get started on the search warrant affidavit."

Ash paused to kiss me on the forehead as both women left the office. By the time they came back, about ninety minutes later, I was hammering away at the affidavit and had it two-thirds finished.

Tina said, "That was one unhappy lady."

"Gage's mom, I assume?"

"Yeah, she got to the jail with the bondsman about five minutes after I delivered the form." Tina slumped into a chair. "Apparently I'm railroading her darling boy."

"Yeah, you cops are all alike."

Ash said, "Did you think we got lost?"

I glanced up from the screen. "No, I just figured you two Amazons had your bloodlust up and decided to go pick a fight at a biker bar."

Ash chuckled. "And after that, we went to Tina's to check on her kids and then to our house. I fed Kitch and let him go to the bathroom."

"That was my second guess."

Ash made a pot of strong coffee and I tossed back two cups of it as I rushed to finish the affidavit. The sun had set and the western sky was pearly gray by the time we left the sheriff's station for yet another trip to Judge Skidmore's house. Once he'd read and issued the search warrant, we headed back to Port Republic. It was fully dark by the time we got to Gage's house. Tina dismissed the deputy who'd been guarding the place, and we went inside.

The county may have reduced Gage's salary, but you sure couldn't tell that from what we found in his living room. There was a big high-definition plasma TV, a DVD player with about fifty or sixty movie discs, a Nintendo unit and more game cartridges than an adult male should admit to owning, and a Sony music system. Not surprisingly, while the electronics were all new and expensive, Gage's furniture was typical single guy décor: a mismatched and soiled collection of thrift store rejects. There was a full ashtray, an oil-stained fried chicken box from a local market, and a carton of greasy wedge fries on the battered coffee table. I could feel my arteries hardening just looking at Gage's lifestyle.

The living room opened on to the dining room and beyond it was the kitchen. Two of the phony antique teddy bears were lying on the dining table next to a computer. There was also a cardboard document storage box on the floor beneath the table, which looked to be crammed full of mail and bills. Next to the box was a paper shredder and the machine's clear plastic storage box was three-quarters full of confetti. It was obvious that Gage had been destroying what he considered incriminating paperwork.

I said, "The more I think about it, the more I wonder if there isn't something significant about the fact you found those bears here."

"How do you mean?" asked Tina

"Gage lawyered up immediately, which tells us he isn't stupid. Yet, he's got evidence in his house that conclusively links him to the counterfeiting operation. That doesn't make any sense, unless—"

"He was going to deliver them to his partner soon," Ash cut in excitedly.

"That's what I think too."

"Maybe the bearded guy was going to come here," said Tina.

"I wish, but we aren't going to be that lucky. By now, Whiskers is going to know Merrit is dead and that we've talked to Gage. He won't come anywhere near this house."

Tina nodded. "So, they were going to rendezvous someplace. Shefford Gap?"

"Unless we find something in here that says otherwise, that would be my guess."

"Then I guess we'd better get to work."

We divided the search into sectors. Tina went to toss the bedrooms and bathroom while Ash took a flashlight outside to search the Forester and the shed. Meanwhile, I'd examine the living room, the kitchen, and the documents in the dining room. After that, we would seize the bears, Gage's computer, and anything else we deemed might have some evidentiary value.

I started with the kitchen and the portable telephone. The base station had a built-in digital answering function, but there weren't any saved messages. I then checked the phone handset for the electronic log of incoming and outgoing calls. Not surprisingly, they'd all been deleted. It was our word against Gage's as to whether Merrit had left a message on Saturday morning.

There wasn't anything else in the kitchen that seemed to be connected with the crimes, but I did find a black plastic trash bag on the stoop outside the backdoor. I tugged at the knotted drawstring and opened the bag. It was full of paper confetti. Gage had been shredding documents like it was the final days of Enron. I grabbed the bag as evidence. True, we'd never be able to identify precisely what papers had been destroyed, but the bag did show Gage was frantically trying to cover his tracks.

I went back into the house and sat down at the dining room table. There was a good chance Gage had installed encryption and security software in his computer, so I turned it off and unhooked the PC from the monitor and keyboard. The machine would be sent to the state crime lab, where the cyber experts could examine it. Then, as I began to look through the stacks of paperwork, I realized we'd caught a rare lucky break. Gage had begun his evidence destruction project by shredding the oldest documents first.

I was shoving some more mail into the document box when Ash came through the front door, holding a small sheet of paper. I said, "Success?"

"Ack! That truck reeks of cigarettes! And everything is sticky with tar."

"It's a glamorous habit."

"Anyway, there was nothing in the shed but a bunch of junk, but I found this tucked behind the clip on the driver's side sun visor." She handed me the sheet. "It's a receipt from the Shefford Gap post office."

I squinted at the faint gray printing. "And he used a MasterCard to ship something to Fridley, Minnesota, by priority mail last Tuesday."

"Twenty-three dollars. Probably he was mailing either bears or a quilt."

"It also may mean that Gage and his partner meet in Shefford Gap."

"Why?"

I nodded at the roomful of expensive electronics. "These guys were doing a huge business, which means Gage has to meet his partner regularly to deliver the merchandise. Yet the bearded guy has only been seen once or twice around town."

Ash nodded. "So they rendezvous at the post office, which is away from town and also where the checks are delivered."

"That's how it looks to me. Excellent work, honey."

Ash dimpled. "I had a great teacher."

Tina emerged from the hallway carrying a couple of grocery bags. "I hope you guys came up with something, because other than a couple more pairs of shoes, all I found was dirty clothes, a dirty bathroom, and even dirtier magazines. Did this guy ever stop smoking?"

"Ash found a receipt from the Shefford Gap post office and I've only just begun to look at this, but it's pretty incriminating." I tapped the side of the document box. "Gage is supposed to be marginally employed, but there are statements from four different Valley area banks that show he's got over twelve thousand bucks."

"Why did he split the money up like that?" asked Ash.

"He had to. Everybody around here knows how badly the museum is doing and that the county had slashed Gage's pay. Twelve grand in a local bank would make folks suspicious and somebody would be bound to talk."

"And it's all profit from the counterfeiting operation." Tina's jaw tightened with frustration. "I wish there was some way we could seize the accounts."

"There may be and we can talk to the commonwealth's attorney about that tomorrow. And if you really want to ruin Gage's day, there's something else you might consider."

"What's that?"

"Drop a dime to the Internal Revenue Service on him. You can bet he hasn't been paying any taxes on this income and, whatever else happens, you know the auditors will get their pound of flesh from him, with interest."

Tina brightened. "Ooh, that's nasty. I'll call them tomorrow."

As Ash and Tina ferried the evidence out to the patrol car, I filled out the receipt and inventory of everything we'd removed from the home. I left a copy of that form along with one of the search warrant on the dining table. It was pushing 11:00 P.M. by the time we left Port Republic and we were all tired. There was little conversation as we drove to the sheriff's station.

We were in Tina's office and in the process of logging the new stuff into evidence when Sergei came in. Either he was wearing a new baked goods–scented aftershave lotion, or there was dessert in the stack of four white plastic foam food containers he carried.

"Oh my, that smells good. Apple cobbler?" Ash asked.

"Your dear mother's recipe as a matter of fact. She was kind enough to share it with me." Sergei handed her a box and a plastic fork. "You've been working very hard and I thought you might enjoy a snack."

"You didn't have to do that," said Tina.

Sergei gave her a dessert and a diffident smile. "But I wanted to, Sheriff."

"Well, thank you, and I'd like it better if you just called me Tina."

"I'd like that too."

Ash flashed me a surreptitious grin. As we ate the delicious cobbler, we took turns briefing Sergei on the investigation. Mostly, he stayed quiet, but when I mentioned following Sheldon Shaw up into the mountains without backup, he called me a "damned fool," which elicited nods of agreement from the women.

When we finished dessert, Tina rubbed her eyes and said, "That was wonderful, but all that sugar is putting me to sleep."

"Me too," said Ash with a yawn.

Tina lazily waved a hand at her. "Stop that or you'll make me start doing it."

"Sorry."

"So, tomorrow." Tina paused to yawn. "See? Anyway, do we have a consensus on Gage? Is he the killer?"

I said, "He's a USDA Prime scumbag, but I no longer think it's likely he murdered Merrit."

"Why not?"

"For starters, when Gage was arrested, his main worry was about what Holly could say about him; not the murder."

"Which means he's more worried about the fraud charges than the homicide," said Tina.

"And maybe one of the reasons he wouldn't say anything or give us the killer's name was because he was frightened of the guy," Ash added.

"Which segues into the other reason I don't think Gage is our murderer. I think it's a safe assumption that whoever capped the round off at me during the burglary also killed Merrit. Yet we didn't find a firearm or ammunition in Gage's house."

"Perhaps he disposed of it," Sergei suggested.

"Professional assassins do that, but not your typical crook. I've never understood why, but they almost always hang on to a gun."

Ash said, "And there's one other thing that tends to rule Gage out—at least from burglarizing our house. The left brake light on his Trooper isn't broken and the lamp cover doesn't look new."

"Then we're looking at the bearded guy as the killer," said Tina. "I guess tomorrow we have to do a stakeout in Shefford Gap."

"Agreed. I think we're only going to get one shot at this, because once the bearded guy finds out Gage is in custody, he'll pull a warp-speed U-FAP."

"Huh?" said Sergei.

"Unlawful Flight to Avoid Prosecution," I explained.

Ash wore a puzzled expression. "Tina, maybe I'm a little confused, but it sounds like you want *us* to do the stakeout. Wouldn't you want some of your regular deputies?"

"I've got some good people, but none of my deputies has even one-twentieth of Brad's experience with surveillances." Tina moved some crumbs around with the plastic fork and then tossed the utensil into the plastic foam container. "Look, this could be dangerous and I have no right to ask, but will you guys please help me with the stakeout?"

"Of course," said Ash.

"And I wouldn't miss it for the world," I added. "Especially since it will give me the chance to introduce myself to the guy who broke into our home, tore up our teddy bears, and took a shot at me."

Sergei cleared his throat. "Tina, I'd like to offer you my services also. The restaurant is closed tomorrow, and although I've never been a policeman, I do possess some talents that might be useful for this operation."

"Oh, like your time spent as a raven?" I nonchalantly asked.

"Bradley, you are a bloody wretch."

"What's a raven?" Ash asked.

"A rabid Edgar Allen Poe fan," I said quickly, deciding it was probably best for my long-term health not to tell the women that a "raven" was the spy-craft label for a secret agent whose primary function is to serve as a gigolo. Not that I thought Sergei had ever performed that function during his espionage career, but guys like to tease each other unmercifully.

"I'm happy to serve in whatever capacity you wish . . . so long as you do not make me sit for hours with him." Sergei gave me an exasperated look.

Tina shyly said, "I'd like your help very much, Sergei. Maybe we could team up together in one vehicle while Brad and Ash are in the other."

I said, "So, you've got your surveillance team. Now we're going to need two unmarked cars. We can use our SUV."

"And I can get a plain-wrap sedan from the county motor pool." Tina turned to her computer and, after clicking the mouse a couple of times, began typing.

"So, what time do we meet tomorrow morning?" Ash asked.

"The post office opens at eight and it's an hour to Shefford Gap. Six-thirty?" Tina asked as the printer began to spit out a sheet of paper.

Ash twisted my wrist slightly to look at my watch. "That's less than seven hours from now. I guess we'd all better go home and get some sleep."

I said, "Actually, I think it might be a good idea if maybe we did a quick recon of Shefford Gap tonight. It'd be useful to know the lay of the land and whether there's mail in our suspect's post office box. What was the box number again?"

Tina flipped through the pages of her notebook. "Twenty-seven and it's registered to Adam Mumford. If you really think it's necessary, we'll go, but I have to check on my kids first."

"And we have to let Kitch out of his crate," Ash yawned.

Sergei said, "Look, there's no point in all of us driving up there. So, why don't we do this? Tina can take Ash home, while Bradley and I scout Shefford Gap. We'll be back before you know it."

"Sounds good to me," I said.

"But I should be doing that," Tina said half-heartedly.

"You need to check on your children and get some rest for tomorrow, boss," I said.

"I suppose."

"And you'll come right home?" Ash asked.

"Don't I always?" I asked and then quickly added, "Don't answer that."

"Don't worry, Ashleigh. I'll keep him out of trouble," said Sergei.

"Before you go . . ." Tina took the sheet from the printer, signed it, and handed it to me, saying, "Here."

"What's this?"

"It's your permit to carry a concealed firearm."

"I don't think I'll need that tonight."

Tina looked solemn. "Probably not, but tomorrow may be a different story. This guy has already taken one shot at you and I want you to be able to defend yourself if he tries it again."

Twenty-three

No sooner had we slammed the SUV's doors shut, than Sergei said, "You and your bloody smart mouth. Are you trying to make things more difficult for me?"

"Sorry about the *raven* crack," I replied while starting the truck.

"You should be, especially since your wife promised that you'd be on your best behavior."

I gave him a look of astonishment. "And you believed her? When did you talk to Ash?"

"When she picked up your dinner. She pulled me aside and quietly told me that I should stop wasting time and let Tina know how I feel about her. That's why I brought dessert over."

"Again, sorry. She didn't get the chance to say anything to me about that . . . just like she didn't mention her interest in going into police work."

It was Sergei's turn to gape at me. "What?"

"Yep. Apparently I've infected her with the cop virus

and Tina wants her as a deputy—not that I blame her. I'd hire Ash as a cop in a hot second."

"But how do you feel about that?"

"Proud, surprised, kind of scared. It's a violent world, even here in the Valley."

"But she'll have the benefit of your mentoring," said Sergei, in what sounded like an artificially hearty tone. "She'll be fine."

"I hope you're right."

We headed westward across the valley, but not at my customary breakneck speed. Deer often cross the unlit highway at night and if you're traveling too fast, you can't see the animal until it's too late to avoid a collision. And sometimes the deer isn't the only one who meets its maker in the crash.

Shefford Gap was about thirty miles southwest of Remmelkemp Mill, on the other side of the Shenandoah Valley, in the hilly farm country beneath the Allegheny Mountains. We drove through Harrisonburg and into a rural area primarily populated by Amish families. The combination of a new moon and no streetlights meant that it was as dark as the inside of a closed coffin. We had to stop several times to shine a flashlight at street signs.

Turning on to Vaughn Quarry Road, we drove through gloomy apple orchards and at last arrived in Shefford Gap. It was after midnight and the place was like a ghost town. The community consisted of two churches—one Baptist and the other Mennonite; an abandoned fruit and produce shop; a combination convenience store and gas station, which was closed for the evening; and a brick post office the size of a two-car garage. As I expected, there was a light on inside the post office, providing illumination for late visitors wanting to drop off mail or check their PO box.

"I've seen worse places to conduct a surveillance," I said.

Sergei grunted. "True, but we'll have to set up awfully close to the post office."

"Yeah, but if we move any farther out, we'll be on the edge of the orchards and still be conspicuous as hell."

"I know. Hopefully, this place will look a little less deserted tomorrow morning, when the store is open and there are some people around."

Pulling into the post office's gravel parking lot, I said, "We'll make sure there isn't a back door to this place and take a quick look at the P.O. box to see if there's any mail. Then we'll head home."

"Suits me. It's been a long day."

Despite appearances, someone must have been up and astir in the village. As we climbed from the SUV, a car horn beeped twice from the direction of the gas station. Then a vehicle engine roared to life. Obviously, the horn was intended as some sort of signal. I glanced at Sergei who nodded in silent agreement.

We froze in our tracks as the post office door flew open. Two men bolted outside and charged down the steps toward us. Since I was looking into the light, the only thing I could initially tell about them was that one was a little shorter and heavier than the other. Meanwhile, a pair of headlights flashed on in the convenience store parking lot and the vehicle began to race toward the post office. I didn't know what we'd interrupted, but the odds were that it was illegal.

"Hold it there!" I yelled.

I grabbed the taller man's bicep, but he twisted from the hold and a split-second later I was staggered by a punch to my left temple. At the same time, I could hear the sound of a struggle as Sergei tackled the other guy. Shaking my head to clear my vision, I swung my cane at my assailant.

He dodged the blow, but made no attempt to escape to the orange Hummer, which had skidded to a stop on the side of the road. Instead, he dove at Sergei, who had the other man in a rear wristlock.

Recognizing the vehicle, I shouted at Sergei. "Watch yourself! These guys are Yakuza!"

By now, I recognized the man who'd clobbered me was one of Ota's *kobun*, and I delivered a vicious backhand blow with my cane to his right knee. He gasped with pain and fell to the pavement, but immediately bounced back to his feet as he continued his frenzied efforts to free his companion. That told me he was trying to rescue his boss.

When I didn't hear or see any other vehicles heading in our direction, I understood that the Yakuza must have shaken the FBI surveillance team. We were on our own and I fearfully wondered if the feds had failed us in another way. Could they have been mistaken about Merrit being alive when the Yakuza left the museum?

The third gangster jumped from the Hummer and ran toward us and I suddenly regretted my decision not to carry my pistol tonight. Unfortunately, at least one of the Yakuza *had* come prepared for action, because I heard the unmistakable metallic snap of a gun's hammer being cocked. Trying not to panic, I considered shouting for help, but knew it would be useless. As I recalled, the nearest home was almost a quarter of a mile away.

Then Ota stopped struggling and I saw why: Sergei was standing behind the *oyabun* and had him in a tight chokehold while pushing the business end of a small revolver into his right ear. I'd had no idea Sergei was carrying a gun, but considering his background in the deadly universe of espionage, I really shouldn't have been surprised, even if he'd produced a flamethrower.

Sergei said, "No more games. Tell your lads to stand down or I'll kill you and them."

Ota licked at dry lips and after a long pause half-shouted something in Japanese to his goons, but it didn't look as if they were ready to surrender. They split up and it was clear they were hoping to flank Sergei. Brandishing my cane, I moved to cover Sergei's unprotected left side. Then Ota glanced at me and blinked in surprise. He shouted at his *kobun* again and this time they stopped, but didn't relax their combat stances.

Ota said, "Mr. Lyon?"

"That's right, Mr. Ota, and I guess you *are* just nothing but a *gurentai*—a freaking hoodlum. You lied to me."

The gangster's jaw got tight. "I did not lie! You warned me not to come back here, but I never said that I would submit to your instructions. I want my money back, or the real teddy bears."

"I think you're missing the bigger issue. You came sneaking back here to find Adam Mumford—or whoever he really is—and you probably intended to thump him like you did Merrit."

"We did not kill Mr. Merrit! The other policemen can prove that."

Ota was right, but I wasn't in the mood to make concessions. I snapped, "As easy as it was for you to elude the other policemen tonight, it makes me wonder if maybe they just weren't paying attention at the museum. By the way, where *is* F Troop?"

"Please?"

"The FBI. Where are they?"

"I don't know. We crossed some railroad tracks just before a train came and they could not follow us."

"Which provided you with the opportunity to come up here and try to murder the right guy this time."

Ota scowled. "I was not lying. Mr. Merrit was alive when we left."

Sergei apparently noticed one of the *kobun* move slightly. He quickly pulled his gun from Ota's ear and aimed it at the thug, saying, "Tell your man that if he continues to slide his hand toward his back pocket, I'm going to shoot him and that's my last warning."

Ota yelled at the gangster, who sullenly nodded.

I said, "Okay, let's pretend I'm stupid and I buy your story that you didn't kill Merrit. Why the hell *did* you come up here?"

There was a long pause before Ota answered, "We *were* trying to find Adam Mumford's home address in the administrative office, but I only wanted to talk to him."

"Right. So, you broke into the post office?"

"No. You arrived before we could get in. You can check."

"We will. But, I'm confused. If you're the boss, why didn't you stay in the truck while your *kobun* committed the burglary?"

"Regrettably, I am the only one who can read English."

"You didn't happen to look in box number twenty-seven, did you?"

"Yes. There are letters in the box." Ota glanced over his shoulder at Sergei. "You are hurting my throat. Can you please let me go?"

Sergei glanced at me and I nodded. He released Ota and shoved him toward his *kobun*, while keeping the gun trained on the trio.

I said, "You say you were just going to talk if you found his home address?"

"I was going to urge Mr. Mumford to give me the bears I paid for or refund my money . . . without violence, of course." Ota gave me a chilly smile.

"Yeah, I'll bet. That explains why you fought with us when we tried to stop you from leaving."

"I regret that. We saw from your truck that you were not the FBI and we were just trying to escape."

Sergei slowly released the revolver's hammer so that it was no longer on a hair trigger, but maintained his aim at the Yakuza. "So, what are we going to do with them?"

"Let me check inside the post office to see if there's any evidence of a burglary." I headed for the steps, keeping a wary eye on the Yakuza. "If not, we don't have any evidence they actually tried to break in."

Opening the door, I quickly scanned the interior of the post office, which reeked of fresh cigarette smoke. Everything looked normal and the wooden door leading to the administrative section of the building showed no signs of forced entry. I also noted that there wasn't a back door for postal customers.

I came back down the steps and said, "Mr. Ota, I want your word that you and your *kobun* are going to get the hell out of here and never come back."

Ota gave me a curt yet formal nod. "I give my promise."

"You're not going to just let them go?" Sergei sounded incredulous.

"I don't like it any more than you do. But there's no proof they've committed a crime, so we can't arrest them. And I sure don't want to call the FBI. They won't find us before morning."

"You've got a point." Sergei lowered the revolver and slipped it into the waistband of his pants.

"Thank you, Mr. Lyon," said Ota.

"You're welcome. Now, get moving before I change my mind."

Ota spoke to his thugs and they hustled to the Hummer and began to climb into it. Suddenly, in the near distance

I could hear what seemed like several vehicle engines. I looked eastward down the road and saw the bright glow of headlights. A moment later, three sedans and a van sped into Shefford Gap. One of the cars shot in front of the Hummer and skidded to a stop, while another pulled up right behind the Yakuza's vehicle. The gangsters were trapped.

I recognized the white van from Boyds Bear Country and allowed myself to relax a little when I realized that the newcomers were FBI agents. For once, I was impressed with the feds. Somehow, they'd actually found us. Flashlights danced and shone in the darkness as the agents pulled Ota and his *kobun* from the Hummer.

Someone approached us from the van and I recognized Special Agent Bartle. He shook his head in resignation when he saw me. "You, again?"

"I missed you too, Agent Bartle."

"FBI?" asked Sergei.

"I thought you could tell that from the dull look on his face," I muttered.

"And who're you?" Bartle demanded of Sergei.

"Unless you have an Umbra clearance, that's none of your business," Sergei said in an equitable tone. Most people have never heard the term, but "Umbra" is a security classification several stages higher than "Top Secret."

Bartle looked as if he'd just bitten into a lemon. Turning to me, he said, "What in the name of God was going on here?"

"We were following up on a lead in our murder investigation and interrupted them before they could burglarize the post office."

"Why were they doing that?"

"Like I told you in Gettysburg, Ota is a teddy bear collector. A couple of months ago, he purchased a pair of antique bears over the Internet and later found out they were counterfeit. The check was mailed to a P.O. box here. Long story short: He either wants his money back or the genuine bears."

Bartle glanced at the Hummer. "And he was going to break in and get the seller's residence address?"

"Yep, and then do a little bill collecting. So, where have you guys been?"

Bartle grunted with frustration. "We lost them in Winchester behind the longest damn freight train I've ever seen."

"That's almost a hundred miles north. How did you manage to find them here?"

"We put our own GPS device on the Hummer before they picked it up at the car rental agency."

A Chevy Suburban now rolled into the hamlet and I watched as the agents ushered Ota and his *kobun* into the vehicle. Ota was insisting that the feds transfer his luggage and new teddy bears from the Hummer to the Suburban, but nobody seemed to be paying him any attention.

I asked, "What are you going to do with those guys now?"

"Take them back to Washington and keep them in protective custody until their flight leaves tomorrow night. We're done chasing them over hell's half acre."

"Good idea, but can you do me a favor?"

Bartle gave me a suspicious look. "That depends on the favor."

"This is an easy one," I said. "Let him have his new teddy bears. You and I both know that sometimes a prisoner's property can be misplaced and I don't want to give him *any* reason to come back here."

Twenty-four

It was just after one-thirty in the morning by the time I got home, and it took twenty minutes to tell Ash what had happened and assure her that I really was uninjured. Then I pulled off my clothes and climbed into bed. Even though I was dog-tired, I didn't sleep well. I never do before an arrest operation, because I'm focused on role-playing successful solutions to every possible tactical scenario, no matter how improbable. But this time my brain was working overtime. Ash had to be factored into the series of potentially lethal equations and that changed everything. Curiously enough, she'd gone back to sleep quickly and I resisted the urge to touch her cheek, for fear of waking her. It wasn't until after the old long case clock downstairs chimed three o'clock that I drifted off into a restless slumber.

We awakened to an Andrea Bocelli CD in the alarm clock. It was 5:30 A.M. and the sky was already gray. Ash went downstairs to let Kitch outside and make some coffee and hot cocoa, while I got into the shower. I felt like death warmed over and my eyelids were sandpapery, but I perked up a little once I'd had a couple cups of strong, black coffee. After getting dressed, I pulled my gun, shoulder holster, and handcuffs from my sock drawer and experienced a powerful and unpleasant sense of déjà vu. The last time I'd worn all this equipment, I'd been shot.

Later, I stood in front of the freestanding mirror in our bedroom, frowning at my image. I was wearing jeans, an Anchor Steam Beer T-shirt, and my shoulder holster, which felt oddly constraining. Partly because I weighed a little more now than I had when I was a homicide inspector, but mostly because over two years had passed since I'd worn the black nylon harness and I'd simply forgotten how it felt. I slipped the seventeen-shot Glock pistol into the holster and secured the safety strap. The gun felt strange under my arm.

Ash finished buttoning her blouse and came over to join me in staring into the looking glass. She said, "So, are we looking for Alice?"

"No . . . but does this outfit make my butt look big?" I asked in an artificially worried tone while pivoting for a profile view. The last thing I wanted was to infect her with my own anxieties.

She laughed, kissed me on the cheek, and grabbed the baggy short sleeve button-down shirt that was hanging from the bedpost. "Here, this will cover your shoulder holster and tush, which, by the way, I think is perfect."

I tucked the handcuffs into the back of my pants and got my old binoculars from the top shelf of the closet. Going downstairs, we put an unhappy Kitch into his crate, I grabbed my cane and my old San Francisco Giants ball cap from the coat rack, and we went out to the Xterra. It was already in the low-seventies and promised to be another hot and muggy day.

Tina and Sergei were already at the sheriff's department, sipping coffee from disposable cups and standing beside a white Ford Taurus four-door sedan. Both were dressed in casual clothing and I noticed that Tina was also wearing an oversized and unbuttoned blouse to conceal her gun. Unfortunately, the same thing couldn't be done for the Taurus. The county motor pool vehicle screamed unmarked cop car, but I didn't say anything, because I knew it was the best Tina could do. As I pulled up beside them, she picked up a portable radio from the trunk of the Taurus and came over to my open window.

Handing me the radio, she said, "Good morning, you guys. Sergei was just telling me about your run-in with the Yakuza last night. Why didn't you call me?"

"I couldn't see any point in waking you up. We ready to roll?" I asked.

"Yeah. We'll operate on channel two. My call sign is Mike One, and yours is—"

"Mike Tyson? That way, I can also be like McGruff the Crime Dog and take a *bite* out of crime . . . or someone's ear," I said in a gravelly voice.

"It's a little too early in the morning for your insanity," Tina said with tired laugh. "Your call sign is Mike Fourteen."

"Heck, you're no fun. So, how do you want to make the arrest?"

"Sergei told me there was mail in the P.O. box, so let's let the suspect go into the post office and get his mail. We'll nail him when he comes back out. That way, we'll catch him with evidence and also avoid a hostage situation."

"Good thinking. Did you let the locals know we'll be operating on their turf?"

"Yeah, I talked with both the Rockingham County Sheriff and the state police. They've agreed to stay out of the area, unless they get a service call or we shout for backup. You can do that on channel five on your radio."

"And will these work back in the foothills?" I held up the radio.

"I wouldn't want to bet my life on it," said Tina, her demeanor suddenly verging on grim. "That's why I wanted you armed."

"And on that cheerful note, let's go to work."

It was just a little past 7:30 A.M. when we arrived. Shefford Gap didn't look much different by daylight, although I did notice a road sign just past the post office that said the West Virginia state line was nine miles away. We had nearly a half hour before the post office opened, but as much as I craved another cup of coffee, we decided to stay out of the convenience store. We were strangers up here and once word got out that cops were watching the post office, the news would spread like a wind-driven brushfire. Inevitably, our suspect would learn about the stakeout and then disappear faster than good judgment at an office Christmas party.

We exchanged some brief messages over the radio. Tina opted for a surveillance spot near the large propane tank on the west side of the convenience store, while Ash and I parked next to a couple of abandoned vehicles on the east side of the empty produce market. When the post office opened, Tina radioed to tell us to maintain our position while she and Sergei went to speak to the clerk. We watched as they walked across the road and went inside the post office. They came out a few minutes later and once they were back in the Taurus the radio crackled.

Tina said, "Mike One to Mike Fourteen, the clerk won't give us the guy's name until she checks with the postal inspectors."

I keyed the microphone. "Which I hope she's doing right now."

"Affirmative. I gave her my cell number to call me directly."

"Was she *any* help?"

"As much as she could be without endangering her job. She confirmed the suspect's description and that he drives a black SUV. Also, that he ships packages about twice a week and receives mail from foreign countries on a pretty regular basis."

"How often does he come here?"

"She said every day, but the times vary."

"So, we wait."

Ash said, "Don't we already know that the P.O. box is registered to Adam Mumford?"

"Yeah, but we want to get the guy's residential address and to make sure there're no other people, or even businesses, receiving mail at that box."

Forty-five minutes passed and during that time three vehicles stopped at the post office, but none of them even remotely resembled the suspect's SUV. It was getting hot and I couldn't keep my window down because a behemoth yellow jacket kept trying to fly inside the Xterra. Between the boredom and discomfort it was a pretty routine stakeout, but Ash was still completely alert and from the tenor of her comments, seemed to be enjoying herself immensely.

Tina's voice sounded from the radio. "Okay, we've got a name. The postal inspectors just called and confirmed that the P.O. box belongs to our old friend, Adam Mumford. The box rental card says he lives on Kimsey Pond Road."

"Is that a Richmond address?" I asked.

"Negative. It's a little west of here, near the state line."

"Well, with any luck we'll know his real name soon."

Over an hour passed and the sun was turning our SUV into an oven. During that time, seventeen cars passed the post office and our only entertainment came from watching some tourists from New Jersey puzzle over the fact that there wasn't a credit card scanner on the gasoline pump.

Ash shifted uncomfortably in her seat. "I'm not complaining, but my butt is starting to hurt."

"Me too. Welcome to the wonderful world of police stakeouts, honey."

"Do you think he's going to come?"

"I don't—oh, hell, it's showtime."

With our view to the west, we were the first to see the black SUV coming down the road toward the post office. I raised the binoculars and saw the vehicle was an older model Mercury Mountaineer, which looked very much like a Ford Explorer. Although the windows were tinted, it looked as if the driver was the only person in the SUV.

Raising the portable radio, I said, "Mike Fourteen to Mike One, I think we've got the suspect vehicle eastbound on Vaughn Quarry Road. You should be seeing him in a second."

Tina replied, "Okay, we've got him. One male occupant . . . can't see the plates yet."

"I copy," I said and handed the radio to Ash. "Honey, when we go mobile, I'm going to need both hands, so why don't you take over on the radio?"

"Got it."

I fired up the Xterra's engine in preparation for swooping down on the post office. We watched in silence as the truck slowed and made the left turn into the gravel parking lot of the post office. A tall bearded man climbed from the truck and I lifted the field glasses to get a better look at him. He had the seedy look of not having washed recently, longish stringy hair and wore mirrored sunglasses. Still, there was something about him that seemed vaguely familiar.

Tina's voice came over the radio: "I don't know if you could see it from your angle, but there's a hole in his left rear brake light."

"Ten-four," said Ash. Lowering the radio, she asked, "The man who broke into our house?"

I said, "Yeah, and this just keeps getting better and better. What's wrong with this picture?"

"What?" Ash said.

"It's as hot as the hinges on the gates of hell and he's wearing a freaking windbreaker? The guy is carrying a gun."

The radio crackled and this time it was Sergei's voice: "Brad, he's probably armed."

Ash raised the radio. "We know—I mean, ten-four."

I handed her the binoculars. "We've seen this guy someplace. Who is he?"

She looked through the binoculars for a few seconds and then gasped, "Oh my God! He's gained a lot of weight, but I'm almost certain that's Marc Poole!"

Suddenly, the circumstances of our Farnell bear being stolen and the other teddies being vandalized made sense. Pastor Marc Poole had been an occasional guest in our home, up until Ash and I had uncovered and terminated his secret career as a crook. He had plenty of reasons to hate us. Knowing that he was about to be arrested, he'd fled town with nothing more than the clothes on his back. It was only natural that Poole would want revenge on us.

With an unsavory chuckle, I said, "Oh, I must have been a very good boy that Santa would bring me *this* present."

"Hey, you wouldn't let me hit him last time, so *I've* got first dibs on dismembering him," said Ash, who had neither forgiven nor forgotten the clergyman's treacherous behavior.

"That's fine, but keep one thing in mind: He probably killed Merrit, so we're going to approach him like we would a copperhead."

Poole stood in the parking lot for a second, scanning his surroundings like a chubby deer preparing to move from the safety of the forest into naked pastureland. Then he stared across the road at the gas station and almost dove back into the Mountaineer. Obviously, he'd recognized his former neighbors from Remmelkemp Mill, Tina and Sergei.

"He's made them! Hang on!" I slammed my foot down on the accelerator.

As I sped toward the post office, Poole threw the SUV into reverse and backed up onto the highway. The Mountaineer's brake lights flashed for a second and I noted the damage to the left red plastic cover. It was definitely the same vehicle I'd seen the night our house was burglarized. With tires squealing, the black SUV took off the way it had come, toward the West Virginia state line. Meanwhile, the Taurus, which now had one of those magnetized flashing blue lights on its roof, was careening from the gas station parking lot. Since hers was the only vehicle with emergency lights, I hit the brakes for a second to let Tina take the lead in the pursuit. A second later, we were both rocketing down the road after the SUV.

"He spotted us," said Sergei over the radio.

"No kidding," I said.

"Ten-four. Did you notice that it was Marc Poole?" Ash replied into the radio.

"Affirmative. He's changed a lot since October. We didn't initially recognize him in his Rasputin disguise."

It wasn't long before we were in the foothills of the Alleghenies and the road became increasing serpentine as it began to parallel a mountain stream on our left. We passed through a dense grove of trees and then, ahead, I could see a long straight section of highway. Here was our chance to close some of the distance on the Mountaineer. Then suddenly the SUV's right turn signal began to blink and the vehicle slowed down. It appeared that Poole had decided to pull over and abandon his bid for escape. The SUV came to a stop on the right shoulder and Tina pulled up almost right behind it. Suspicious of Poole's abrupt and inexplicable surrender, I stayed back about four car lengths.

Then I realized that Poole hadn't turned the Mountaineer's engine off. It was one of the moments when you know exactly what's going to happen next, but you just can't react quickly enough to prevent it. I yelled, "Call and tell them they're too close!"

Ash keyed the microphone, "Move back, you're—"

But it was too late. Suddenly, the Mountaineer's backing lights flashed on and Poole hit the gas. The back of the SUV slammed into the front of the Taurus with an enormous crash and pushed it backward along the shoulder for about fifteen yards. A second later, Poole was again headed westbound toward the state line. I drove up and stopped so that we were parallel to the wrecked Taurus. Sergei looked furious, but was otherwise uninjured. However, Tina was bent forward and cradling both her wrists against her stomach. I realized that she'd probably broken them while clutching the steering wheel during the collision.

I yelled out Ash's window, "Are you guys all right?"

Sergei shouted back, "Don't stop! Get that bastard and bring him back so I can geld him!"

Hitting the gas, I said to Ash, "I guess Sergei's got first dibs on Poole now."

"He can have my place in line and I'll loan him a dull knife." Ash's voice was stiff with rage.

The Mountaineer was perhaps two hundred yards ahead of us, but it wasn't going as fast now and I wondered if it had sustained major damage also. We closed the gap pretty quickly and were soon on the SUV's tail as we began winding our way up into the Alleghenies. Meanwhile, I heard static-distorted messages from the police radio that told me Tina had called for the cavalry. I hoped the cops would hurry and that we'd remain on the main road so that they could find us. But if Poole decided to go four-wheeling in this wilderness, we might lose him for good and I couldn't let that happen.

I said, "Ash my love, do me a favor and hang on tight, because I'm going to PIT Poole the next chance I get."

"Pit?"

"It's some sort of acronym for me hitting his SUV with our vehicle and making it spin out. With any luck, he'll hit a big tree, be crippled for life, and forever after talk like he has a mouthful of cat food."

Ash glanced at me nervously. "Have you ever done this before?"

"Once."

"Did it work?"

"No, but the theory is sound and I'm not going to let Poole get away."

"You're damn right you aren't."

"But if this does work, I want you to stay behind the Xterra and out of the line of fire."

"I will. Now ram that rotten monster!"

"God, I do love having you as a partner."

We crested a tall hill and I could see that the road ahead curved lazily to the right. This looked like a promising spot to play roadway Russian roulette. Offering a silent prayer that the road would remain free of oncoming traffic, I jammed my foot down on the accelerator, veered to the left, and made as if to pass the Mountaineer. Poole sped up, but not quickly enough and I jerked hard on the steering wheel to the right. There was a crunch of metal as the Xterra's bumper collided with the left rear quarter-panel of the SUV and I resisted the impulse to hit the brakes. Instead, I buried the gas pedal in the floorboard and pushed the Xterra against the Mountaineer.

Suddenly, Poole's SUV was in an out-of-control rotating skid and I hit my brakes to stay out of the way. The Mountaineer slid laterally across the highway and was facing eastward when it slammed sideways into some pine trees lining the opposite side of the road. I parked on the other side of the highway and realized that I'd have to leave my cane behind, because I was going to need both hands. I threw the door open and came as close as I ever will to jumping from the Xterra.

Yanking the Glock from my shoulder holster, I glanced to make sure that Ash had taken cover behind our truck. The Mountaineer was partially wrapped around a tree and looked immobilized, but I wasn't going to take any chances on letting Poole go mobile again. I took quick aim at the back tire of the Mountaineer and fired a round to flatten it. A second later, the front tire was also resting on the metal rim and then I swung the gun upward so that it was pointed at the driver's window.

Although my ears were ringing from the gunfire, I heard Poole yell from inside the SUV, "Don't shoot! I don't have a gun!"

"You aren't going to have a freaking head if you lie to me again! Take your gun by the barrel and throw it out the window, now!"

"All right! I'm sorry! Please don't hurt me!" Poole slowly extended his left hand from the vehicle. He was holding a little semiautomatic pistol by the barrel and tossed the weapon onto the asphalt. "There! I'm cooperating!"

One of the first things drilled into your head at the police academy is to never assume an armed and dangerous suspect is only carrying one gun. That sort of assumption will earn you the place of honor at a police funeral. What's more, I had a tangible reason for believing Poole had a second firearm. The weapon he'd thrown out the window was a small caliber pistol, but the gun he'd used at our home had been a large bore revolver. It was obvious that Poole was waiting for me to approach the SUV's window so that he could open fire.

"Poole!" I shouted. "You are going to throw that other gun out right now or I'm going to give you a Viking funeral!"

Poole sounded shrill. "You have my gun! Ashleigh, I'd never hurt you! Tell your husband not to kill me!"

"Shut up, you fraud!" Ash screamed back.

I hollered, "You've got three seconds, or I'm going to start ricocheting rounds off the pavement so that they hit the underside of your SUV! Once I hit the gas tank, you're going to get a sneak peek at hell! One!"

"Please, I surrender!"

"Two!"

"I'm unarmed!"

"Three!"

Taking careful aim at the roadway in front of the Mountaineer, I began slowly cranking off rounds and saw coppery metallic sparks as the bullets struck the vehicle's frame. I fired four times, but before I could shoot again, I saw Poole hurl a large blue-steel revolver from the SUV. It clattered to the pavement about ten feet from the vehicle.

Poole screamed, "You are goddamned crazy! I give!"

I yelled back, "No more guns, knives, or tactical nukes?"

"No!"

"Biblical weapons, like plowshares turned into swords?"

"No!"

From somewhere down in the Valley, a siren began to wail and I hoped Poole heard it too.

I said, "Then here's how we're going to do this. As you get out of that SUV, you're going to move so slowly that I'm going to think you're a government employee. Then you're going to lie facedown on the pavement and extend your arms. Got that?"

"Yes!"

"And here's where the jokes stop: Poole, if you so much as even glance at those guns, I'll kill you."

"I won't!" Poole's voice quavered with terror.

"Ash, come here!" I hissed.

She slipped around the rear of the Xterra and joined me. "What?"

In a quiet voice, I said, "Once I get him proned out, I want you to take the Glock and cover me as I handcuff him. If he tries to fight, I'm going to fall down and I want you to shoot him. Can you do that?"

"You've seen me at the range."

"This isn't a paper target."

"I know. When you're ready, give me the gun."

Turning back to the Mountaineer, I shouted, "Okay Poole, let's do this. Open that door very slowly."

Poole pushed the door open and cautiously stepped away from the SUV. Everything seemed to be going fine, until he shot a furtive glance to his right at the dense forest bordering the road. He turned to take one step to run and I fired a round in his path. Poole stumbled to a stop and stared at the neat hole at belly button height the bullet had just created in the fender of the Mountaineer.

Poole looked accusingly at me. "I can't believe you'd shoot me in cold blood."

I said, "Pal, the only downside to shooting you is that Ash will be angry, because I didn't let her drop the hammer on you. Now, lie down!"

A moment later, I was kneeling on Poole's upper back and neck, tightening the handcuffs around his wrists. Then I searched him for weapons and was a little surprised not to find any. There were more sirens now and they were getting closer. Ash gave me the gun back and then we pulled Poole to his feet.

As we walked him over to the Xterra, Poole sniveled, "I'm sorry about crashing into Sheriff Tina's car. It was an accident."

"Right, and isn't it interesting that you knew Tina was elected sheriff. Gage must have been keeping you very well informed of what was happening in town."

"The crash *was* an accident."

"Just like how you and Gage murdered Merrit?"

"I don't know what you're talking about."

"Yeah, that's real convincing. But you might want to keep something in mind before you start lying and denying: Gage has already dimed you off as the killer. That's how we knew where to look for you," I lied.

"But *he* killed Merrit!"

"It's your word against his and he's cooperated fully."

Poole snarled, "The little bastard! Fine, I'll make a full statement when we get back to the sheriff's department."

"Wise decision."

Ash turned to give Poole a wicked smile. "And when this is all finished, you can look forward to joining the Vienna Boys' Choir. Oh, and don't worry about hitting the high notes. Sergei Zubatov will fix your voice."

Twenty-five

The first cruiser to arrive was a state police unit. It skidded to a stop and a big trooper helped us shove Poole into the backseat of the patrol car. I asked the cop how Tina was doing and he told me she was being transported via ambulance to Rockingham Memorial Hospital in Harrisonburg. The initial prognosis from the EMTs was that she had at least one broken wrist.

"What about the man that was with her? Is he okay?" I asked.

"As far as I know he's fine. He insisted on riding to RMH in the ambulance with your sheriff and everybody decided it was best not to argue with him." The trooper nodded toward Poole, whose chin was on his chest. "What do you want me to do with this guy?"

"You'll be doing us a big favor if you transport him to the Massanutten County sheriff's office and tell the deputies to lock him in an interview room," I replied.

"My pleasure."

"And can you also get a wrecker en route? We need this thing towed down to the crime lab in Roanoke." I hooked a thumb in the direction of the Mountaineer.

"I'll radio my dispatch and get it arranged."

"Thanks, and be careful with Jerry Garcia there. He's a definite escape risk."

"And I'm a definite ass-whupping risk. Got that, buddy?" the trooper shouted at Poole, who nodded sullenly.

Once the state trooper was gone, Ash gave me a hug and said, "Wow, look at how well you're getting around without your cane."

I grimaced. "Thanks love, but don't get used to me being fully ambulatory just yet. The adrenaline is wearing off and my leg is really starting to hurt."

"Let's get your cane. There's ibuprofen in the center console."

"Yeah, and it might be a good idea to make sure the Xterra isn't so damaged that we won't be able to drive out of here."

I grabbed my cane from the backseat of the Xterra, while Ash got the pills and I swallowed them dry. Then we went to check out the front of our vehicle. The right front bumper was a little mangled, but otherwise the SUV looked drivable.

After that, Ash went to search the Mountaineer, while I collected the two guns lying on the pavement. The wheelgun was a rusty Smith & Wesson .41 caliber magnum revolver with the serial numbers obliterated by some sort of grinding tool—a not-so-subtle clue that it was stolen. It was loaded with hollow-point ammunition, which I was confident the crime lab would positively match to the bullet removed from our living room wall. The other firearm was a .32 automatic that looked as if it was Czech-made.

No doubt, it was stolen too. I secured both guns in the Xterra and then returned to the Mountaineer.

I asked, "Have you found anything, honey?"

Ash put a largish cardboard package on the hood of the SUV. "He was going to mail that to someone in Florida."

"A teddy bear?"

"I think so. There's also a checkbook from a bank over in Franklin, West Virginia, in the same name he gave for the post office box."

"Any shoes?"

"Why?"

"We're going to want all of Poole's shoes for analysis."

Ash stuck her head into the vehicle again and called, "None that I can see."

"Then grab that stuff and let's head ten-nineteen," I said, using the old California police radio code for the sheriff's station. "There's no telling how long Tina is going to be at the hospital and I need to interrogate Poole before he changes his mind about talking."

As we drove down the mountain, Ash said, "I know this is going to sound strange, but even though I despise Poole, I find it hard to believe he might have killed Merrit. I mean, I've known him since we were kids and he never showed any signs of violence then. And, my God, he was a preacher."

"And Josef Stalin was once a seminary student," I said. "People change, sweetheart. I'm convinced Poole is the murderer."

"Why him instead of Gage? Like you said, maybe Gage went back to the museum to give himself an alibi."

"That's possible, although I don't think he's a good enough actor to have faked the look of shock I saw on his face. But the more important thing is to contrast their criminal profiles. Gage is a conman and a sneak thief, but he hasn't shown any predisposition toward violence."

"And Poole has?"

"On more than one occasion. He tried to shoot me while robbing our home, thirty minutes ago he committed felonious assaults against Tina and Sergei, and he was prepared to use those handguns if he'd lured me close enough to his truck. By any definition, he's now a violent criminal."

"And the kind of person who would hit someone else on the head with a hammer." Ash looked sad. "I see what you mean. So, how are you going to get him to confess?"

"The only thing I can do is to keep pretending that Gage rolled on him and offer Poole the chance to get even. Maybe if he tells enough lies, he'll trip himself up."

Ash rubbed my arm. "You sound a little worried."

"I am. He knows how I operate, and that's going to make things much tougher."

Later, as we were approaching Harrisonburg, I asked, "Hey, how would you like me to drop you off at the hospital?"

"No. They probably won't even let me into Tina's room and I want to go to the station and help you interview Poole."

I put my hand on her knee. "Honey, you're going to have to trust me on this, but I really don't think it's a good idea if you're in the interview room while I interrogate him."

"Why?"

"Because unlike me, you're an honest and decent person who's easily outraged by a scumbag like Poole."

Ash sighed. "That's true."

"And considering our last conversation with him, back in October, he already knows you hate him. So, if you're sitting there, all he's going to do is spout excuses and we don't have time for that. We need the truth."

"And I'd be liable to lose my temper."

"You? Lose your temper?" I gave her a puckish smile.

She put her hand on mine. "You're right. Why don't you go ahead and let me off at the hospital. But do me a favor."

"What's that?"

"Drive a stake through his heart like he's a vampire. I don't want there to be even the slightest chance that he can ever violate our lives again."

"Just call me Van Helsing."

I made the turn into the emergency room parking lot and Ash kissed me before getting out. It took another fifteen minutes to get back to the sheriff's office and Deputy Bressler was waiting for me in the lobby when I came stumping in. He had a message from Tina: I was to proceed with interrogating Poole and that her deputies had been instructed to assist me in any way I deemed necessary.

"Where is Poole?" I asked.

"In the interview room," said Bressler.

"Still handcuffed?"

"Yes, sir."

"Good. Get me a tape recorder and a couple of cassettes."

Bressler trotted down the hall and I went into Tina's office, where I removed my shoulder holster and put it into one of her desk drawers. I also decided to leave my cane behind. Poole was accustomed to viewing me as crippled and the continued absence of the blackthorn would send a disquieting subliminal message that I was now his physical equal.

I met Bressler in the hallway outside the interview room. He handed me the tape recorder, a power cord, and the cassettes. I quietly instructed him to remain outside the door and not to enter unless he heard the sounds of a brawl. Then I opened the door, gritted my teeth, and strode into the interview room. Poole was seated crosswise in a chair, with his back against the wall. He looked up at me as I put the tape recorder and accessories on the table.

Pulling my key ring from my pocket, I said, "Stand up, turn around, and let me take the handcuffs off."

"It's about time." Poole bent at the waist and pushed himself to his feet.

I unlocked the handcuffs. "Sit down."

"What happened to your cane?"

"Don't need it anymore. Sit down."

Poole slumped into the chair while rubbing his wrists. "Before you start recording, we need to talk."

"About what?" I plugged the power cord into the wall socket.

"I'm not going to say anything unless I've got a guarantee that you won't press charges against me."

"Immunity from prosecution?" I snorted with amusement as I yanked the plug back out of the socket. "What, are you on drugs?"

Poole looked apprehensive as I gathered all the stuff up and headed for the door. He said, "Where are you going?"

"You're wasting my time, Poole. I don't need your statement. In fact, I almost *don't* want it, because Gage has already reserved you a window seat on the lethal injection shuttle to hell."

"Don't I have the right to have a lawyer here?"

"Sure, but you and I both know that if you had an attorney, he or she would tell you to remain silent. That means that Gage's story of how you brutally killed Merrit becomes gospel. But hey, if you want to lawyer up, be my guest."

"All right, dammit. I'll talk."

"So long as you understand that I'm not offering any deals."

"I agree—not that you're giving me any choice."

I sat down and re-plugged the power cord into the wall. Then I put a cassette tape into the machine and pressed the record button. I began by stating the date and time. Next, I identified myself and made Poole provide his full name. After that, I recited the Miranda admonition for about the twenty-thousandth time in my life.

When I finished, I said, "So, having those rights in mind, do you wish to speak with me?"

Poole leaned forward to speak into the recorder. "Yes, because I've been falsely accused of murder and I want to help the sheriff catch the real killer."

"Your commitment to civic virtue is an example to us all. But before we get to the murder, I want to cover some foundational material."

"Such as?"

"Such as where you've been since October of last year."

"After the . . . uh, trouble . . . with Sheriff Holcombe, I knew I couldn't get a fair trial, so I went to go live in the mountains."

"On Kimsey Pond Road?"

Pooled blinked, obviously surprised that I knew where he'd been staying. He said, "There and some other places."

"You've been living under the alias of Adam Mumford, right?"

"Yes."

"I'm assuming you somehow got ahold of Mumford's driver's license."

"Yeah, I've had it awhile."

"And you're aware that possessing stolen property and identity theft are both felonies, right?"

"Yes. I'll accept my punishment, so long as I can clear my name of a murder I didn't commit."

I threw an arm over the back of my chair. "Good, then let's move on to some more felonious behavior. Tell me about the counterfeit bear and quilt scam."

"That was something I began talking about with Neil Gage just before everything fell apart in October. I had no idea how valuable antique teddy bears were until I began making the arrangements to auction that Mourning Bear. And quilts? Americana is hot right now." Poole's voice grew unintentionally enthusiastic.

The bear Poole was referring to was from an extremely limited edition of Steiff teddies made in 1912 to commemorate the victims of the sinking of the *Titanic*. Back in 2003, one of the black bears had been sold for a cool $165,000 at a London auction. And he was also on the mark about the skyrocketing value of antique quilts.

I asked, "Whose idea was it to make counterfeits?"

"Gage's. I had no money, so I just planned to steal the stuff and split half of whatever I made with him."

"But?"

"But then he suggested combining his access to the bears with my information on the antique bear market."

"By producing bogus antiques. And did Frank Merrit know about this scam?"

Poole shook his head. "No, he would never have gone along with the deal."

I gave him a bland smile. "How old-fashioned. Apparently he thought the Eighth Commandment actually meant something."

"I'm not proud of what I did, but I was out of options. I didn't have any money."

Resisting the urge to say, *Yeah, you're a real victim of circumstance,* I said: "Okay, so you and Gage decided to go into business making counterfeit antiques, yet you waited until March to begin production. Why?"

"The original plan was that Gage was going to use some old lady in Pineville to make the bears and quilts." Poole sighed wearily. "But in December she had a stroke and couldn't sew anymore."

The self-pity was too much and this time I couldn't rein in my smart mouth. "Wow. How inconvenient for *you*."

He glowered at me.

"So, Gage had to find a new seamstress?"

"Yes, and it took him until February."

"Did you ever meet her?"

"I was outside her house once. We never spoke."

"Her name is Holly Reuss, by the way, and she's a nice, if overly-naive, lady. Were you worried that she'd recognize you?"

"No. One of the first things Gage found out when he met her at that quilt show was that she attended church in Grottoes."

"Who came up with the cover story that she was making the bears for the museum gift shop?"

"Gage. Did she actually believe that?" Poole sounded slightly amused.

"Yeah. Hilarious, huh? She also thought Gage was in love with her."

"I don't know anything about that."

"Of course not. Hey, just to satisfy my curiosity, whatever happened to the antique bears that Gage boosted from the museum?"

"Once the seamstress—Holly, I guess—had learned to copy them, we sold them."

"Do you remember who bought them?"

Poole gave me an annoyed look. "No. It's not like I was keeping business records."

"Just thought I'd ask. Okay, so Holly started making bears while you pretended to be a representative from the

Massanutten Museum of History and searched for potential victims on the Internet. How'd you go about doing that?"

"Online auctions and contacts through some of the collector bulletin board sites."

"And you began selling the counterfeits. How much did you get per bear?"

"Usually around three-thousand. Sometimes a little less."

"Sweet. Factoring the split with Gage, the pittance you gave to Holly, and the cost of materials, that left you with what? Twelve-hundred for each bear sold?"

"At first, but then the prices began to go down."

"Because you got greedy and created a glut in the market."

Poole nodded glumly.

Suddenly, another piece of the puzzle slipped into place. "Is that one of the reasons you burglarized our house? To steal the Farnell Alpha bear?"

"I didn't break—"

"Whoa there! Before you finish that lie, remember the crime lab is going to match the bullets in that revolver of yours to the slug recovered from our house."

Poole snapped his teeth together in frustration. "All right, I broke into your house. We needed a new collectible and I remembered Ashleigh showing me that bear not long after you'd moved here from San Francisco."

"And she undoubtedly told you it was an anniversary gift from me. That must have made the notion of stealing it that much more delicious, right?"

Knowing it could never be perceived on an audiotape, he gave me a malicious smile. "I didn't know anything about that."

Keeping my voice benign, I said, "That isn't a very

clever lie. Your motive wasn't simple theft; otherwise you wouldn't have destroyed those other bears. That was nothing but a little payback."

Poole's eyes lit up with anger. "So, you lost a couple of your precious teddy bears. You wrecked my entire life!"

"You'd already done that, long before we ever arrived on the scene. In fact, you're still evolving as a criminal."

"What are you talking about?"

"In less than a year, you've moved from being a fence for stolen property to a home intrusion robber and maybe even a murderer. Were you hoping to kill me when you fired that shot?"

"That was just a warning shot." Poole leaned across the table and waggled a finger at me. "You'd have been dead if I'd really meant to kill you."

"Kind of like what happened to Merrit?"

"I don't have anything to do with his murder."

I noticed the statement was phrased in the present tense, which told me he wasn't talking about his past actions, but rather how he felt at this very moment. Technically, it was a truthful answer, yet Poole had deflected the question. I said, "Which brings us to Saturday morning. Now, we know you were at the museum, because we have an independent witness that saw your Mountaineer. But where were you before that, when Merrit called Gage?"

Poole sat back in his chair. "I was at Gage's house. I made the money drops on Saturday mornings."

"So, what happened?"

"Merrit was screaming about Japanese gangsters coming to the museum and it was obvious he'd figured out that we'd replaced the original antique bears with fakes. He was going to call the law, but Gage managed to convince him to wait until he could come over to the museum and explain."

"How'd he do that?"

"A variation on the museum gift shop story. He told Merrit that he'd thought of a way to save the museum, but wanted to make sure it would really work before sharing the plan."

"And Merrit obviously bought it, because he didn't call the sheriff. That being the case, why did you go there too?"

"Gage was scared," Poole said scornfully. "And we both knew that the gift shop story was only a stopgap measure. Merrit would figure that out soon enough."

"So, did you go there to kill him or try to buy him off?"

"To offer him a full cut in the operation. There was still plenty of money to be made."

"What happened when you got to the museum?"

"I followed Gage over to the museum and we tried to talk to Merrit, but he got mad because Gage had sold the real bears. He started yelling about it being wrong to sell local historical artifacts."

"Imagine someone being concerned about that. So, Merrit was flamed. What did you do?"

Poole put two fingers against the side of his nose and in doing so, partially covered his mouth. "He said he was going to call the sheriff immediately, so I got out of there."

"Where'd this conversation take place?"

"In that little office of his behind the admission desk."

"Did you ever go anyplace else in the museum?"

"No."

"Did you see Gage kill Merrit?"

"No, of course not! Look, I may have made some big mistakes in my life, but I wouldn't have allowed such a thing to happen."

I nodded in agreement. "So, if you didn't see the crime, why do you think *he* did it?"

"He was still there at the museum when I left. They were arguing and Gage was yelling about how he wasn't

going to go to jail." Poole locked eyes with me, hoping to
convince me that he was telling the truth. "He must have
killed Merrit sometime after that."

"But you weren't there to see it?"

"I told you that once already."

"So you did." I pretended to mull that over and said,
"Do you know how Merrit was killed?"

"No."

"His skull was smashed in with a big freaking hammer.
Do you know what happened after that?"

"No. What?"

"The suspect dumped a huge wooden china cupboard
on Merrit. There was broken glass everywhere. It was in
the old dining room, so you probably never saw it."

Poole folded his arms across his chest. "No, I told you I
wasn't there when Merrit was killed."

"And good thing for you that you weren't, or you'd have
trace evidence on your boots. Why don't you go ahead and
take them off now."

"Why?"

"Because we're going to send them to the crime lab
along with all of Gage's shoes. You see, whoever killed
Merrit is going to have microscopic fragments of broken
antique glass and ceramics embedded in the soles of their
shoes." I sat back, gave him a placid smile, and decided to
spring the trap. "So, go ahead and kick your boots off."

Poole's face began to go pale. "You son of a bitch."

"I don't know what you're so upset about. You told me
you didn't kill Merrit, and if you have a clean sole—get
it?—that'll prove you're telling the truth. Unless . . ."

"All right, I'm sorry for lying! I was scared, because I
knew you wouldn't believe me."

"Believe what?"

"I-I was defending myself."

"Right. From a man six inches shorter than you, who had his back turned when he was walloped on the head with a hammer. And then had six hundred pounds of furniture dumped on him! Oh dear, poor Pastor Poole is a victim again. I imagine the jury is going to snicker at that story just like I am right now. Take off your boots."

"You think you're *so* frigging smart."

"Fooling you doesn't qualify as smart. Take off your boots."

"Hell, as long as I'm going to prison, why don't you come over here and get them?" Poole started to rise from his chair.

"Oh, I've been sitting here hoping you'd say that."

I'd been waiting nine months for what happened next. He managed to clip me on the side of the head with a decent right hook as I waded inside and began punching. By the time Bressler got into the interview room, Poole was on the floor and unconscious.

Massaging my sore knuckles, I glanced at my watch and then spoke into the tape recorder, "Time is fourteen-twenty-three hours. Suspect Poole declined to surrender homicide evidence and was physically subdued. End of interview."

Bressler said, "What do we do with him?"

"Handcuff him, takes his boots off, and book him for the murder of Franklin Merrit."

Twenty-six

Later that evening at home, Ash and I cuddled on the couch and decompressed with the assistance of some weapons-grade margaritas.

Resting her head on my left shoulder, Ash studied the knuckles on my right hand. "They're all bruised."

"That's what happens when you're stupid and punch someone in the head with your fist." I swallowed a big dose of Aztec anesthesia.

"You must have done something right. Tina said you knocked Poole out." She kissed my knuckles one at a time. "I wish I could have seen that."

"You'll have more fun watching him sentenced to prison."

"You don't think he'll get the death penalty?"

"No. We just can't prove any premeditation. Still, when you add up all the other felony charges he's got pending, not to mention the outstanding crimes from last year, Poole is looking at decades behind bars before he's even eligible for parole."

"And all because of the great job you did."

"The great job *we* did." I stroked her hair. "If it weren't for you noticing that the bears were fake and then identifying who'd made them, we'd never have broken this case. You're one heck of an investigator."

"Thank you."

"So, when did you talk to Tina?"

"She called for a second while you were outside with Kitch." Ash took a sip from her drink and then gave me a smile of self-satisfaction. "Do you know what's happening at her house right now?"

"While the kids are still awake? Whoa. You go, Sergei."

"No, and you have got a dirty mind."

"It's one of the things you like best about me."

"That's true."

I leaned over to kiss her. "So, what *is* happening at Tina's right now?"

"Sergei is making dinner for Tina and her kids. It's sweet. In fact, he said that he'd take care of all the meals until Tina gets the soft casts off. And you know what else?"

"What's that?"

"He actually asked her to go out on a date."

"The daredevil. I guess that means I'd better finish up on that bear he wants to give her."

Ash studied her empty glass and smacked her lips delicately. "Is there any more of this in the blender?"

"Yeah, let me get it."

I disentangled myself from her and carried both of our glasses into the kitchen. As I poured us fresh drinks, I noticed an ominous-looking envelope in the stack of mail. It's almost never good news when it's correspondence from an attorney's firm. I brought the letter back over to the sofa with the margaritas.

"What's that?" Ash asked, taking her drink.

"I don't know. It came in the mail today." I put my glass down on the coffee table and opened the letter. After a while, I said, "Well, you'll never guess where *we're* going in September."

"The Blue Ridge Craft Show?"

"Nope. San Francisco. The parents of the guy who shot me have filed a police brutality and wrongful death lawsuit against Gregg and SFPD." I flipped the letter onto the coffee table and picked up my drink. "I'm being called back there to testify in a deposition."

"But that man shot you, so how can they sue Gregg?"

"You don't need facts to file a lawsuit. Just a money-hungry attorney hoping for a pretrial settlement."

"Do we have to pay for the trip?"

"Nope. The plaintiffs have to foot the bill."

"Huh. Does it say when in September?"

"I have the choice of a couple of dates. Why?"

"Well, there's a teddy bear show in Sonoma in September. That's just up the road from the city." Ash gave me a shrewd smile.

"And you'd like the ambulance-chasing lawyer to pay for us to attend?" I took a swallow of margarita. "I love it. Find out the date and I'll contact them."

"I will."

"And that might just give me enough time to design and finish my newest cop bear. We could unveil him in California."

"You've already got an idea for another bear?" Ash gave me an amused and adoring look. "Tell me about him."

"Deputy Bearny Fife. But God only knows how I'm going to create those bug-eyes."

"And you're going to have to learn to needle-sculpt his lips."

"Needle-sculpting? I've never done that before."

"You'll learn."

I chuckled uneasily, because needle-sculpting required far more skill than I thought I possessed. "Oh, Lord, what have I gotten myself into here?"

Ash leaned over to kiss me. "As always, nothing you and I can't handle together, my love."

Barbara Burke

My wife, Joyce, and I have learned an important rule for attending teddy bear shows: If you want a bear made by award-winning artist Barbara Burke, you'd better be at the event before the doors open and be willing to race the other collectors to her table. Her mohair bears usually sell out quickly and with good reason: They are among the sweetest stuffed animals ever created. Sometimes they don't even make it to the show—recently, while in transit from her home in Massachusetts to a teddy bear show in Florida, she sold several of her furry creations to enchanted fellow travelers.

The curious thing is that up until ten years ago, Barbara Burke didn't have the slightest interest in making teddy bears, nor was she a collector. She had a degree in fashion retailing and design and devoted most of her time to creating wedding dresses and children's clothing. But in October 1996, she attended a teddy bear show in Vermont and that changed everything.

"I just suddenly knew that this was what I'd wanted to do all my life," said Barbara. "I was suffering from carpal tunnel syndrome in both wrists at the time and immediately scheduled two operations to correct the problem. I knew that once I started working on the bears, I just wouldn't be able to stop."

By May 1997, Barbara had made enough bears to attend her first show as an exhibitor. Unknown and new to the bear community, she only sold one bear, but was ecstatic. Things have changed quite a bit since then. Barbara is now one of the premier bear artists in the United States and has won a multitude of artist awards, including two Teddy Bear of the Year (TOBY) Industry Choice awards, and one Golden Teddy. However, she maintains a down-to-earth attitude regarding such honors. "I'm pleased and humbled by the awards, but they're not nearly as important as the pleasure I get from watching someone fall in love with one of my bears," she said. "That's the real payoff."

Barbara's bear designs come to her in a most intriguing fashion. Typically, she dreams about them and so she keeps a sketchpad and pencil next to her bed to immediately capture the images upon waking. The bears have also come to her in another form of unconsciousness. Earlier this year, she was diagnosed with breast cancer and had to undergo a surgical procedure. As she emerged from the anesthesia, Barbara told the nurse that she wanted a pencil and paper to sketch some bears she met in dreamland. They've turned into her newest teddy project.

A self-described "perfectionist," Barbara dedicates hours to creating each individual stuffed animal and doesn't consider it finished until the bear has "talked" to her. This happens when she holds the bear as she would an infant and gazes into its face. "The eyes speak to you and it's almost as if it has a soul," she explained. As the owner of several of her bears, I understand exactly what she means.

Not surprisingly to the people who know her, Barbara's breast cancer diagnosis hasn't slowed her much at all. She still attends shows all over the country and is famous throughout the bear community for the long hours she spends working on her bears in her hotel room on the night before an event. Barbara attributes her success in fighting the illness to her work with teddy bears and interacting with bear artists and collectors. She told me, "You've got to have a joyful attitude to make a teddy bear and the hobby attracts some of the nicest people you'd ever want to meet. Above all, I've been blessed."

The only thing I'd add to that is that my wife and I are blessed to call Barbara our friend.

Barbara attends teddy bear shows all over the country. If you'd like to learn more about her schedule, she can be contacted via email at *BBwuvncuddles@aol.com*. And if you decide to go to one of those events, remember: Arrive early and be prepared to race me to her table.

Afterword

Don't look for Remmelkemp Mill, Massanutten County, or Shefford Gap on a map of Virginia. They exist only in my imagination. However, the other Virginia locations mentioned, such as Port Republic, Barboursville, and Elkton, are real places. The two teddy bear emporiums mentioned in the book are also genuine. Boyds Bear Country is in Gettysburg, Pennsylvania, and My Friends and Me is in Leesburg, Virginia.

The Michtom, Bruin Manufacturing, and Farnell bears described in the tale are authentic, as are their monetary values given in the story. In addition, the account of how the teddy bear received its name back in 1901 is accurate. Finally, Serieta Harrell, Joanne Mitchell, Masako Yoshijima, and Gary Nett are all real teddy bear artisans. I thank them for making our world a better place.